FAME ADJACENT

Also by Sarah Skilton

Club Deception

FAME ADJACENT

SARAH SKILTON

GRAND CENTRAL
PUBLISHING

NEW YORK BOSTON

This book is a work of fiction. Names, characters, places, and incidents are the product of the author's imagination or are used fictitiously. Any resemblance to actual events, locales, or persons, living or dead, is coincidental.

Grand Central Publishing

Hachette Book Group
1290 Avenue of the Americas, New York, NY 10104
grandcentralpublishing.com
twitter.com/grandcentralpub

First Edition: April 2019

Grand Central Publishing is a division of Hachette Book Group, Inc. The Grand Central Publishing name and logo is a trademark of Hachette Book Group, Inc.

Library of Congress Cataloging-in-Publication Data has been applied for.

ISBNs: 978-1-5387-4798-8 (trade), 978-1-5387-4799-5 (ebook)

Printed in the United States of America

LSC-C

10 9 8 7 6 5 4 3 2 1

For Kiana and Sarvenaz, of course

God, make me famous.
If You can't, just make it painless.
—"Creature Comfort," Arcade Fire

PART I

1

House lights up.

Enter stage right.

Test the microphone.

Find an audience member, lock eyes.

Connect.

"Something weird happened to me when I was a kid. I was on a TV show, and afterward, everyone on it became famous except for me.

"I don't mean 'famous in their hometown' or, like, 'runs a successful blog.' I mean global-domination famous. Sold-out stadium tours. Oscar nominations. Golden Globes. Emmys. Grammys. MTV Music Awards. Number-one hit singles. Unauthorized biographies. Clothing lines. Perfumes. Paparazzi."

That got their attention.

"Anyone know what I'm talking about? It was the early 'nineties, and the show took place at the San Diego Zoo. It had song-and-dance numbers and comedy sketches, except educational because it was on PBS..." (Switch to announcer voice.) "... 'filmed in front of a live studio audience.'

"Even if you never saw it, you've probably heard of it, because it's where *this* little girl got her start."

Music cue: The instantly recognizable opening chords from "Sock Me in the Face (Right Now)" burst forth. A blistering piano riff, followed by a drum kick and low bass. The beat, tempo, and pop vocals—aye aye aye aye—*sent everyone back to the late '90s. (Even if they hated the song, it would now run through their heads the rest of the day. Heh-heh.)*

"What does that song even *mean*, right? 'Sock me in the face'? Right now, by the way. Not later."

The audience laughed, warming to me.

"Fun fact: Melody Briar didn't write the lyrics. I know, you're shocked. The song was written in Sweden, by Swedish people who thought they were using American slang. That's why it doesn't make any sense. They tried to play it off as an homage to Goldie Hawn on *Laugh-In*, because, you know, they're both blondes. Or, wait—no, how did they put it? A callback to Aretha Franklin. That's right. 'Sock it to me, sock it to me, sock me with the truth.' Anyway. Here's another person who was on the show with me..."

Multimedia cue: 15-second film clip from the Journal, *in which a baby-faced Ethan Mallard in a World War II uniform kisses his beloved in the pouring rain.*

A passionate speech: "I know I'm just a farm boy and I can't give you a big house or fancy clothes, but I can give you my heart, and my soul, and they will be yours forever."

"Everyone knows who that is, right? Ethan Mallard single-handedly resurrected cheesy romances for a new generation. And after he got his first Oscar nomination, he announced he was quitting show business to buy a llama farm. Which, to be fair, he did. For about six months. Let's see, who else? Anyone used to watch *Honeypot*, with Kelly Hale, on the WB?"

Multimedia cue: 10 seconds of Honeypot, *a coming-of-age TV show about a college student at Virginia Tech who moonlights as a CIA agent. The heroine of the show has endless spirals of curly hair and an introspective voice-over that suggests nostalgia in present time, for events that are currently happening.*

In every episode Kelly runs like a jacked-up cheetah, down a long hallway, chased by goons from the Russian mob, her elbows stabbing the air.

Voice-over: "It was then I realized... the code to the safe was in me. It always had been."

"And then there's Brody Rutherford..."

Multimedia cue: Pop vocals again, this time male. Although the singer might be the whitest boy ever, he sings and dances as though he's the fourth coming of Michael Jackson, while the chorus for "Bubblegum," an early-2000s number-one hit, plays. "You're stuck on me, I'm stuck on you..." Pivot, stomp, drop to one knee like a proposal, hop back to both feet and stick the landing.

"And lastly, don't ever call her 'the token African American' of the show. Tara Osgood is *British*, ladies and gents, and she could out-sing *all* those white kids."

Multimedia cue: An attractive black woman gives a powerhouse vocal performance in Broadway's Dreamgirls. *Cut to: Her clothing line for Target selling out.*

"With this chic and affordable new look, everyone's in the spotlight."

"This year marks the twenty-fifth anniversary of *Diego and the Lion's Den*. In two months, there's going to be a celebration, with live music and a Q and A at the place that started it all: the San Diego Zoo. Tickets go on sale next week and it's expected to sell out within minutes because it's the first time the entire cast will be together in one place since becoming superstars."

At that point, I paused and gasped for air.

Dizziness washed over me, making my insides roil. I feared I would fall off the stage. For good or ill, whatever remained of the child actor I once was insisted on a proper conclusion to the tale I wove.

"Well, almost the entire cast. One person was overlooked. One person didn't get an invite. Can you guess who?"

Awkward silence.

A cough, followed by the rustling of a chair.

Then a lone voice from the crowd shouted "Booooo" between cupped hands.

It was that guy: the one who told me, "Pretend it's your nightclub act," before I got up to speak.

The guy with short hair and a three o'clock shadow: three o'clock of the following day. He leaned back in his chair, long legs in ripped jeans stretched in front of him, hands behind his head, with medical-grade, black-Velcro wrist guards strapped on tight.

His idea had worked, for a while. I'd practically seen my name on a marquee. *Live, one night only, at the Comedy Club in Redondo Beach. Two-drink minimum.*

I sliced the air with my finger. "They may not want me there, I may not be good for ratings, but *I'm going*. Ohhhh yes. I'm showing *up*. I'm not going to be written out of the story. Not this time."

I breathed hard, thirsty for air, trying not to sway.

The facade had slipped, the spell was wearing off.

1. It was not nighttime
2. I was not in a nightclub
3. I was not even onstage
4. I was in fucking Minnesota
5. In a windowless room, standing in front of five patients and a therapist, who sat around a long table
6. I had just impersonated my former friends and castmates, possibly twisting my ankle during the "Brody's dance routine" component
7. I wore sweatpants without drawstrings because drawstrings represented a threat to myself and others
8. I couldn't cue any music or multimedia presentations because my iPhone was in lockup on the other side of the country
9. Most importantly, this was how the "nightclub act" ended:

"So, yeah. Learning about the anniversary sort of messed with my head. I spent a little time—okay, a lot of time—online when I should have been working, or taking care of myself, or, you know, showering and leaving the house. My name is Holly Danner, and I'm an internet addict."

2

Reddit/AMA

I'm the "missing" cast member from *Diego and the Lion's Den*. I grew up with Kelly Hale, Brody Rutherford, Ethan Mallard, Melody Briar, Tara Osgood, and J. J. Randall. AMA.

(self.AMA)
submitted 34 days ago by HollyD
5,073 comments
share
best
*[–]**DevilOmelette** 3 points 7 hours ago*

Why aren't you famous? Are you ugly?

The one thing everyone on Reddit wanted to know (besides which rumors from the last twenty years were true, which I wasn't touching) was, "What were they like, before? How did they change?"

That was tricky to answer. As far as they were concerned, they were normal before and they had stayed normal. (Villains never see themselves as villains.) It was everyone else who changed. Everyone else who got weird.

Except me, they liked to say. I never treated them differently. I knew them before and after, and I never sold a single article to the tabloids about them. Everyone else turned against them, including their own family members.

I alone stayed the same.

3

What I wrote down on my Prevail! Individualized Internet Treatment Plan Intake Form:

Name: Holly Danner

Occupation: Former freelance writer, former nanny, former actor

Age: 36

Why you are here: Lost my job due to internet use

What I *wanted* to write down on my Prevail! Individualized Internet Treatment Plan Intake Form:

Name: Irrelevant

Occupation: Day Cryer

Age: Middle

Why you are here: I am afraid I have wasted my life

If you wound up at Prevail! you were probably sleep-deprived. I slept for twenty straight hours when I arrived, like a cat. That was part of the treatment plan. Sleeping, and learning about sleep. How to do it better. How to get enough of it.

Our sleep lecturer, Tiaran, looked a little *too* well rested. He wore a black-and-white Adidas tracksuit and bounced on the heels of his feet, as though he might bolt outside and run a marathon at any moment. It made me nervous.

He had smooth skin, no bags under his eyes, and loads of energy. It was enraging, like sleep was his superpower and he'd learned to harness it while the rest of us were, ironically, too lazy to do so. Internet addicts like myself tended to sit around all day doing nothing much physically while our brains got scrambled, toggling between six screens and even more identities. We were internally frantic and externally slothful.

It was sad because I used to love sleep. For a long stretch in my early twenties, before I flunked out of showbiz for good and decided to give college a try, it was all I wanted to do. This eventually became known to whomever I was dating. I probably lost three boyfriends to my sleep habits, and even more jobs since I only scheduled auditions after two p.m.

But I digress. Before we could start cognitive therapy and group sessions at Prevail!, they wanted to build us back up to functioning humans from the shells we'd become, or the rest of our therapy wouldn't take. Rebuilding us included an all-day seminar on the concept of objective truth, catfishing, and how to disengage from trolls and bots, which eventually led to a discussion about the psychological toll of being collectively gaslit by the US president. Those whose primary addiction was hate-reading Trump's Twitter feed were siphoned off into a different treatment plan altogether. The rest of us stayed at Prevail! and tried our best to become sleepologists.

"In an average lifetime," Tiaran explained, "a person will spend approximately twenty-five years asleep..." (Pretty sure I'd been on track for at *least* thirty.) "...and will have three hundred thousand dreams."

Even with that many dreams to draw from, I couldn't recall a single time I'd dreamed about my own stardom. I dreamed about *them* all the time. (Yeah, I know: me and half the world.) Not even in my dreams was I the famous one. My brain couldn't imagine a world in which our fortunes were reversed.

Tiaran taught us about circadian rhythms, the twelve-hours-on, twelve-hours-off light cycle, and how electronic screens had disturbed our natural ability to induce and regulate sleep. Even forcing ourselves to pass out via alcohol or drugs didn't count because it wasn't truly restful; it was the kind of sleep that came on like suffocation.

But illicit substances had never been this group's problem. We were separated from the drug addicts because our treatment was experimental, full of trial and error. As the head counselor, Lisa, had explained it to me, "Our program is the first in the country to address internet addiction as a separate category of addiction. We don't subscribe to the Twelve Steps utilized by AA or NA. While that's effective for many, we don't share their goal of abstinence. How could you function in today's society if you *never* used the internet?"

What it boiled down to was that the substance abusers had a TV and we didn't. The sun-faded game room walls in our wing of the hospital boasted a tacked-up Monet haystack poster where a flatscreen used to be, but it was lopsided and I could see the original color behind it. Way to taunt us with screens we couldn't have.

If you find yourself idly wishing you were a drug addict, it's safe to say something in your life has not gone according to plan.

Not that I ever really had a plan.

To pass the time before bed (lights out at nine), we were encouraged to write letters.

The only person I could imagine writing was Renee. Besides our parents, no one else knew I was here. My social circle had dwindled to immediate family the last several years. She'd booked the flight and sat beside me in the exit row and when we landed at Minneapolis/St. Paul, she bought me paperbacks, a thermos, a neck pillow, and a lavender-scented eye mask. ("I'm so sorry I won't be able to send care packages! Pretend these showed up at regular intervals with the most amazing thoughtful notes attached.")

I think it made her feel good, looking out for me for a change. To be the capable big sister again, handling all the details and assuring me everything would be okay.

Dear Renee,

Welcome to the Twilight Zone. I know you were curious about this place when you dropped me off, but there's not much to see. Devoid of any and all computer, laptop, iPad, or iPhone screens, the general theme is Empty. For the first time in years, we're not looking down, but in the meantime, everything to look at got up and left. Probably due to neglect.

I've been here more than a week, but it's hard to tell because my cohorts aren't adjusting well. Two days ago, I saw a woman swipe her finger across the window to change the view. She burst into tears when it didn't work and I was at a loss for how to comfort her.

You know that moment when you can't find your phone, and even though you don't need it right that second, you're going to need it eventually, possibly soon, and the fact that you can't feel it in your pocket or see it in your purse, and you can't recall where it is, and whether you might have left it at the store, or in a public restroom, or at a friend's, sends you into a preemptive panic? Imagine that sensation of dread, times a thousand, and you'll understand how it feels to be at Prevail!

The only way to combat it is to not be conscious anymore. My bedroom is sparse, with only three things in it: a dresser/desk, a mirror, and a king-size bed with all the Posturepedic, memory foam trimmings. It's glorious. It's sateen. Best sleep I've had in years.

On the con side, here's a mystery for you: Our entire hospital wing smells like meat loaf, but I've never seen them serve it. Unnerving.

This morning, day nine, was my first time to talk. When I got up to introduce myself, some jackass told me to pretend it was a nightclub act. I ended up talking about Mel, Kel, Brody,

Ethan, and Tara instead of myself. I may have... impersonated them. Somehow, I don't think I'll mention this when I see them at the anniversary.

I asked my Prevail! tour guide why our beds were top-of-the-line but the rest of the place was... less so, and she told me a key part of our treatment was to associate our bedrooms with sleep and nothing else. Supposedly, if we can learn to keep our screens out of that "sacred area," we'll feel much better rested on the outside.

(Also, they're waiting for more funding to spruce up the place.)

Remember that Simpsons episode where they visit Grandpa in the old folks' home and the sign says PLEASE DO NOT SPEAK OF THE OUTSIDE WORLD? That goes double for us. I feel like I'm on Reverse Rumspringa. The magazines are several years out of date. I almost read a Better Homes and Gardens with Mel on the cover from her "housewife, kids, and cooking" rebrand.

I wear my wrist guards at night and that helps with my tendinitis and repetitive stress syndrome. Speaking of hands, mine are killing me writing this. I wasn't sure I'd even remember how to write in cursive. Can you read this? Or does it look like the walls in A Beautiful Mind?

How is Lainey? Are you getting her all packed and ready for Belgium? If you need suggestions for books on the plane, she's been *into the Descendants (kids of supervillains) lately. And don't forget to pack her Ollie Owl and sticker book/checklist. She says she doesn't care, but she'll want it with her for when she sees certain monuments, etc.—she'll be bummed if she can't check them off.*

I crumpled up the sheet of paper and started over. This time I didn't mention Lainey. It was none of my business. Not anymore.

Besides, by the time the letter reached them, they'd be gone.

4

When she was four, Lainey went to half-day preschool three times a week. After her first fire drill, she returned flush with information.

"If you are in a fire," she advised me, "turn yourself into a turtle. Then you'll be flat and can squeeze under the door. You have to check for smoke first, though."

"Turn myself into a turtle," I repeated, with utmost seriousness. "Got it."

5

Despite the cafeteria being filled to capacity, mealtimes were eerily quiet. No one seemed to remember how to talk to each other. The only sounds were plastic forks and knives tapping against each other in a futile attempt to cut the food. There were no smartphones to hide behind when the conversation lulled, and anyway, for a conversation to lull, it had to have been there to begin with.

I didn't have anywhere to sit yet so I trudged over to the meds window for my daily dose of D. Some of us were being simultaneously treated for obsessive-compulsive behavior, depression, or anxiety, but all of us received vitamin D because it was assumed—correctly—that we rarely ventured outside. I was also allotted one Dixie cup of Coke Classic to curb my caffeine withdrawal. Coffee was verboten, but chamomile tea was available as a sleep aid before bed.

The window-swiping woman got up to bus her tray, so I commandeered her seat, noticing too late that it put me across from Mr. Pretend It's Your Nightclub Act.

He stood and held out his hand. "Thom Parker."

We shook. "Hi."

No one had stood for me at a table in years.

I was at the earliest dinner shift, five p.m., so it was still light outside, and the sun filtering in through the windows gave me a better look at him than I'd gotten that morning at group. He looked like a CW actor's mug shot, his face full of scruff because razors were only allowed under close supervision. His short, dirty-blond hair stood in ragged tufts because he regularly gripped pieces of it in his fingers and tugged. (Most of us had restless hands, now that we were mouse-less and click-less.)

It would've taken a stylist in LA a few hours to achieve that look with mousse, but clearly it wasn't something he'd planned; it was something that had *happened* to him. In fact, nothing about him seemed deliberate. He looked to me like the kind of guy who didn't realize he had a big dick. He just went about his swingin' dick day, dopey and oblivious, having assumed long ago that everyone else's was the same size.

It always bugged me in my auditioning days when women in screenplays were described that way: "Sasha, 22, has no idea how beautiful she is." (God forbid she be aware.) But in real life I found it fascinating.

"Great show today," he said, stretching his arms behind his head. "Have you thought about taking it on the road?"

Har. Har.

"Um, thanks."

"I mean, your performance was manic, and your moonwalk needs a little work, but your singing's decent. You captured each star's essence in a short period of time."

Did I *ask*?

He grinned. One of his top teeth pressed down on his lip like a little fang. His teeth had their own ideas about whether he was good looking. In Hollywood, they'd have shaved it down.

"At the risk of sounding like a reality show contestant, I'm not here to make friends," I replied, and picked up the pace of my eating. He wasn't going to trap me there a second longer than necessary. Without screens, there was no reason to be awake. As soon as I finished eating, it was off to dreamland on my ten-thousand-thread-count, Posturepedic masterpiece.

He slurped from his straw, loudly, undeterred. "How come you left out J. J. Randall?"

I stabbed my lettuce leaves with my fork. "I think people got the gist of it by then."

He leaned back in his chair, tilting it precariously on its hind legs, the way he did at group. Not a care in all the world. It was annoying as hell.

"You talked about everyone else, but not him. Why?"

"A real connoisseur of 'nineties boy bands, are you?" I asked.

"Oh, definitely. It's extraordinary how they figured out you could rhyme the words *girl* and *world* like that. And how they notice things like the way someone *walks* and *talks*."

"Are you serious right now?"

He rolled his eyes, which were a startling light blue. "I had to watch my kid sister every day after school back in Ohio and the only way to get her to come to the skate park with me was to bribe her with *Total Request Live*. Every day for six months my senior year of high school, the number-one video was..." He aggressively hummed the opening bars to OffBeat's "Girl (of Mine)."

Parenthetical song titles were big in the '90s.

"Yeah, well, I actually *was* J. J.'s 'girl of mine' so imagine how that earworm felt *my* senior year."

His jaw fell open. "You dated J. J. Randall?"

"Not publicly, but I like to think that, in an alternate universe, the press nicknamed us 'Jolly.'"

He scanned my face, as though trying to recognize me, but it wasn't going to work. "Why not publicly?" Then: "What's your name again?"

"Didn't you hear?" I asked. "I'm nobody."

He looked me straight in the eyes. "I very much doubt that."

His words, and the certainty with which they were delivered, sent an unexpected spear of longing through my gut, until he added, "You've lost your marbles if you think crashing their high school reunion is going to make you feel better."

"I'm in internet rehab. How many marbles do you think I have? And it's not a high school reunion."

"It might be on a red carpet but it's still a high school reunion. Why torture yourself? I myself never..."

I myself? Really?

I took a calming breath and released it. I was at a distinct disadvantage; because of my impromptu musical introduction that morning, he knew far more about me than I did about him. "What brought you here, Thom?"

He tilted his chair precariously up on its back legs again and crossed his arms. "Guess."

"Porn."

"Then I'd only need one wrist guard," he pointed out.

I walked right into that one.

And now it's time to walk out.

Before I left, I nudged the front of his chair with my foot, covertly under the table so he wouldn't see. Just enough to tip it off balance.

His eyes widened, and he leapt away before it crashed to the floor.

"I'm okay," he announced to the indifferent cafeteria.

I smiled, not even a little sorry.

Because I may have pegged him all wrong. It occurred to me he knew *exactly* how big his dick was.

6

Unfortunately, sleep had to wait.

Lisa the head counselor stood outside my door with a clipboard. She wore glasses, a wide variety of bracelets, triple-hoop earrings, and a scoop-necked blouse.

Lisa and her jangling circles asked, "How was dinner?" but didn't wait for an answer. "I wanted to go over your IITP—Individualized Internet Treatment Plan—and see if you have questions about it."

She led the way to her office, settled into her desk chair, and motioned for me to take a seat on the couch. It was difficult to concentrate on her words, because every cell in my body hungered for the computer sitting on her desk.

Screen. Screeeeeeen. If I could hop online really quick and check Reddit…

"Holly, did you hear me?"

"Hmm?"

"I need to feel that you're listening to me."

I forced my gaze away from temptation. "I am, I swear."

I'd already missed out on so much since I arrived. Literally *millions* of updates. How would I ever catch up? What if I never did?

My iPhone was thousands of miles away in California, under lock and key at my sister's house. By separating me from it, I'd been separated from my *self*. I was lost. Floating, untethered to reality. In some far recess of my mind I knew there used to be other realities—for me and everyone else—and that those realities shrank in importance around 1994, when email came into existence.

Just in case, I reached in my back pockets, my fingers scrabbling.

Oh God.

There was nothing there.

I leaned down, put my head between my knees, and breathed.

In.

Out.

In.

Out.

Lisa perched beside me on the couch's armrest and placed a gentle hand on my shoulder. "Your phone's not gone forever. Just a few weeks."

"*Six*," I rasped, as though they were my last words before dying. "*Six... weeks...*"

"Not six. Three."

My head snapped up like I was possessed by a demon. "What?"

"I'll explain. And I'm going to add a meditation session to your schedule tomorrow." She made note of this in her pad. "As I mentioned, abstinence is not our goal. *Our* goal is to gradually reintroduce you to your screens so you can eventually enjoy them again in moderation, at fixed times, and under fixed circumstances. After an initial transition period of three weeks, which is generally regarded as the amount of time it takes to change a habit, you'll be allowed fifteen minutes online, supervised, once per day. In the meantime, would you like a talisman?"

I'd seen those around: squeeze balls and smooth stones, any type of small object to be kept in pockets and clung to until panic abated. One guy had crafted a cardboard rectangle the exact shape and size of an iPhone XS and decorated it with puffy stickers for the apps and buttons. It was begging to be 'Grammed and mocked, and made the rest of us irate that its batshit existence would never be documented. The tension it caused only ended when it was stolen and presumably ripped to pieces on the sly.

WHO IS THE TALISMAN BANDIT???? the dry erase board in the hallway demanded for half a day, until a staff member erased it and rewrote the day's activities.

Lisa's continued explanation interrupted my thoughts. "When you arrived, you signed a contract stating that in exchange for free treatment you would allow us to track your progress and keep a file of the results—names blacked out, of course—for our board members to use when requesting grants. It's important that each patient fulfills the terms of the agreement. Any questions so far?"

Three weeks without internet isn't so bad. I can do that. The dizziness subsided. I slowly uncurled and sat back up. "And the whole thing is free?"

"Yes. Because Prevail! is a new program, we're continuing to update our research regarding which types of therapy are most effective for which patients. In the future, the treatment will not be free, but since you're in the inaugural group of—"

"Lab rats?"

"We like to say 'volunteer test subjects.' You'll also receive a per diem of ten dollars a day upon completion of the program."

"Is that more or less than I'd get for jury duty?" I was going for humor but she either didn't get it or didn't think it was funny. Likely the latter.

"Okay, Holly, I'll see you at ten tomorrow for our first counseling session."

"K. Good night, and thanks for your help."

That night I slept like a log stuffed with sleeping pills. I dreamed I was home in San Diego, and I was desperate to get online, but I couldn't because I had no hands. When I opened my mouth to scream, the only sound that came out was the interlude rap from "Girl (of Mine)."

7

When Lainey was fourteen months old, she would only fall asleep for naps or bedtime if she had two binkies: one in her mouth, and one in her left hand. Her right hand was pinned to her side in a diagonal swaddle. The thin linen blanket had baby elephants on it. In the mornings, it was dry, but it would become wrinkled with drool as the day went on. She looked like a caterpillar in a cocoon. When she yawned, her mouth took up her entire face.

I couldn't simply lay her in the crib and leave the room. First, I had to put on a recording of a blow dryer noise, then wait for her eyelids to flutter closed, and then crab-walk backward out of the room, praying she wouldn't see me, sense me, or wake up right as I reached the hallway.

When her nap was over or morning came, she would yell something muffled and incoherent until I arrived, at which point she would say, clear and crisp as an instructor teaching a foreign language, "Other binkie."

At some point during her rest, she'd inevitably throw the mouth binkie over the side of her crib and shove the backup binkie into her mouth to replace it. Now that someone had arrived who could do something about it, she'd remove the mouth binkie long enough to repeat the urgent words: "Other binkie."

I'd search for it on the carpet, often finding it near the closet—she got good distance—wipe it off, and place it into her grasping fingers.

If there's a lesson in there somewhere, I think it's this: Life is never about the binkie you have; it's about the binkie you don't. The one you threw, the one that's gone, the one that's out of reach.

8

I nearly didn't make it to meditation. Although we're allowed three missed classes in any category before we're kicked out (and replaced with better-disciplined test subjects, presumably), I didn't want to use any of my skips this early—better to keep them in reserve. As I wove down the hall trying to beat the clock, I was brought up short outside the gym.

A lean male figure in butt-hugging red swim shorts climbed out of the exercise pool like Bond-movie Daniel Craig emerging from the ocean.

The closest I came to clearing my mind during meditation five minutes later was to rewind his cameo at the pool and replay it behind my eyelids. His blond-ish hair dark and wet across his forehead, his broad shoulders straight and strong as he leaned down to scoop his towel off the chair.

Okay, so Thom's a verified Handsome. It wasn't like it mattered. There would be no souvenirs from this "vacation."

9

Reddit/AMA

I'm the "missing" cast member from *Diego and the Lion's Den*. I grew up with Kelly Hale, Brody Rutherford, Ethan Mallard, Melody Briar, Tara Osgood, and J. J. Randall. AMA.

(self.AMA)
submitted 34 days ago by HollyD
5,073 comments
share
best

[–]Bleeeeeeeeet

3 points 7 hours ago

[Kiwifroot]: Are these really written by Holly Danner? She was my favorite! Whatever happened to her?

[MiZterPEE]: LOL holly danner wasnt anyones favorite

[Kiwifroot]: Holly, a technical question if you don't mind: Why was the boom always in the shot?

[HollyD]: I wouldn't say it was "always" in the shot, but our production values were certainly compromised due to the unpredictable nature of the cast. (The showbiz adage "Never work with children or animals" went double for us.)

[SARGHoov]: Whoever chose the songs in the first season was high, right? Why were they so weird? (When was the show supposed to take place?? Some things were modern and some things were like super old)

[HollyD]: If I may read between the lines, I believe what you're wondering is, "Why didn't we sing contemporary music, especially since we were supposed to be an aspiring band?" Here goes: After the crew, set designers, writers, choreographers, dance instructors, singing instructors, tutors, craft services, room and board, promotional materials, and rehearsal spaces were paid for, our PBS affiliate didn't have enough money to secure the rights to modern pop music. Our only option was to use songs from the public domain, which is where "Little Brown Jug" came in. Other songs from the inaugural season were "I Don't Want to Play in Your Yard," "Bells of St. Mary's," "I Ain't Got Nobody and Nobody Cares for Me," "In the Good Old Summertime," "Camptown Races," and "Hard Times Come Again No More." Mercifully, "Cabbage-Leaf Rag" was cut because of time constraints. In seasons two through four, we had a higher budget, which allowed us to cover such timeless ballads as "Jump" by Kriss Kross.

[Kat1976]: Did the San Diego Zoo even give them permission to film there? It sort of seemed like they wanted no part of the show. And it was never referred to by name.

[HollyD]: Kat1976, you're clearly an observant individual. It's true we only ever alluded to it. (Diego: "Let's go home, everyone." Everyone: "Yeah, let's go back to the place.") There was a mild controversy over the fact that the characters were orphans/runaways who *lived* at the zoo; fear of actual child copycats kept the legal department up at night. We did have permission to shoot on location, but only after the zoo closed for the day, because it was too difficult to get release forms signed by every visitor who might appear in a shot. Mornings were out because that's when they sprayed the place down. So all the exterior shots took place at night. We had to run into frame, record our lines as fast as possible (usually in one take, flubbed lines be damned; you're welcome, drinking-game players) before the sun went down. It was sort of guerrilla-style filmmaking.

10

At my second therapy session with Lisa, she covered her desktop computer with a crocheted blanket and repositioned the couch so it faced away from the screen. It worked; I was better able to focus on our conversation. I sank into the brown pleather couch with a sigh.

"Let me see if I've got this straight. Before you found out about the show's anniversary special, you had a healthy relationship with the internet?"

If I'd been drinking something I would have coughed. "I wouldn't go *that* far, but a much better one. I could still function. I could still get work done."

She peered through her bifocals at a sheet of paper. "You wrote on your intake form that you lost your job because of internet use. As a writer?"

"No—that came later."

"I'm not sure I understand."

"Sorry, I know it's a bit confusing. First, I left my job as a nanny." She tilted her head curiously, and I rushed to add, "Nothing bad happened. It was just time."

"So, you left the nanny position and became a writer?"

"Well, I'd been doing freelance on and off for years."

"What sorts of things did you write?"

"Articles for online magazines, a few print—mostly obscure, niche publications."

"And was that... able to pay the bills?"

I cleared my throat. It didn't take a genius to question the profitability of "obscure" writing.

"Well, I was living at my sister's house, so I didn't have to worry about rent or groceries or anything. It was—the girl I nannied for was my niece. *Is* my niece. I was planning to move out when..." (I gestured with sweeping arm movements.) "... *this* happened."

She nodded encouragingly so I kept going, tripping over my words as I attempted to explain myself. "The truth is, leaving the nanny position had me thinking back over my other jobs, and it hit me that I'd never *had* any other jobs. I booked *Diego and the Lion's Den* when I was eleven, and I stayed for all five seasons, then I graduated high school and went on my gap year."

"Oh? How'd you spend it?"

I looked down, cringing. Why had I called it a gap "year"? It had been *seven*. "In Hollywood, going out for parts. When I hit the quarter-century mark with nothing to show for it I decided it was time to become San Diego State's oldest freshman, but that didn't last long before the, uh, nanny thing opened up, so..."

I lacked an identity. I had no core. I was a mushy apple all the way through; no seeds inside to plant something new.

"It makes sense that when you quit one job, you'd think back to the job you had prior to it, to the life you had, and you'd wonder, 'What if…?' Did you find yourself revisiting your past? Your former castmates?"

"Yup." *And let's leave it at that, shall we?*

"How so?" *Dammit.*

"I set up a few Google alerts, and it sort of…spiraled. As I'm sure you can imagine, they're written about frequently."

"You're not in touch with them, though?"

"It's been a few years. Anyway, within a week, I discovered the anniversary announcement. No one noticed I was missing from it."

"That must have been extremely frustrating."

"I had to channel my feelings somewhere. On a whim, I set up an account on Reddit and started an AMA thread."

"What's AMA?"

There was a reason so many alcohol counselors were recovering addicts: so they wouldn't need shit explained to them. How was Lisa going to treat internet fiends if she wasn't versed in their culture?

"It stands for 'Ask Me Anything.' It's a subreddit thread."

"Got it." She jotted this down.

You're welcome, Reddit-related patients.

Then I chastised myself. *Relax. The treatment's free, and you get what you pay for.*

"I explained my situation—that I was on a show in the 'nineties with a bunch of people who went on to become famous—and offered to answer any questions people had. It was something to do while I figured out my next move.

"At first the collective response was WDGAF, and the usual 'pics or it didn't happen.' And of course, someone asked what kind of soup I like."

Lisa seemed perplexed. "I'm not sure I…"

"WDGAF. 'We don't give a fuck.'"

"Right, and the soup?"

"I know, it's dumb, there's this one guy who always asks that. Anyway, after a few days of crickets, someone posted a link to it at the *Daily Denizen*—that's a fan site devoted to *Diego and the Lion's Den*—and the floodgates opened. I was inundated with questions." An involuntary smile slithered onto my face as I reminisced about the initial rush of attention.

Lisa picked up on it. "How did that feel?" she asked.

"Good. Really good. People were talking about the show with such fondness, sharing their memories of watching it after school and how crazy it was that so many big stars got their start on it. They were dying for information, and they LOL'd at everything I said. It was nice to be at the center of it all. I found my old scrapbooks and *TV Guide* clippings and scanned a bunch of photos. At one point it was Reddit front page."

"Sounds fun."

"Yeah, it was. At first. But it used to be I had a life of some sort. I'd get up early every day, go for a jog before it got too hot, shower, eat breakfast, write for a few hours, break for lunch, work on a freelance assignment—and *then* go online. There was a whole reward system at play. Around three I might pick up Lainey from school—my niece—and help her with homework or make dinner with her. But once I quit, and all I had was the occasional magazine article to write, there was nothing stopping me from being online all day, so I decided to answer them *all*. Unless it was a repeat question or blatantly inflammatory." I swallowed. "I blew two deadlines and didn't even notice; just completely forgot about them. And after that, there was no reason to stop, you know?"

My eyes misted up and I coughed into my hand.

Lisa's face was open and relaxed, and she gave me time to continue my train of thought, but when I didn't, or couldn't, she prompted me with, "When did you realize you needed help?"

"Renee, my sister, brought my parents over and held an intervention. If they hadn't I'd probably still be staring at my computer. One of them saw an article about Prevail! and thought it would help." I perked up slightly, remembering how I'd marked my desk calendar and circled the date of the anniversary in a red circle, the way characters always did in movies. "The timing's actually great—I'll finish this program, get cured, and be home with two weeks to spare before the anniversary."

"And you're determined to . . . disrupt it in some manner?" She spoke in a carefully neutral tone, like a hostage negotiator.

"Why, do you have to report my intentions? I'm just going to talk to them. And any reporters milling around. I won't be *violent.*"

"What do you think that will accomplish? Sorry. Let me rephrase: What would you *like* it to accomplish?"

"Honestly?"

"Yes, please."

"The only thing I want it to accomplish is saying, *Eff you. I'm not dead, and you can't erase me.* I get that they're on a whole different level, but the fact that they didn't invite me? That they didn't even let me know about it? It's . . . " I clenched my fists, the tendons along my wrist popping out. "Unbelievable."

Lisa was quiet, mulling things over. Her eyes flitted to the wall clock and back to me. I followed her gaze; we had gone five minutes over our allotment.

"We're done for today," she confirmed, "so this is off the record, so to speak . . . "

A low, heavy feeling settled in my belly.

She turned her back and conducted a search on her phone, which was basically like snorting lines in front of a coke addict. I envisioned myself snatching the phone from her hands, locking her in her office, and running down the hall, phone raised high like a trophy kill. The other patients would make me queen if it meant internet access for all.

Lisa's chair swiveled back around. "Is this you?"

In a clear violation of my Individualized Internet Treatment Plan three-week rule, she flashed me a glimpse of her phone screen. A photo culled by Google image search showed me sandwiched between J. J. and Brody at Brody's twenty-seventh birthday party at Soho House. In the picture, I'm smiling and blushing, being hugged on either side and kissed on the cheeks simultaneously by the guys, who'd just been named number one and number seventeen on Celeb.com's "30 Most Powerful Hawties Under 30," respectively. Given that my identity was unknown, it caused paroxysms of rage to detonate throughout the fandom. The twitterati referred to me as a "random skank-ho."

Random? I'd huffed.

"Yeah, that's me," I muttered. "Did you think I was making it up?"

"No, no... I wanted to make sure we treated the *correct* underlying condition. We weren't sure at first, if you felt a fan-related kinship to the group or if you truly knew them. It would be tempting to claim that you were friends with so many prominent, very, very famous people."

"Right," I deadpanned.

She shut down her phone. Then, eyes gleaming, she planted her heels on the carpet and propelled her rolling chair closer to me.

"What was it like to work with Brody?"

11

I would never live it down.

At group therapy the next week, people were still speculating about the possibility of an encore performance from my first day.

Or at least, *one* person was.

"Who wants Holly to sing 'Copacabana'?" asked Thom, as he did every day, swapping in new titles each time.

"This is not the Holly Danner Variety Hour," Lisa remarked, as *she* did every day. She sounded only slightly irritated; she was no longer sore I'd declined to tell her anything about Brody. To her credit, she'd apologized for her unprofessionalism and promised it would never happen again.

"Agreed," I told Lisa. "It's someone else's turn."

The pervasive meat loaf smell of our hospital wing had been replaced by something treacly and sweet I couldn't identify. Ice cream? Cotton candy?

I didn't know how many people were in the overall program (rumor had it the Trump-Twitter group was the largest, and totally sequestered), but my group therapy consisted of six.

It was a relief to hear about other people's fuckery. In my current state, I could barely remember their names but had zero problem memorizing their addictions.

First up was Wikipedia Avenger, who was in agony speculating about the damage his opposite number—an honest-to-God archnemesis—was doing to his entries while he was trapped at Prevail!

The next person to speak was a woman around my age who referred to herself as a Popaholic. She used to pick at her skin and hair until she discovered popping videos on YouTube: people popping zits. Apparently, there were hundreds of channels devoted to this, and she found that, by watching the videos, the urge to pick her own skin was reduced. The downside was that she became inured to the pops and needed more and better videos to achieve the same sedating effect. Soon she'd ventured into tumor removal, cyst draining, and hard-core surgeries. She was terrified to find out what came after that.

Twitter Fiend didn't hold my attention for long. He averaged three hundred tweets per day, blah, blah, blah, he retweeted articles he hadn't read (didn't we all), shot off competitive tweet threads in the hundreds, and had been blocked by countless accounts. Twitter itself finally put him on probation and he decided to give treatment a shot while he'd lost access.

Then, of course, there was Thom. In contrast with the others, I remembered his name fine, but still had no idea what had brought him here. It had been over a week since our cafeteria chat.

Abruptly, Lisa clapped and stood. "As some of you know, today is a special day. Marjorie has reached her first milestone."

Murmurs of excitement filled the room.

Just kidding; none of us reacted. Lisa would have to do *a lot* better than that.

Whoever Marjorie was, she was celebrating three weeks of treatment.

"Which means…" Lisa did a drumroll on the tabletop. "After group today, she will be going online."

Now we cared. All eyes swiveled toward Marjorie. We deemed her suspicious and undeserving of such a reward.

"It'll be a letdown," Thom said, leaning back in his chair. (Did he learn nothing from my attempted maiming?)

"Thom," Lisa warned, "we've talked about this."

I was afraid she'd make us repeat the Prevail! mantras but she was as eager to move on from that quasi-rebellion as the rest of us.

"I'm saying, I've had access for two weeks now. It's not that great. You know what's great? The hike we took last Saturday at Elm Creek Park. And swimming in the pool."

Couldn't argue with him there. From my vantage point, swimming had been *very* worthwhile.

"Listening to music," he continued. "Having a goddamn conversation. You know, things people did *before* the internet."

I thought about how he and I were the only people who spoke to each other at dinner eight days ago.

"Moving on," said Lisa. "For the newcomers, please remind everyone what brought you here, Marjorie."

Marjorie looked to be in her forties, and she had a sad, droopy mouth. Pliable. Maybe with a tiny push, it could change shape, recover from its sadness. She wasn't a fan of the spotlight. Her soft face calcified with fear and her hands twisted together in her lap, as though trying to pin each other down before they mimicked the motions for mouse movements and clicks. Once she got started, though, her feelings fueled her voice, which rose in volume and strength. "My main problem was Instagram," she said, her eyes wet.

"What about Instagram?" Lisa asked.

She blinked. "The other moms."

"How so?"

"At first, it felt like friendship. Long distance, maybe, but still friendship. Until I noticed they're all perfect, and I'm not. Holidays are the toughest. Everyone's dressed in designer costumes, coordinated, frolicking in the autumn leaves, dancing in the pumpkin patches, eating homemade ice cream, or making seasonal arts and crafts..." She winced, as though she'd been pelted with the crafts. Which was probably how it felt for her. "They have so many kids, four, five, even six sometimes. I only have two, and I'm lucky if I can get them to school on time with their underwear facing the right way." Her voice cracked and reemerged as a whisper. "I don't know what I'm doing wrong. My photos come out blurry, or someone's closing their eyes or running out of frame and even with all the filters we never look good. Maybe I'd be better off on Pinterest."

"No!" the rest of us yelled.

"Why do they have to be so perfect?" she asked, bewildered. It hurt my heart to see. She reminded me of Renee when she was in the midst of postpartum depression.

A dewdrop of a tear slid down her cheek, drawing attention to the shimmer of blush across her cheekbones. It was clear she'd put effort into her appearance, had gotten dolled up for today's milestone.

"Newsflash: They're not perfect. They're liars and frauds," said Thom.

"Thom..." Lisa repeated.

"She needs to hear this." Thom swiveled in his chair so he faced Marjorie. When he spoke, he was forceful but kind. "A lot of those accounts are making money. They get paid to post, in ad revenue, clothing, and products. It becomes their *job* to promote an 'aspirational lifestyle.' The dads are usually Ivy League grads who buy expensive photography equipment and use their MBAs to build a business with their family as the brand ambassadors. The way they present themselves online is not real. It's painstakingly crafted, well lit, and *not* spontaneous. They have time to do this because it's the only thing they do all day. And they try to pass it off as real so you'll buy the stupid shit they're wearing and the stupid gourmet meals they're making together in the kitchen. They make money every time you view their videos or 'like' their photos. Their kids are posing for content, and while it's impossible to say whether they're enjoying it, I know for a fact that *your* kids are running around and taking blurry photos because they're having fun."

Marjorie looked hopeful for about a millisecond, then doubts overtook her again. "Are you sure? Because sometimes they'll show a messy room or something and hashtag it 'real life' or 'parenting fail,' and—"

"Just as staged as the perfect stuff," Thom interrupted. "Only more insidious, because it's there to make them seem down-to-earth and relatable, so you'll believe their life would be attainable if you'd try harder. But it's not. It's really not. And that's okay."

Lisa's assistant from the University of Minnesota wheeled in a tray of party food that consisted of a frightfully cheerful cake and mugs of lukewarm decaf. I wondered if the cake was the source of the sickly-sweet smell I noticed earlier. Spread between layers was raspberry jam instead of icing. Lainey called that a "fake-out."

After we ate, Marjorie left the room with an Internet Supervisor to an undisclosed location where she would presumably gorge on Instagram for fifteen minutes. I hoped she wouldn't, though. I hoped she went to a different site, or FaceTimed her kids or something. She seemed like a good egg.

After they left, Lisa split us off into pairs.

"Everyone has a piece of paper with questions on it. Alternate who asks and who answers, and when the timer goes off, move to your right."

"Wait. Is this speed dating?" asked Thom.

Lisa's jaw twitched. "Think of it as a chance to practice the art of conversation."

I was initially partnered with Twitter Fiend, who didn't bother with any conversational pleasantries. He picked up the scratch paper and read aloud, "What's your goal for treatment?"

I stopped chewing on my fingernail and looked up. "To leave."

"It says you should be specific."

"To leave triumphantly," I revised.

Popaholic's goal was to reduce her video watching to five minutes a day, and to watch videos in a wide range of topics instead of one. It seemed to me she was self-aware enough to turn the Good Ship Pimple Popper around. I had many, many questions for her, but they had to wait, because Wikipedia Avenger was next on my rotation. We swapped tales of poor eating habits and what we'd do differently once we left, such as eat meals at tables instead of snacking all day at our desks or in bed.

Thom and I were paired last. He crumpled up his list and tossed it over his shoulder.

"What are you doing?" I asked.

"My questions are better." He cleared his throat. "Why'd you and J. J. Randall break up? Did he cheat on you?"

What was *wrong* with him? "No! Next question."

I could tell he didn't believe me, but it was true.

"When you were on the show, did you get recognized a lot?"

"Not really. It was on PBS but it didn't air in all markets, and it was for kids who were younger than us, so we rarely met them. When we weren't rehearsing or filming, we had to perform at parades and street fairs to hype the show. There was a fan club you could join if your parents donated money to the station. Every month you'd get a signed eight-by-ten glossy and a handwritten questionnaire that one of us had filled out."

"Please tell me you kept them."

I shook my head. "Sorry. I remember wandering into the subscriber phone bank once and seeing a huge stack of them in the recycling bin. Apparently, it wasn't a hot-ticket item for the *Masterpiece Theatre* crowd."

He chuckled and I smiled back. I loved it when someone thought I was funny; it made me feel calm. Like I didn't have to be a real person so long as I made other people laugh.

"Have you done any other acting?" Thom asked.

"Yes. Brace yourself. Are you ready?"

He slapped his hands together. "So ready."

"Do you remember that show *Fowl Play*?"

He cringed, which was the only reaction that made sense.

"About the... parrot who..." He trailed off. "Don't make me say it."

I giggled. "Come on, you can do it."

"The parrot who solved crimes," he finished in a pained, embarrassed rush.

"Ding-ding-ding, we have a winner."

"God, that show ran forever. You were on it?"

"I was the daughter."

His eyes widened. "That's huge."

"I know. I think it ran for ten years. But I was only in the unaired pilot; they recast my role for the series."

Thom frowned. "That sucks. I mean, I wasn't exactly a fan of *Fowl Play*, but..."

"Not even the creator was a fan of *Fowl Play*."

"That must have been frustrating."

He sounded like Lisa. According to them, my life was one big frustration.

I waved him off. "It's all right. It was a long time ago."

Every episode hinged on whether the damn bird overheard and mimicked exculpatory or incriminating evidence. They stole a page from *Murphy Brown*'s rotating cast of secretaries and hired a different guest star to play a quirky judge each week. (Some of the actors *were* former *Murphy Brown* secretaries.)

"The kicker was I'd done this whole extravagant makeover at the producers' request to book the role, but when they fired me, the person they got to replace me looked exactly the way I used to."

He covered his mouth and moaned, "Nooo."

"Honestly, it was for the best. I figured out there was no winning. The next time, I would've been too tall or too short or too skinny or too fat or too smart or too dumb, or too much of whatever it was they didn't want. I couldn't keep putting myself through that, so I quit show business for good."

Outside of Reddit, which I only started posting to a month ago, I hadn't thought about those experiences in years. Thom seemed safe to talk to; he didn't care about fame, as his blistering takedown of Instagram influencers made clear. But he seemed genuinely interested in *me,* which made it easier to open up.

Of course, we were supposed to be alternating who asked and who answered. I'd been treating his questions like an interview for *Star* magazine instead of a conversation. I felt like a self-absorbed asshole.

"How about you? What job do you go back to when this is over?" I asked.

"I design skate parks," he replied simply, proudly, letting his chair fall forward with a thunk. Even his chair-thunking was confident.

"You don't still *ride* a skateboard, do you?" I asked, my nose wrinkling. I pictured him wearing a suit and tie and holding a briefcase while he zigzagged around pedestrians on the sidewalk.

One of his eyebrows went up. "I'm an adult, Holly."

"Weekend Warrior, huh?"

"No, really. I hung up my wheels a long time ago."

"And this is in...Ohio, did you say?" I mentally high-fived myself for remembering, because it proved I wasn't a frenzied narcissist.

"I grew up in Ohio, but I'm on the East Coast now."

"Small-town Ohio, or like, Cincinnati?"

"Small town that gradually became a hellhole." His mouth twitched.

"Like, the Rust Belt where 'real Americans' live," I joked.

"No, I mean a hellhole."

I sighed and continued my attempt to pry information out of him, because we couldn't go back to me until I'd put forth a reasonable effort. "And you design the skate park structures? Like an architect?"

"Urban planner. Upstate New York."

His reticence to talk about himself surprised me. Every other time we'd interacted, he couldn't shut up.

"I thought about applying to Cornell," I offered. "It's beautiful there. But I ended up at San Diego State. That's one good thing that came out of *Fowl Play*: It paid for college."

"That's cool."

"Until I dropped out," I added sheepishly. No sense tricking him into thinking he chatted with an educated person. Not that I thought he'd care, necessarily, but it seemed important to me that he knew.

"Why'd you drop out?"

"My older sister needed me."

"What for?"

"She had a nasty bout of postpartum depression and her husband was serving overseas. I moved in with her so I could help out with the baby."

"That was thoughtful of you."

I couldn't tell if he was being sardonic or genuine.

Out of habit I reached in my back pocket for my iPhone so I could show him pictures of Lainey, but obviously, my phone wasn't there. Thom used this momentary distraction to dig further.

"What's the *real* reason you left college?"

Jesus Christ with this guy. "What do you mean?"

"Your sister could have gotten outside help. She's not your responsibility."

"I *wanted* to help."

He tilted his chair back on its hind legs, looked at me, and waited.

I had nowhere to be and nothing better to do, so I waited, too.

"What if you'd said no?" Thom pressed me.

"I couldn't have said no!"

"It's a mental exercise."

"Okay, okay, it wasn't the only reason. There might have been other factors."

He smirked. "I knew it. Such as...?"

"Midway through sophomore year I realized that even if I worked my ass off, got a 4.0, graduated summa cum laude, earned a degree, got an upper-middle-class job, and basically did everything right for the rest of my life, it would still take me seventy years to make as much money as Melody did in a *week* from 'Sock Me in the Face (Right Now).'"

"Huh. I can see how that would be demoralizing."

I readjusted my ponytail. "Yeah."

He studied my face, his clear blue eyes penetrating mine. "I believe you."

"Well, *that's* a relief." I wiped my brow with exaggerated movements. "I wasn't sure I'd be able to sleep again if Thom from Prevail! didn't buy my sincerity."

"Thom from Prevail! is the best damn question-asker on the planet."

"You must be doing something right," I admitted. "I never talk about them and here I am spilling my guts."

"Really? Why?"

"Most people have no idea I was in show business. It's not something I tend to bring up."

"How come?"

"I don't want it to be the only thing they think about when they're with me."

"It's not what *I* think about."

My stomach flipped. I'd always been fairly good at telling whether someone was interested in me, or interested in my connections. The easiest way to find out was to watch how they introduced me to others. Was I their friend Holly, or was I *their friend Holly who was on that show with all those people, can you believe it?* Thom's questions had focused so tightly on my experiences and not those of the so-called Denizens (the *Daily Denizen*'s nickname for *Diego* alum) that it was clear which category he fell into.

"I read somewhere that whatever age you are when you become famous is the age you stay the rest of your life," he said. "It traps you because you never have a chance to mature beyond it."

A shrug was all I could offer him.

"I've decided to interpret your shrug as full and total agreement."

I slapped him lightly on the arm.

"What?" he laughed. "It props up my high school reunion theory."

"It's not a—"

"What do you do when you're not on Reddit?"

Smooth, Thom. At least he agreed a change of subject was in order.

Was he undercover? Was he secretly a counselor going incognito so he could confront us about our personal lives when we least expected it? It would explain his persistence, and why he wouldn't tell me his internet addiction; maybe he didn't have one.

"Freelance writer. I'd love to sell a book someday, but it's hard to find the time."

"You're here for six weeks with no distractions," he pointed out. "Hundreds of hours of uninterrupted writing time, a king-size bed, meals prepared. It's practically a writing retreat."

"Pshaw. Have you *met* any writers? How am I supposed to write if I don't have the internet to procrastinate with?"

His lips quirked in a half smile. The little fang I noticed earlier made an appearance.

"What kind of freelance?" He sounded genuinely curious.

"Have you heard of *Living* magazine?"

"*Southern Living*?"

"Just *Living*. They usually have a vibrant fifty-five-year-old on the cover, smiling so hard you'd swear there's a gun against her head that's been Photoshopped out."

"I think I've seen it at the doctor's."

"Well, I wrote for its chief competitor, *Dying*."

He sputtered. "That's not a thing."

"Oh yes. It's a niche market. Although technically everyone's in it," I finished spookily.

"You're totally messing with me right now."

"It's real, I swear. Look it up next time you're online."

"And waste my precious fifteen minutes?"

"Holly Danner: Contributing Writer."

"What kind of articles would that even entail?"

"Wills, power of attorney, Is Hospice Care Right for *You*?, plots. Riveting, I know."

He looked disturbed. "Plots? Like, how to fend them off, that sort of thing?"

"Not plots *against* you. *Cemetery* plots. *Final resting places.* Paranoid much?"

"Sorry," he guffawed. "I didn't—I couldn't figure out if..."

"Anyway, it doesn't matter now. They fired me. I got fired by *Dying* magazine."

For the first time since it happened, the hilarity of the situation overcame me. How bad did things have to get, to be fired by *Dying* magazine? I guess he wondered the same thing because we couldn't stop laughing. A tear of unhinged delight poked at my eye. We leaned toward each other and I even smacked the table, helplessly.

"Ow," I lamented.

He pretended to check on my injury. My body didn't understand he was joking, and little tendrils of joy shot up my arm from his touch as he examined my palm. Our faces scrunched up with more laughter and my ribs hurt. I couldn't figure out why nobody had shushed us or glared at us yet. Come to think of it, the room was a little dark, too.

That's when I noticed we were alone. Group ended twenty minutes ago and everyone else had left. I thought about pointing it out to him, but stopped myself in time. If he hadn't noticed, why ruin the rapport we had going? And if he had noticed but kept it to himself, all the better; that meant he was as protective of the bubble that had formed around us as I was. We were safe, here. Together.

A comfortable silence settled between us as we caught our breath.

"All right, let's get into it." I elbowed him gently. "Why are you here?"

"I don't want you to know," he replied quietly.

It was an abrupt end to our hysteria a moment before.

"A hint, at least?"

He shook his head.

"I won't judge you. Probably." I winked, trying to draw him out.

"That's because you don't know, and I'd like to keep it that way."

"Were you going to leave next week without telling me?"

"Ideally." He smiled, but it wasn't the lazy, sunshine-and-mimosas smile from earlier. It was tense.

He'd been going online for two weeks already, starting after the third week, which meant he had only one week to go.

Who would I talk to after he left?

He mimed finding his phone in his pocket. Pretended to swipe and unlock it, and widened his eyes. "Would you look at the time?"

"Yeah, yeah."

"I need to hit the pool before they close it for the night."

I blushed, remembering what he looked like in those butt-hugging red swim trunks. If I'd noticed his impressive physique, surely other people had, too. Depriving him from swimming was like depriving the population of the hospital at large.

"Don't let me keep you," I said.

Despite the downturn of the conversation at the end, I felt a vague, humming sense of contentment for the connection we'd made and what tomorrow might bring.

12

I had to wait a few days before we had the chance to speak again. With all his prep work for "returning to IRL" he missed a couple of group sessions. At midnight on the second day, I slunk out of my room carrying my backpack, to buy a snack from the vending machine.

When she'd dropped me off, Renee gave me a Ziploc bag of quarters for precisely this purpose, but the choices were distinctly unappealing: ramen noodles, protein bars, white cheddar popcorn, and Sour Cream & Onion Tato Skins.

I reluctantly punched in the code for the Tato Skins, which got stuck above the exit flap. *Of course.* I reared back and—

"Don't kick it," said a voice. Startled, I whirled around, heart pounding.

"Here, just sway it," Thom told me, and wrapped his arms around the sides of the machine like they were dancing.

"If you guys want to be alone, I can give you some privacy."

He pushed on the machine a few times until the Tato Skins fell through. He stooped and retrieved them.

"Thanks. The sad part is, I don't even want them. Whatever happened to *plain* Tato Skins? Original style. Those were so good. Why does everything have to have flavor dust all over it?"

"Old Lady Danner has a lot of opinions. I think someone could use a subscription to *Dying* magazine."

I snorted. "What are you doing up?"

"Couldn't sleep. Thought I'd take a walk, and then I saw you about to lay down some violence."

We sat together at the plastic picnic table, passing the Tato Skins back and forth like a flask.

"You want something else to eat?" I asked.

"Sure."

I reached down to open my Ziploc bag, and the movement knocked over my backpack. It fell off the picnic bench, and its contents scattered across the floor, including a rectangle of cardboard with puffy stickers strategically placed on it.

Thom's hand flew to his mouth and his eyes went big.

"Shhh," I begged, and looked around for witnesses.

"It's you! You're the bandit!"

"No, I—I found it—"

"You're the bandit!"

"Shh! It just, it made me so mad."

"It made all of us mad, but we didn't feel the need to *steal* it."

"You won't tell, will you?"

"Can I see it?"

I pressed it into his palm. He examined it, stroking his thumb over the stickers. "Why did it make us so mad?" he wondered.

"I don't know. Maybe we were jealous he thought of it and we didn't?"

"And here we all thought you'd be more moral, somehow, or that you weren't as fucked up as the rest of us," he mused.

I stuffed the stolen talisman in my pocket. "What do you mean?"

"You've only had 'poor internet habits' for two months, right?"

"Right..."

"Most of us are going on years. Didn't you think it was a little strange they let you in the program right away?"

"I didn't give it much thought. I figured it was a rolling admission."

"It is, but the only reason they had an opening was because Carl got kicked out."

"Oh." Great, I was an outsider in real life for having an addiction, and an outsider in rehab for not being addicted *enough*. I shook off the self-pity and focused back on Thom. "Why did Carl get kicked out?"

Thom's face radiated excitement. He could barely wait to tell me. "You're not going to believe this."

"Tell me, tell me!"

"He smuggled in a phone. Huge scandal."

"He smuggled—how?"

"Uh...well..." He scratched the back of his neck, and the tips of his ears turned pink.

Now I *needed* to know. "Is that why we aren't allowed to bring in stuffed animals from the gift shop?" (Renee had purchased a SEE YOU BEAR-Y SOON bear for me as a joke, and it was promptly confiscated.) "Is it because of Carl? Did he gut one and shove the phone inside?"

I'd seen that plot on more than one TV show, albeit to hide jewels.

"Getting warmer..." Thom said. His discomfort should have clued me in, but in a testament to my not-quite-so-addicted addiction, I couldn't fathom the lengths some people would go to, to keep their phones.

"Just tell me."

"He, uh, used his 'prison pocket.'"

"Prison pocket? What's that?" Then it hit me. "Oh my God. Ew! How does that even...ow!"

"It's a tough act to follow," Thom sputtered. "You'll never live up to that."

"Jesus."

"We should throw this out," he said, referring to the cardboard iPhone.

We tore it into unidentifiable pieces and scattered it like ashes into several different trash cans throughout the wing so as not to arouse suspicion. It felt like disposing of a body.

The hospital was peaceful in the middle of the night. The only sounds were the tap of our shoes, our hushed giggling, and the droning hum of the vending machine.

I don't know if it was the late hour or if he felt like opening up, but once we finished our task, we kept walking through the dimly lit hallways. It was the closest we could get to an evening stroll.

"Did you like slumber parties when you were a kid?" he asked. "Staying up late, raiding the fridge?"

"I hated them, actually. Being trapped at someone's house, not knowing where anything was, being forced to watch movies I didn't like."

"Like what?"

"Let's see, when I was ten, my friends were into John Hughes movies because of their older sisters. *Ferris Bueller*,

Sixteen Candles. I thought they were appalling. They had so many bad words."

"They did?"

"Oh yeah. My tender ears."

"I was traumatized by the Pinhead movies," he admitted. "Freddy and Jason, too. All that shit gave me nightmares." He gave a courtly bow. "Pardon my language."

I swatted him lightly, rolling my eyes. "Do you keep in touch with any of your school friends from Ohio? I know you don't go to reunions, but..."

"Nah. My junior high friends were dicks. I had some decent ones in high school, but we've mostly drifted apart."

"What made them dicks?"

"I remember one of the birthday parties at my neighbor's house. Alex. We'd been close since kindergarten, and we both loved *Calvin and Hobbes*. This was '93, '94, when it was still syndicated. I cut out and saved every Sunday strip—so they'd be in color—all year so I could make wrapping paper out of them. I taped the strips together and if you were careful when you lifted the biggest flap on the present, you'd be able to keep them together, have a poster for your wall. Everyone put their gifts on the kitchen table when we arrived, so you didn't know whose was whose. One of his other friends made fun of it all day, like 'Who was too cheap to buy wrapping paper? Who used this shitty baby cartoon from a newspaper?'"

"Fuck that kid."

He feigned shock. "*Sixteen Candles* was a bad influence."

"Yeah, it was all downhill from there. Did your friend come to your defense?"

"Nah, he acted like he was just as confused as everyone else, and when it was time to open them up and see what he got, he ripped the whole thing into pieces while everyone laughed, to show how cool and above it he was." Thom swallowed. "Last I heard, he's been in and out of rehab for opiates. Happened to a lot of guys I used to know."

"Oh man. I'm sorry."

He explained that the neighborhood where he grew up in Ohio was considered one of the first pill mills. When he was a sophomore, a cabal of greasy-haired, red-eyed doctors with expired licenses and marks on their records slithered in from other states to set up shop. They handed out Oxycontin prescriptions like taffy, the slow-release ones that kept patients either perpetually stoned or perpetually vomiting from withdrawals, and when the crackdown on scrips came, people turned to black tar heroin, which was actually cheaper to buy. Thom's parents still lived there but he rarely visited them; instead, he flew them out to New York every Christmas and Fourth of July.

I still didn't know what his addiction was.

13

Reddit/AMA

[WickedBlintz]: I'd like to address the most troubling aspects of the show. Why was Brody Rutherford cast in the role of DIEGO? I know it was the '90s, but how was that okay?? He was vaguely ethnic, in a Freddie Prinze Jr. kind of way, but **obviously** coded white, and **obviously** not Latino, which is problematic on so many levels, especially when San Diego is, like, one mile from the Mexican border and the Studdards could have easily found someone who more accurately represented what the name Diego implies!! Secondly, the "token black girl" was BRITISH. Why couldn't she be an AMERICAN black girl? Was that somehow too threatening? Too controversial? And from a logical standpoint, WTF? We are talking about runaways who lived at the zoo—why and how did a girl from England get to California on her own??

[HollyD]: I hear you! I'll do my best to answer, but keep in mind I was in middle school at the time and didn't have a clue how offensive some of the choices were; also, there really is no good answer to your questions. I'm glad you brought up the Studdards (the show's producers/financiers) because everything stems from them. The first thing you have to understand is that they had more money than sense and had never worked in entertainment before. Mrs. Studdard, a grain-processing heiress and philanthropist from Point Loma, happened to be at the San Diego Zoo with her bird-watching group when the idea for a kids' show came to her. She and her husband funded the program primarily as a tax shelter and relied obsessively on focus groups of children to supply the show's content. If you visited the San Diego Zoo in the summer of 1989, and you were 5 to 9 years old, you were handed a piece of paper upon admittance that asked what you'd like to see in an animal-themed upcoming PBS show. The problem was, from what I can tell, they used every concept they received. Nothing was too ambitious or bizarre. What if the kids adopted a different zoo animal each week and took care of it, learning all the details of its life, habitat, and eating habits? What if there were different themes each day to determine which animal got the spotlight? What if the kids spun a wheel like on *Wheel of Fortune* and it landed on different categories like Leapin' Lizards, 'Mazing Monkeys, and Rockin' Rhinos? What if our characters were orphans who lived and worked at the zoo? What if we hid in the bathroom stalls at night and survived off coins thrown in the fountain? (That part was flat-out stolen from *The Mixed-Up Files of Mrs. Basil E. Frankweiler*; luckily it never made it to air, and our "dorm/house" became the titular lion's den instead.) And then the biggest, splashiest suggestion: What if we weren't just orphans, we were orphans who'd formed a *band* and were looking for our big break? As for the deeply flawed casting decisions, they were based on the Studdards' premade travel plans; they held open calls wherever they happened to be on vacation. Tara was discovered in London, and they didn't bother to give her (or any of the other kids, to be fair) any sort of backstory. We emerged whole cloth in the lion's den, without parental supervision until midway through season 2 when the roles of zookeepers Ed and Martha were added. If the Studdards had visited Mexico instead of Texas that fall, perhaps we'd have found a Diego who better fit the name. The only reason they even called him that was so we could refer to the location of the zoo. The Studdards' cluelessness doesn't excuse the issues, but it all starts there.

Essentially, if you pull any thread—plot, characters, casting, setting—the whole thing falls apart.

[AngBee]: First impressions of the ***original*** cast, please. (Only Brody, Tara, Kelly, and J. J., please. Don't care about Melody or Ethan.)

[HollyD]: Sure. Brody and Tara were always paired together for duets, partly because they could be counted on to hit the high notes, and partly because Brody tried much harder when Tara was around because he wanted to impress her. She was the only one of us with bona fide musical theater chops, having appeared in a West End production of *The Wiz* as one of Glinda's court girls prior to being cast. Both of Tara's parents flew to San Diego to help her settle in, but only her mother stayed for the long haul. Her dad traveled back and forth to Merry Old on business. If Tara was homesick for Britain, she never let on, though she did receive regular shipments of Fry's Turkish

Delight bars that she hid from everyone except Brody.

They were always huddled together laughing and practicing, although they were given much less dialogue than the rest of us, because their speaking voices were...concerning. Tara's British accent was difficult for her to shed, but because she kept trying, she sounded like someone from a fake country, like Balki from *Perfect Strangers*. Brody couldn't memorize a single line of text, let alone any Spanish words. Also, he laughed through every sketch. I'm not saying that to be mean. *He laughed through every sketch.*

Kelly Hale was a Botticelli painting come to life. She was also four years older than the rest of us and we all wanted to be her, because (a) she could drive, and (b) she made it *cool* to be nice, and that set the tone for the set and everyone who worked on the show. The first time we met she told me I looked like Cindy Crawford. Probably because of my bushy eyebrows. She drew a mole on my face with eyeliner once, and she told me that toothpaste, dotted on problem areas, would nuke zits. She was our hero.

As for J. J., he was skinny, with curly brown hair and large glasses. The Carolina Panthers football jersey he wore swallowed him whole; a stiff wind from the Pacific would've sent him into orbit, with the enormous jersey serving as a parachute. If the kids at my school had heard him speak ("Ah'm hankerin' for a Coke. Y'all got any?"), they would've eaten him alive. His birdie wrists were smaller than mine. His Reebok high-tops were unlaced, a pratfall waiting to happen. He was eleven, like me, but he looked about nine. His speaking voice was piping high, but when he opened his mouth to sing, a gorgeous baritone came out, shocking us all. He was small, vulnerable, open. His parents wanted nothing to do with Hollywood and tried to yank him off the show after the first week.

14

Friday evening I planned a wild night of reading an *Elle* magazine from 2009 when a knock sounded on my door.

"Holly?" called a bright voice.

"Be right there."

The only pajamas I had brought to Prevail! were a thick gray flannel with pink polka dots on them. I finished buttoning up the top and opened the door.

Lisa's assistant stood in the hall looking young, adorable, and helpful.

"Sorry to bother you, Miss Danner, but you have a phone call."

"It's no bother."

Only one person had my number here. After thanking Lisa's assistant, I practically skipped to the private phone room when a chilling thought hit me: Why were they calling from Belgium? Wasn't it three a.m. there? Was something wrong?

Renee traveled there every other year with Mom and Dad for research—her Belgian bistro, Gaufre It, specialized in *gaufre* (waffles) and *pommes frites* (fries). This was the first time

Lainey had gone on the trip. She would be celebrating her eleventh birthday there.

"Hey, you guys okay?" I asked breathlessly. My concerns poured out nonsensically. "What's going on? When did you get in? Did you find the children's melatonin? Did you have her drink a glass of water for each hour of the flight?"

Turning off the part of my brain that worried about Lainey was easier said than done. I craved information. No one answered my greeting. Had we lost the connection? When Lainey was younger our phone calls had abrupt endings—when she learned to talk on the phone, instead of saying goodbye before hanging up, she'd say, "The end!"—but this was different.

"It's me."

Oh.

Shit.

No.

My heart beat so rapidly it seemed to make my entire body shake. My hands tingled and I thought I might throw up. It was about a thousand times worse than the feeling I'd had in Lisa's office when I realized my iPhone was so far away.

It took me a moment to recover my voice. "How did you find me?"

I sounded quiet, and timid, and I hated him for it.

"I saw Renee at church and she gave me the number."

"Oh. You're in San Diego right now?"

"Has it really been five years? What have you been up to?"

I couldn't possibly dignify that with a response. What was I supposed to say? *While you traveled the world in a private jet, I staged a coup at the local bookstore and took over the Saturday Storytime so my niece wouldn't have to listen to mumblers who couldn't enunciate or emote? And it was an honest-to-God highlight?*

He sighed at my lack of response. It did not move me.

"I thought it was just me you weren't talking to, but Tara and Kelly said they haven't heard from you, either. And I saw Ethan and Melody at the—" (He was about to say something impossibly obnoxious, like *the Golden Globes*, or *the McGregor fight in Vegas*, but cut himself off.) "Anyway, even Brody was like, 'Where's Hol-Hol at? It's been a minute, yo.'"

His version of Brody used to crack me up.

"I didn't realize you weren't talking to *anyone*," he added quietly.

"What do you want?" My voice quivered, which only made me feel more helpless and angry. I'd had no time to prepare for the possibility of him contacting me.

"I'm sorry you're not doing well. I kept expecting to hear that you sold a novel or something, I look for it whenever I'm in a bookstore, and—"

"Nope."

"Can I... Will you let me pay for your rehab?"

"What? No. Why?"

"Whatever it costs, I'll wire it to your bank—"

"I don't want your *money*," I said.

(No way in hell was I telling him the program was free.)

"It's nothing, let me do this for you."

"I would never accept it from you." My words came out in a rush. They felt harsh in my throat, like they'd been painstakingly scraped from it.

The shock of hearing his voice after so long made it hard to breathe. I had to remind myself to do it; my brain was no longer capable of performing automatically.

"Come on, Holly. Don't be this way. I'm trying to reach out."

"And now you have, so..." *The end!*

"Wait, there's something else I—"

I hung up before I lost the strength to do so.

The entire conversation was forty seconds, max, but I felt as though I'd landed after an eighteen-hour flight. I would've loved that to be true. I would've loved to be in Belgium right then. Unreachable.

I stood there in a daze, light-headed and dry-throated.

Eventually I staggered back to my room, hugging the walls and keeping my head down. My hairline and underarms were slick with sweat, and my heart blasted so hard in my chest it turned my pulse into a bass drum. I'd been ready for bed before I spoke to him, but now it seemed unlikely I'd ever get to sleep. Frustrated adrenaline would keep me up for hours while I parsed his words and my dumbfounded responses for meaning.

Why the fuck had Renee given him my number?

The humiliation hit me like a wave. I didn't want anyone to know I was here, but especially not them. Not *him*. The whole point of showing up at the anniversary was to surprise them. I hadn't wanted to be in their thoughts prior to that.

On the plus side, *Prevail!* was a vague term, creamy with hope; it could mean anything.

If they found out I needed to be *separated from society* for Googling the shit out of them, stalking their social media accounts 24/7, and writing essays on Reddit about the old days, I would crumble into dust and blow away.

Maybe I should do that anyway. Maybe it would be a goddamn relief to disappear.

Why, oh why couldn't *they* be the ones to disappear, for once?

I was awash in memories, pain, and regret when another knock interrupted my racing thoughts.

"Who is it?" I warbled through tears.

"Thom. Can we talk for a sec?" he asked. I didn't remember his voice being that low. It was oddly soothing.

I cracked the door open. "You can come in, but I don't feel like talking."

He hesitated in the doorway, eyeing my full-body flannel pajamas. "Expecting some gale-force winds tonight?"

"What's up?" I muttered.

He ran a hand through his messy hair. "I, uh, I was just..."

I was intrigued. In the two weeks I'd known him, he'd never tripped over his words. I wasn't in the mood to make things easy, though. I stared back, blank-faced and expectant.

"Yeah, so there's a field trip, for lack of a better word, at the Mall of America tomorrow. I wasn't sure if you heard about it."

I didn't give an inch. "Uh-huh."

He slipped his thumb into his empty belt loop (no belts allowed) and returned to his usual cocky self. "And I was thinking: you, me, a slice of pizza at Sbarro..."

I leaned against the doorframe, monotone. "Are you asking me on a date?"

"I wouldn't call it a date, exactly, but we have to travel in pairs when we're out in public. Prevail! policy, so nobody sneaks off to an internet café or asks a stranger to borrow their phone," he said. "No arcade games, either. You know, screens..."

We looked at each other in silence. I let my gaze drop to his jeans, and the thumb that was so near to his zipper.

"Why wait? We could have a date right now," I said.

I barely registered the look of surprise on his face as I grabbed a fistful of his shirt and pulled him into my room. The heavy door slammed shut behind him.

It was true, what I'd told him a moment ago. I didn't feel like talking.

My fingers deftly undid the first two buttons of my flannel ensemble.

Thom's baby blues went wide and it was nice to have rendered him speechless.

I tugged his hand forward and placed it around my waist. Tilted my head up toward his and gave him a soft kiss.

He froze. "Isn't this…against the rules? I've been here longer than anyone, and I'm pretty sure that, uh, there's no fraternization."

" 'Against the rules'?" I mocked. "Look at these beds. They're enormous. It's practically an invitation." I kissed him again, and teased his bottom lip with my tongue. He tasted like an after-dinner mint, with a hint of chocolate.

Thom glanced nervously behind him. "The room doesn't have a lock."

"You could always push me up against the door. That'll keep people out," I suggested. I licked my lips, enjoying the flavor I stole from him. "And I can be quick."

"…I'm not sure this is a good idea."

I opened the remaining buttons of my top.

He watched my every movement. I could feel his hot, fluorescent gaze on my pale skin.

"Is there a Mrs. Thom?" I asked.

"What? No. But there's a—"

"Then what's the problem?"

I tried to lift his T-shirt off but he gripped both my wrists in his hand, halting my progress.

"Is that what you like?" I whispered. "I can be down with that." Wrists still pinned together, I climbed his body and curled one of my legs around his hip. I wanted him to know how certain I was, how much I'd like for him to help me forget all about the phone call with J. J.

I reached for his zipper, letting my fingers brush against his denim-clad hardness.

"Oh," I murmured appreciatively. "You'll do nicely."

"I'll 'do'?" he repeated.

"Hmm?" I asked dreamily.

He pulled away.

"So if Ryan or someone had shown up tonight instead, you'd have invited *him* in?"

"Who's Ryan?" I racked my brain. "Do you mean Wikipedia Avenger? Yeah, no. He's crazy."

"The people here have names, you know. You've been here long enough to know them."

"I know *your* name. Don't you want to hear how it sounds on my lips when you're—"

He shook his head. Squeezed my hand. "I'm sorry. This doesn't feel right."

"We're never going to see each other again. You leave in, what, three days? Don't worry, I'm not going to come after you, I'm not going to *look you up*—"

"That sort of makes it worse."

He bent over, scooped up my flannel top, and handed it to me without looking me in the eyes.

"Get some rest," he said, and walked out the door.

Alone again, the tears I'd been holding in since the phone

call filled my eyes and sluiced down my cheeks. I brought the flannel to my face and cried hard for a few minutes, the kind of crying where you make noises you don't recognize, noises that don't correspond to words or sense or logic. The only thing left to do was feel the pain in its entirety and hope I could move through it.

After I exhausted myself and fell, limp, on the bed, my thoughts cohered into a damning realization:

I almost had unprotected sex with a stranger in rehab.

There was a term for that, according to Melody: Rehab Roulette.

After Mel crashed her Mercedes into the Beverly Center nine years ago, she'd dried out at a drug and alcohol treatment center and engaged in Rehab Roulette with a few different guys. (This was during a break from her latest contractual faux-mance.) Upon release, she spent the entirety of her pregnancy scare at my parents' house in San Diego, hiding from the paps. Renee and I bought her pregnancy tests and stayed up watching '80s movies and talking until the wee hours. No one knew the location of the "halfway house" she'd retreated to or the fact that a select handful of her peers used it whenever they were in trouble. (Which was frequently. Suburban anonymity cured a variety of fame-related ailments.)

When she'd had her fill, she took a helicopter back to LA.

Back to live-in chefs, masseuses, personal assistants, and stylists.

"You're so lucky, Holly," she told me once, in her oblivious way. "You don't have to worry about how you look, or what you do, or what you wear, because nobody cares."

For all I knew, J. J. had already told her I was in treatment. For all I knew, he'd already texted everyone, and they were all "smh" over it, because what was more pathetic than somebody who wasn't rich having rich-people problems? What was more pathetic than Holly Danner, former nanny and failed writer, acting like her behavior even mattered?

Texting the others didn't sound like J. J., though. He always knew how to keep a secret. Especially when the secret was me.

Having wrung myself dry emotionally, I slipped a fingertip between my legs to test out my slickness. There was an ache to go with it, that empty feeling that ballooned inside me when I thought I was going to get laid. Without Thom or anyone else to fill up the emptiness, that ache felt like rejection and neediness. Yup, miserable and horny. Gee, why did Thom possibly turn me down?

Maybe Thom was right about child stars never growing up. None of my relationships lasted long, apart from J. J. And that relationship had been conducted in short bursts that happened to be repeated many, many times.

I wish I'd had the wherewithal to bitch him out on the phone.

You don't get to do this anymore, I should have said. *You're not allowed to pop back into my life as though it were on pause, waiting for you to give it meaning.*

You may think losing your virginity to a pop star would be all sexy slow-mo, soft lighting, and pristine, tangled sheets. Instead it was confusion and soreness and tenderness and laughter, breaks for water, a leg cramp or two, and more love than a hundred lovesick puppies could muster. My parents had maintained it was puppy love but I knew it was the real thing, intense and authentic and painful, like a mixtape with only one song on it. A song that dared you to prove your devotion by listening to each possible version (a cappella, instrumental, and EDM remixes), over and over, both sides. A song designed to slowly drive you mad.

Our first time was in London over Christmas. We were seventeen. He was touring with OffBeat for their first album. The group's manager, Pamela, had corralled the boys together in Texas, but they lived and worked in pop-friendly Europe for several years while they honed their sound and experimented with different group members before debuting Stateside. She flew me out a few times to make up for the fact that J. J. couldn't travel home and escort me to Renee's wedding. You might think that was an extravagant apology—a trip to Merry Old on Christmas break, all expenses paid, a hotel on Marylebone Street, the Covent Garden Christmas tree, ice skating at Somerset House, Victorian funfair rides at Kew, glamour shopping at Harrods—but in my teenage brain, grudges were nurtured not assuaged. I was still pissed I'd be flying solo as maid of honor the following month, when Renee said her vows at Camp Pendleton with Ian, her marine fiancé.

Our reunion was passionate, and for the first time we didn't stop at kissing. We were both nervous. I bled. More than was expected; I'd gotten my period early. It looked like a crime scene. The white satin sheets were smeared with red; like the pure white snow outside, dotted with red holiday lights; or the thick clotted cream speckled with raspberry jam on the scones we ate at the Three Wishes café.

Afterward, we clung to each other, sticky and sated and shaking in our small, love-wrecked bodies. I twisted my fingers around the damp tuft of hair on the small of his back. It felt like it belonged to me and no one else.

When he spoke, he was solemn and earnest: "If we go to hell, it'll be worth it."

I thought it was the most romantic thing anyone would ever say to me.

In a weird way, I still did. He truly believed he would burn in eternal hellfire because of what we'd done with our bodies and hearts. That was intoxicating to a teenage girl. It made me feel powerful. But it was something else, too: the beginning of guilt trips and emotional manipulation I endured for years to come. Hot-and-cold running J. J.

When I returned to San Diego, he cut off all contact for a week, including on New Year's Eve when I rang him about twenty times in desperation.

When he finally returned my call, the long-distance echo messed with our ability to hear one another as he tried to explain his guilt-fueled absence.

He had sinned. He had allowed himself to be led astray.

"But it's okay since we love each other," I told him. I should've known there was no argument he couldn't bat away; he'd been going to church twice a week since birth.

"True love waits, Holly," he said between tears.

("What did he mean?" I asked Renee at three in the morning, my voice hoarse from crying. We did a lot of crying, J. J. and me. "Was he saying he wasn't in love with me? That if it was true love we would have waited? Or was he saying he *was* in love with me, and that's why we *were supposed to* have waited?")

As though a bookish seventeen-year-old girl who'd tap-danced her way onto a TV show and now only tap-danced to the fridge, who still slept with a stuffed animal and came in first at Speech Camp, was a temptress. A siren.

To blame.

Unlike J. J., I didn't need to die to experience hell. I was already there. Every time he boarded a plane, or sent a postcard, or cut a phone call short from some exotic locale while I stayed behind, was hell. Being separated from him was hell, like functioning with half a heart, only nobody else could see what was missing, so they couldn't understand why I was mopey all the time. To be fair, most of our breakups over the years were due to misunderstandings, hurt feelings, or poor communication—nothing that couldn't have been fixed by maturation or simply staying in the same city for a while. When our final breakup came, five years ago, there was no mistaking our reasons for saying goodbye. The relief was palpable; just in time for my thirty-first birthday, our breakup gave me a freedom I hadn't experienced since I was eleven, right before I landed a role on *Diego and the Lion's Den*.

I didn't confuse freedom with happiness. But it was still freedom.

Until today.

I pushed my hips into the mattress, determined to get off if only to prove he couldn't hurt me anymore. My movements sped up and I allowed myself a small, muffled cry.

I didn't want to but I thought of Thom, and how, the first time we talked, he said, "I very much doubt that" in a low, knowing voice when I told him I was "Nobody." And I was so full of shame for thinking about him and so full of anger toward him for acting as though he might be interested and then leaving me wanting that I covered my face with a pillow and screamed into it until my throat felt rubbed raw with sandpaper.

15

Reddit/AMA

[mehcrocs]: which of the boys in BeatOff are gay

[HollyD]: What a clever nickname. Never heard that one before. ***rolls eyes***

[mehcrocs] come on don't play dumb what about this from 2004: (source: Gossip Blinders)

"Overheard at an industry cocktail party: 'Try marketing a teenybopper group to girls' parents when at least one of them is in the closet and one of them is stoned 24/7.' Okay, Blinders, which member(s) of this popular band are Lyin'?"

Lyin' = lion = Lion's den, obviously

So?????

[HollyD]: I can't and won't speak to anyone's sexuality but there are a staggering number of fanfics out there for every type of fan, so go nuts

I kept to myself the next few days. Lisa thought I was depressed, which I was, but mainly I was avoiding Thom. If I missed more than three group sessions, though, I'd be out of the program.

At one thirty-seven a.m. of the third day, I was banging on the vending machine to release the Tato Skins I didn't even like when footsteps pattered behind me.

Alarmed, I turned to see who it was. Phew. Only Popaholic.

A part of me was disappointed. A part of me thought he'd find me here, like last time, and we'd walk the quiet halls together.

"I can't believe Thom's leaving tomorrow," she remarked, stifling a yawn.

"I know. Hey, do you know why he was here?" I asked, succumbing to my own yawn and hoping the action made me sound ambivalent and casual.

Don't let it be 4chan.

Don't let it be men's rights.

Neither of those fit him, of course. He was too chivalrous. The way he reassured InstaMom—I mean, Marjorie (*see,*

Thom? I know people's names)—that she shouldn't berate herself for not measuring up to other people's photos had been kind, albeit wrapped up in arrogance.

Also, if he'd been a 4channer or men's rights activist, he probably would've taken me up on my cringe-worthy offer. And then doxed me and posted revenge porn of me topless in my granny pajamas.

Popaholic jabbed her finger on the button for a Diet Coke. "I'm surprised you don't know, given how much you two *linger* after group."

I fisted a bunch of Tato Skins in my mouth. The vile powder clung to my lips and fingertips. "He kept things pretty close to the vest."

She pulled her can of soda from the slot and popped the tab. "I don't know the details, I just know it was bad."

My pulse jumped. "Oh? In what way?"

She sipped and considered my question. "We're all afraid we ruined our lives in some way, but he actually did. Lost his kid…"

"He has a kid?" I was stunned. Had he tried to tell me? Had I been too self-involved to listen?

"Yeah, his son's living somewhere else while he gets help. He's been counting the seconds until he can leave. Before you showed up, we had a running bet he'd take off in the middle of the night."

16

A ritual commemorated Thom's last day. It was optional, so I watched from my bedroom window, on the ground floor, like a coward. I had a straight view of the courtyard, where everyone gathered to release forty-two balloons, one for each day of his stay, symbolizing, I dunno, letting go of his journey. At one point, he looked in the direction of my room and I crept back into the shadows.

When the last balloon disappeared, Lisa handed him his phone and the group stared at it hungrily. I feared Wikipedia Avenger (Bryan? Ryan?) would lunge for it. To my surprise, Thom didn't boot it up in front of the others. He slid it in his back pocket and walked inside the building. Maybe the treatment had worked. I couldn't imagine being so blasé about having my phone back; I would have been flaunting that shit. But for now at least, it didn't seem to have any sort of hold over him.

I pressed my ear against the door so I could hear what they all said in the hallway. Today's breakfast was apparently fiesta eggs with avocado and salsa (dammit, my favorite), and then

Marjorie announced she was heading off to her fifteen minutes of screentime. I was only a day away from joining her, which you would think would make me happy, but instead made me grind my teeth with impatience.

As I waited for everyone to go their separate ways, I re-read the postcard I'd gotten from Lainey and Renee yesterday. Lisa had slipped it under my door, along with a note reminding me I couldn't skip any more sessions if I wanted to stay in the program. The instant Thom left today, I'd rejoin every activity.

The postcard depicted a carnival-looking place in Brussels called Bruparck! ("Aunt Holly, we are both at places with exclamation points in their names," Lainey wrote in her small, messy handwriting.) Renee's part of the message admitted that Lainey was homesick, so they'd visited an amusement park with a Cineplex so they could watch an American movie. Only, the movie had subtitles in three different languages (German, Flemish, and French), which took up more than half the screen, so it was hard to watch.

Surely enough time had passed that it was safe for me to emerge. If I was quick enough, maybe I could snag some of those fiesta eggs.

I cautiously twisted the knob, counted to three, and pushed the door open. Thom waited for me on the other side.

"Woah." I jumped back.

"Sorry, just came to say goodbye." He held up his duffel bag, looking chagrined.

"I'm the one who should apologize," I said, briefly meeting his eyes. For the first time since I'd met him, his hair was combed and parted. Of course. He was finally going home to his son.

"It's okay."

My instinct, when faced with an awkward situation, was to make jokes. "Are you by any chance a devout evangelical? Because I get it, more than you know."

"No, I'm not religious, and before you ask, I'm not gay, either."

"You weren't repulsed by me in the abstract, you were repulsed by me, *specifically*. Glad we cleared that up."

"I wasn't repulsed."

I held up a hand to stop the onslaught of embarrassment. "You don't have to explain."

"It sort of sounds like you want me to, though," he pointed out.

"I asked *one* question. I wasn't demanding a play-by-play." *The end!*

"Okay, no more talking. Only typing." He handed me his phone.

"What are you…?" Was this a peace offering? Was he smuggling me a screen? OH MY GOD. I slid my thumb across the lock bar. Where did I even BEGIN? Email? Reddit? Definitely email. Only a psychopath would go to Reddit first. "Real people" from "life" should get priority. *But Reddit might have new questions. Questions only I can answer.*

Thom watched me paw at the lock screen like a bear.

"Whoops." He keyed in his password and opened his phone contacts. Scrolled to the name he wanted to use and handed over his phone again.

The contact was listed as "Somebody."

My throat went dry.

"Phone number?" he prompted me.

"What for?" I asked.

He looked taken aback. "I thought we could keep in touch, maybe check in with each other."

"We're on opposite coasts, I'm not sure I see the point." I knew from my years with J. J. that long distance was crap and never worked.

He swallowed. "Just a thought." He held out his hand. For a second I thought he wanted to shake, and the formality made me sad. Then I realized he wanted his phone back, which reminded me of how ludicrous his request was; he'd wanted nothing to do with me the other night, but now he wanted to keep in touch?

"It seems a little hypocritical, your sudden interest," I mumbled.

He rubbed his forehead. "Ohhh-kay, you know what, Holly…?"

"Was I not romantic enough for you? Because I'm never going to be the kind of person who says, *I have baggage and you have baggage but somehow, together, we're a matched set.*"

"Except that you *are*, because you *just did*," he replied.

His I'm-calm-you're-crazy routine was maddening, especially because he knew what I meant.

I was about to tell him that when InstaMom cannonballed between us, splashing with news.

"Holly, there you are. I have to tell you something!"

I expected Thom to flee at her girlie drama, but his eyes darted between us, curious.

"Are you okay? What's wrong?" I asked, placing a hand on her arm. Her excited motions flung me off.

"Whoops, sorry, I was online, at the *Daily Denizen*."

I was instantly on edge. "Why? That's *my* addiction."

"Yeah, you can't have it." Thom waggled his finger mockingly.

"I just mean—I'd hate for you to get sucked into a different problem when you're supposed to be treating your Instagram habit," I clarified lamely.

"You're territorial over your addiction," Thom chided me. "Lisa," he fake-whined. "Holly's not sharing."

I wanted to stomp my foot at him.

"No, listen," Instagram Mom cried. "I did it on purpose. It was relaxing, checking on yours instead of mine. It's a technique they call cross-pollination; you'll learn about it soon."

Her anxious frivolity was contagious. My heart thrummed and my body tensed.

"What'd you want to tell me?" I asked.

"Didn't you say the reunion is in a month?"

"Friday, May twenty-sixth."

"It's actually on Friday, *April twenty-fourth*."

Today was Wednesday, April 22, according to the dry erase board of announcements in the hallway. If Marjorie was telling the truth, that was two days away. Which was *impossible*.

My throat constricted and I frantically swallowed. "No, it can't be. It's in May. After I leave here."

"The *Daily Denizen* has a countdown clock up, and it said two days, ten hours, and five minutes."

"No, that can't be right."

" 'La la la, I'm not listening,' " Thom impersonated me.

"Don't you have somewhere to be?" I exploded.

Everyone in the hallway—and cafeteria—gaped at us. Thom slung his duffel bag over his shoulder and marched out of my life. Regret washed over me.

There was no time to dwell, though. I clutched InstaMom's arm, tightly this time so she couldn't flail me off. "Are you absolutely sure about this?"

She nodded vigorously. "It's at Rockefeller Center, eight p.m."

"New York?" I squeak-screamed. "Not San Diego?"

"It was moved because of a scheduling conflict."

"No, it's supposed to be in San Diego. In a month. After I leave here."

"Tara has a Broadway show opening the next night, so they moved it up a month and changed it from West Coast to East Coast."

"The whole point was it would be in San Diego, where the show was filmed. Near my house."

"I'm only telling you what I read."

"But—"

"You can believe me or not."

"Right. Yes. Thank you," I responded by rote. My voice sounded far away, distant, hopeless.

I paced in an ever-widening circle, muttering denials to myself.

The others observed me, moving back as one unit as the circumference of my path widened. They probably wondered if they were witnessing a full-blown mental collapse. *Was this what happened to Carl after his iPhone was discovered in its "hiding place"? Am I the new Carl?*

I broke the loop I was in and ran to Lisa's office. I told her I had an emergency and needed to leave right away. She was not thrilled.

"*You* came to *us*," she reminded me. "You wanted to make changes in your life, and you will, but only if you give the program a chance to work."

"Maybe I'm not even a real addict," I said. "Thom told me I was a replacement for a guy who got kicked out."

"You may not have been struggling as long as the others, but I saw the potential for it to get much worse. Why not stay and prevent that from happening?"

"I'll come back, I swear. You can hold my spot for me. I'll even start over from scratch. But I need to go to the reunion—I mean, anniversary." *Stupid Thom, getting in my head.*

"How will you possibly travel to New York?" Lisa asked, her eyebrow raised, her bifocals inching down. In fact, all her circles—from her necklace to the sun graphics on her whimsical blouse—looked like they were frowning at me.

I ticked off the possibilities. "Rent a car, catch a flight, ride a bus, take a train, does it matter?"

"When your sister dropped you off, she took all your personal effects with her for safekeeping."

Fuckity-fuck.

Seeing the eerie blankness to my face, she tried a gentler tack. "What you're feeling is perfectly normal. The panic, the withdrawal, the desire to escape, everyone goes through it. Everyone. But it's going to be okay. And hey, tomorrow you get fifteen minutes online. You're so close. The second phase is about to begin, and you don't want to miss it. The first thing we'll be teaching you is cross-pollination..."

My brain entered hyperdrive. There had to be an answer, there had to be a way. True, Renee had all my stuff. Besides my laptop and iPhone, she had my purse, which she couldn't FedEx to me because she was out of the country, and my parents couldn't use their spare key to get it because they were with her. No one else could get in the house—I'd always been the backup. *Who was my backup?* Without my credit card or ATM I couldn't buy a plane ticket, and without my license I couldn't board the flight anyway. Nor could I rent a car. I could hitchhike—if I didn't mind ending up in a bunch of jars.

"If you leave the program early, you'll forfeit your per diem," Lisa blathered on.

"Oh no, not the ten bucks," I moaned sarcastically.

That's when I remembered.

Thom lived in upstate New York.

And he's driving there right now.

"I'm sorry, that was rude, but I do have to go," I told Lisa. "Um, could I have *part* of the per diem? No? Okay, no, I get it..."

I signed myself out "against counselor's advice" and grabbed my backpack of clothes and my notebook from my room: all my earthly possessions.

I gazed longingly at the massive, comfortable king-size bed. I would miss that bed. The past twenty-odd days with it had given me the longest, most luxurious nights of sleep I could recall.

I raced to catch up with Thom in the parking garage, which smelled like wet paint. He was piling his stuff into an ancient Volkswagen Passat. It was the color of rust. No, wait, it was actually rusted. All over.

"Thom!"

His back went rigid and he turned slowly to face me. "Come to yell at me one more time before I go?"

"The anniversary got moved to New York."

"I heard. The entire hospital heard."

He went to shut the trunk. I tossed my backpack inside first.

"Take me with you," I pleaded.

"No can do, buckaroo," was his reply, and the single most irritating phrase I'd ever heard. He retrieved my backpack and placed it on the ground, slammed the trunk fast this time, and moved to get into the driver's seat.

I placed my hand on his arm. It was warm and firm. He tensed slightly and looked at me.

"I will find a way to get there, with or without you, but if I'm sliced up by the Minnesota Mangler, or whoever, they're probably going to want to interview you."

My hand still rested on his arm. A partial tattoo peeked out from beneath his shirtsleeve. I wondered what it was. Thom gently extracted my hand and placed it back at my side. It felt like the rejection in my room all over again.

Tears of frustration stung my eyes. "Is it so horrifying that I kissed you? It's all right if it is, but then you probably shouldn't have been flirting with me all week."

His eyebrows flew sky-high. "Flirting? When did I flirt?"

"I seem to recall an offer of pizza at a certain Mall of America?" I hated that those words lived in my brain and found a way out.

His baby-blue eyes bored into mine. "If I were to flirt with you, there would be no confusion about it. You would know."

His words, and the anger in his voice, gave me a little thrill. God knew why.

His voice lowered, and his eyes darted around. "Look. It's *because* I like you that I'm not going to take you with me."

I couldn't decipher his logic. He *wasn't* flirting, but he *did* like me? How did that work, exactly?

"Thanks, nice, that's helpful," I said in clipped tones.

"Why are you so determined to go?" he asked. "The fact they moved it up is a gift. Now you can forget about it and focus on yourself." He nodded back toward the hospital.

"You wouldn't understand."

"Try me."

I closed my eyes for a second, loathing what I was about to admit. Loathing how pathetic it would make me sound. "I don't have a 'self' without it. It's the only thing I've ever accomplished, and it happened when I was eleven. I peaked when I was eleven. Do you have any idea what that feels like? I'm thirty-six now, and what do I have to show for it? I never finished college, I forgot to marry and have my own kids because I was raising my sister's daughter, and now that I finally told them, 'It's time for *me*,' it's probably too late. What was the point of anything in the last twenty-five years?"

I waited for him to interrupt, or contradict my words, but he simply looked at me, so I kept going.

"See, when I was eleven... anything was possible. Anything could have happened after that. I was on *fucking TV*, back when that *meant* something. I auditioned and I was chosen and I was *good at it.* I did photo shoots, I got fan mail, gifts and letters, like the rest of them. But after I turned sixteen and the show got canceled, that's where it stopped for me. Everyone else, that was the beginning of everything, their *lives*, but for me it was the end. It's the only thing in my life I can look at and say, 'I did that. That really happened, that was mine,' and now they want to take it from me, pretend I wasn't there, that it *didn't* happen. I can't let them do that. It's all I have," I repeated, my throat sore. "It's all I will ever have."

He absorbed my words. I struggled for breath, and my neck flared with heat.

"I'm sorry," he said at last. "But I'm not taking you."

"I can get you home faster to your son," I blurted out. I felt gruesome saying it. "If we take turns driving while the other one sleeps, we'll get there twice as fast."

Thom looked surprised, but then his eyes narrowed. "How do you know about Sammy?"

"A few of us were talking, and someone mentioned you were in a hurry to get back to him."

"Yeah. I am."

He climbed in the driver's side and slammed the door shut. Jammed the key in the ignition. If he left, all hope of crashing the anniversary went with him.

"Please?" I begged. "*Please?*"

Thom rolled down the window. Slowly, and with effort.

Dear God, it's a crank handle. That's how old and decrepit his car is.

He pushed his closed fists against his eyes for a second. When he pulled them away, his face looked wrinkled and pained.

"Get in."

PART II

1

COLD OPEN

INTERIOR LION'S DEN—DAY

(HOLLY, TARA, KELLY, J. J., DIEGO)
HOLLY rushes in, her arms and legs flailing madly. She jerks her limbs and throws her hips side-to-side.

HOLLY

(whisper-screams)

Skunk!

TARA

What's going on?

KELLY

I think it's her new dance move. Remember she was saying we never let her come up with routines?

J. J.

Is this your new dance? I dig it!

HOLLY

Skunk! Skunk!

She frantically points to the den's exit. The others think this is part of her dance move and start to copy her, pointing in rhythm to the exit.

J. J.

Sweet moves, Holly! Let's all do 'The Skunk'!

TARA, KELLY, J. J., and DIEGO mimic HOLLY's increasingly bizarre movements.

DIEGO

Yeah, that's one funky skunk!

Audience laughter. HOLLY waves her arms and legs again, trying to get them to understand: There's a skunk outside! A sudden splash and poof of skunk juice shoots into the den. The others scream and flail at the horrible stench. The room fills with smoke (fog machine).

KELLY

Holly, why didn't you tell us there was a skunk?

Audience laughter. As the smoke clears, DIEGO waves his hand in front of his face.

```
                DIEGO
    That really IS one funky skunk . . .

            END OF COLD OPEN
```

I'd told Thom that being recast in *Fowl Play* made me realize acting was a fool's game, but that's not exactly how it went down. That *should've* been my response, and I wish it had been. I wish I'd stopped playing then and there.

Lesson One: Actors are not known for their self-respect.

When *Diego* got canceled, most of us were sophomores in high school, except for Kelly, who, at twenty, was long emancipated and immediately headed to Hollywood. Over the next year, everyone's pen-pal game was strong. Then OffBeat formed and took everyone with it, beaming them into outer space from their collective hometowns, as though raptured into Boy Band Heaven. Brody was the first one signed. An eccentric woman who claimed to be an entrepreneur in Sugarland, Texas, realized boy bands were making a comeback. Via an ad in the local paper, she recruited three twenty-something guys to form the initial lineup. They needed two more singers, preferably younger, to complete the band. Texas-born-and-bred Brody fit the bill and called J. J. in North Carolina to join him; and for a time, Melody and Tara appeared as the group's opening act as a short-lived duo named Manchot (literally "penguin" in French. Because they were black and white. I know, it's horrifying). Around the same time, Kelly got the lead in *Honeypot*.

While our friends jumped aboard the Fame Express, Ethan and I kept our heads down. He'd returned to his regularly scheduled life in Iowa and I relied on him to justify my inaction. He was the other "normie," and his blasé attitude about the entertainment world seemed the healthiest, the one I most wanted to emulate, of the bunch. But then he, too, got swept away, in an indie film about neo-Nazi youth that would earn him a Golden Globe nomination.

By senior year, I was the only one still enrolled in public school, or any kind of school, but I shrugged it off. What was the rush? Why not enjoy the break from early call times and constant rehearsals? Besides, if I decided to go back to show business, it would be waiting for me, like a puppy.

Lesson Two: Show business is not a puppy.

My teenage self believed it was my choice whether I was on TV or not. I didn't realize it was something other people had to agree to.

Nearly every casting director, producer, and director who received a copy of my reel immediately crossed me off the list for roles that required *subtlety*. On *Diego*, I'd been up for any joke, pun, song, silly costume, or waka-waka moment you could think of. In retrospect, it was obvious I'd been drunk with power. *Clowning power.* While in clown-mode, backed up by the indiscriminate, torture-induced laugh track, I hit my marks and my lines well enough, but in no way had I demonstrated range.

Fowl Play was in my wheelhouse (that is, a comedy taped live with animal co-stars) and didn't require its cast to behave like a human ever would, so I fit right in. For the pilot, at least. The night before I was supposed to shoot episode two, I received the call from my agent that ripped my heart out and set it on fire.

To help me recover, J. J. flew me out to Iceland to watch the aurora borealis with him.

I tried to stay positive, telling him it was worth losing the gig to see those lights. (I was still operating under the assumption that other jobs were around the corner. It hadn't dawned on me yet that it might never happen; that what had worked for me as a kid didn't work for me as an adult.)

If I'd run out of money, I might have given up sooner, but the *Fowl Play* checks kept me solvent enough to continue auditioning.

Fowl Play had screwed me over, but not as badly as it appeared; the pay-or-play contract my agent had negotiated meant the network had to pay me for the episodes I would have done (all nine, the length of the original buyout) had they not replaced me the day before the series started shooting. (I still get tiny residuals each time an episode from those first nine airs. At this point it's not worth the paper cuts I get opening the envelope, but for a while it was my sole income.) The fact that it became a hit later didn't help me, but the original six figures stretched far and wide when I was eighteen to twenty-four.

By 2001, when I was twenty, OffBeat had managed to escape the clutches of their first, deranged manager and *Bubblegum*, their first album post-liberation, had first-day sales of a million units. Though the title was intended to be tongue-in-cheek, and music scholars eviscerated the lyrics "You're stuck on me, I'm stuck on you" ("Like something stuck to the bottom of my shoe," read *Pitchfork*'s angry headline), there was no denying that bubblegum pop was back for good, and OffBeat was its poster child. The world's obsession with the group hit a fever pitch when Mel and Brody got together as a publicity stunt. Not even "viewers like you" were immune; PBS threw together a compilation DVD of *Diego* skits and songs called *The Best of J. J., Melody, and Brody* as a new-subscriber perk.

The so-called Diego Darlings, with their status as the show's most famous alumni, captured the hearts and allowance money of teens and tweens by the truckload.

Since I appeared in one of the sketches, I received a small cut of the DVD profits. Everyone else donated their portion back to PBS. I took the money and ran.

Lesson Three: Dignity is overrated.

For a while I shared a studio apartment with a girl who did closed captioning for daytime TV shows. She worked *and* slept on the couch, headphones on, special caption keyboard at the ready. At night I had to climb over her sleeping form on the couch to get to the bed, which was mashed up against the wall behind it. I stepped on her face once when she reversed her positioning without telling me.

I spent most days nursing a bottomless cup of coffee at Denny's on Sunset Boulevard, going over lines and counting the days until J. J. would swing through town again on tour. We broke up and got back together more times than I could count, and the only person I could talk to about it was Tara.

Brody and Melody's fauxmance dominated the tabloids, and it was surreal for me to witness. He and Tara had been best friends during *Diego*, and she'd been his first choice for fake girlfriend, but she'd turned him down, refusing to tie her career and prospects to his dating life. She wanted to be taken seriously as an artist, as well as an artist of color, which was challenging enough after the debacle that was Manchot. No way would she be a beard for a white pop star, regardless of their friendship. Melody's rise was stratospheric after that; she launched a solo career and Tara could only watch as opportunity after opportunity went to high-profile, blond, and perky Melody instead of her. Leaving her to wonder whether her integrity or her skin tone was the cause.

I had failed as an actor, but at least I didn't have to watch J. J. slobbering over someone else for the cameras, and reaping all the benefits. OffBeat's PR machine pretended J. J. was single so fans could imagine themselves in the girlfriend role; with Brody so publicly "taken," they needed to present J. J. as an alternative. Ironically, this led to rumors that J. J. was "the gay one."

I wish I'd said, *Goodbye forever, Hollywood! Have fun shattering people!* Instead, I continued chasing fame until I had almost no money left, and only then did I apply to college.

(TL;DR: I spent five years on a TV show, and seven years trying to get it back.)

At twenty-five, I was the oldest freshman in my dorm. I purchased wine coolers for the kids on the floor and studied psychology and musical theater. I nabbed the role of Little Red Riding Hood in the campus production of *Into the Woods*, but the weekend of dress rehearsals, I got an emergency call from my parents that my sister had survived a perilous labor but didn't believe the baby belonged to her. She told the doctors who examined her that she was waiting for the baby's real mother to show up.

2

Having left Woodbury, Minnesota, we took I-90 east going sixty-five miles an hour, not a mile more, not a mile less. Have I mentioned the speed limit was seventy?

"Is this how we're doing this?" I asked. "Slow and steady wins the race?"

"I don't want to get pulled over. And when it's your turn to drive, you'll do the same," he replied gruffly.

Still prickly I forced myself on the road trip, then.

The Volkswagen's air conditioner seemed to be in a death spiral. It rattled and hissed, and one of its vents appeared to be melted shut from some long-ago heat wave. *Very* long ago. The radio was broken, by which I mean it wasn't there. A tangle of loose wires spilled out from the space it used to occupy. I assumed it had been stolen.

"Had this car awhile, have you? Since high school, maybe?" I had no idea why I kept poking the bear. But arguing was better than silence for two thousand miles.

"It's new," Thom answered vaguely.

I coughed uncontrollably.

"New to *me*," he clarified. "I think it's a '94."

I wiped my eyes. "Right."

"It should take us twenty-five hours to get to Manhattan," he continued. "Though I didn't plan on a passenger and her girl bladder making us stop every fifty miles."

"My girl bladder is top-notch, I'll have you know."

"I'm not—all I'm saying is you can't exactly pee into a bottle. It's not your fault." He dragged heavy fingers through his dirty-blond hair, ruining the side part from that morning. "We can alternate shifts of seven hours each per day, and spend one night in a hotel. I haven't budgeted for meals now that we have to double up, though."

"I'll pay for everything," I assured him, ticking off the list on my fingers. "Gas, food, hotel, Red Bulls. Go nuts."

"I'll cover the gas since I'm driving this way anyway, but if you want to handle the rest that'd be great. Thanks."

First thing we needed was a different car, I thought. Perhaps one that was new to the *world*.

I kept my misgivings to myself. We were still within twenty minutes of Prevail! and who's to say he wouldn't dump me on the side of the road if I annoyed him too much?

"I have one rule," he said.

"Anything." (*Don't spill soda on the car, as it might detract from the stains already there?*)

"Since you didn't finish the program, you have to follow the guidelines at Prevail! I'm not hauling your ass halfway across the country while you stare at a screen the whole time. Once a day, for fifteen minutes, you can use my phone to go online. I'll be your sober companion, so to speak."

I didn't *love* the plan, but I was in no position to argue. Tomorrow would've been my first chance to go online if I'd stayed, so why not? This way, I was getting my treat a day early.

"Done," I agreed.

"I'll get you to New York, but what you do after that is up to you. I'm not going to be part of your little scheme."

"I'm aware of your feelings on the subject. But remember we're on the clock." My eyes strayed to his mileage indicator and its unwavering adherence to sixty-five mph.

"Trust me, I want to get to New York even more than you do."

My tone softened. "Of course you do; you miss your son. Sammy, right?"

"Sammy Bear," he said quietly.

"How old is he?"

"Eight."

I waited for more, but he wasn't forthcoming. When the topic was *my* dysfunction (or InstaMom's, or anyone else's), he was a regular Chatty Cathy, offering opinions left and right. When it was his turn to reveal a weakness of any sort, he clammed up.

Not to mention the verbal gymnastics he'd used to avoid mentioning his progeny the past three weeks.

"Were you able to talk to him on the phone at all?" I asked.

"A couple of times. With school, and the time difference, and his weekend activities, it was sort of tricky to set up. And my parents didn't want us to talk too often because they thought it would disrupt his day, make things harder on him. He tends to... fixate on things." Thom pointedly kept his eyes on the road while he spoke.

We rode in silence. The Volkswagen did not. A mysterious rattle shook the cup holder, even though it was empty, and the car bounced and swayed at random, as if we were flying over dangerous terrain instead of traveling *below the speed limit* on a smooth expanse of highway.

Before my excruciating seduction attempt, I'd have said a road trip with Thom would be a piece of cake, filled with conversation and laughter. Now I found myself staring out the window at passing billboards, most of which were in favor of colonoscopies, Wisconsin Dells, and the Unborn. The past few days without Thom had been isolating and lonely. Now that we had all this time alone together, it was a shame we couldn't return to our old banter.

Eventually, Thom cleared his throat.

I sat up straighter but remained silent. I didn't want to scare him off by appearing too eager.

"When I left New York, it was the first time Sammy and I had been apart since he was three," he said quietly.

"Wait. You didn't have a single night away from him in five years? No overnight trips, no vacations, nothing?"

"He suffers from night terrors. He hasn't had a full night of sleep since he was a baby."

Which meant neither had Thom. "I'm sorry. That sounds tough."

"If I have to travel for work, I take him with me, and if I go out of town during the day I make sure to get back before bedtime. He misses a lot of school that way, but it's easier than trying to find someone who can handle him."

"I bet he loves being with Grandma and Grandpa, though."

He wouldn't give an inch. He was determined to tear himself down. "He needs to stick to a routine as much as possible. We were making progress—at least I thought we were—and I shot it to hell by coming here."

"Hey, you don't know that. Maybe it was good, to get a break from each other. Or if not good, at least necessary. For *both* of you."

He gripped the steering wheel so tightly his knuckles whitened. "Not for forty-five days."

"The important thing is you faced your problem and got help," I pointed out, insipidly, aware of how cliché I sounded, "and, and—"

He shook his head, unconvinced. "You don't get it."

"I do, I really do—"

"I know you helped out with your niece, but it's not the same."

"I didn't 'help out.' I was her primary caretaker."

The skepticism in his voice remained. "For what, a year or two?"

"Until two months ago. She's *ten*."

He looked stunned. "I didn't know."

"At least I mentioned her. You didn't tell me *anything* about Sammy."

He swallowed. "It upset me too much. Being with you—I mean, *talking* with you," he quickly corrected, "it was a break from all that."

"Guess we both kept things from each other," I admitted.

"What'd you say earlier? 'You have baggage and I have baggage, but together we're a...'"

"I didn't say it," I protested. "I used it as an example of something I would never say."

"The fact that you even came up with it..."

"*As an example of a ridiculous line.*"

"That you nevertheless felt the need to—"

I threw up my hands. "Moving on."

He laughed. It felt good to hear that sound again. "Okay, 'Lisa,'" he teased me.

"She hated you."

"She couldn't find her own ass with both hands."

"Come on, she wasn't that bad." I felt a pang of guilt. I'd been unfair to her, ditching the program, but what choice did I have?

"Anyway, you said the show was all you have, but it sounds like for ten years you had a hell of a gig watching your niece. What made you decide to leave? I'm not blaming you, just curious."

I chewed on my thumbnail before answering. "I don't know. It was just time."

"Was it a tough conversation to have with your sister, or did she understand? And what was your plan after quitting? You must have had something else lined up?"

"It wasn't exactly formal," I said uncomfortably. "I asked her to meet me in the kitchen for a talk, and I laid it out as gently as I could, that it was time for me to move out because I wanted to do my own thing now."

I didn't look at him when I said it. The words came out in a precise, self-conscious order but my gaze remained out the window, looking into the windows of other cars. Other lives.

I should've known by then he wouldn't drop it that easily.

"You *lived* with them?"

"Well, I had my own cottage out back. Kitchen, living room, bedroom. I was close by, but not right on top of them. And you didn't have anyone helping with Sammy? No regular sitter, no day care?" I didn't ask about Sammy's mom because I figured he would bring her up if he wanted to. I wasn't about to dig it out of him.

"He got suspended from three day cares before I realized I needed to make a big change in my life. So I set up a home office and worked from home."

"And you haven't spent a night without him ever since?"

"It sounds good when you put it that way, but it's only a technicality."

"What do you mean?"

"I was home with him all the time, but I wasn't really there. You know? When he was asleep, I'd be on the computer, and when he was awake, the only thing I could think about was *How many more hours until I get to go on the computer?* I missed out on so many things, things that were happening right in front of me."

"It's impossible to be fully engaged every second of the day. Everyone's mind wanders. And sometimes kids are..." I lowered my voice as though the words were blasphemous. "*...kind of boring.*"

"I should've done better. I want to."

We drove in silence for an hour, until our first pit stop: a gas station next to a Cracker Barrel in Kenosha, Wisconsin, right near the Illinois border. After Thom flew through a series of complicated maneuvers with the gearshift, the Volkswagen shuddered to a halt.

"Credit card?" He held out his hand and looked at me expectantly.

"Oh. Um, I don't actually...have my credit cards on me."

"There's probably an ATM inside. Should we grab food first, and then fill up?"

I scratched my forehead absentmindedly, trying to stall. "Yeah, about that. I don't have my ATM card, either."

"I don't understand," he said slowly. "You told me you would pay for everything."

"Pay you *back*. And I will. My sister has my cards but she's in Belgium with the rest of my family."

"No, you said you'd pay for everything, which I took to mean 'while it's occurring.'"

He exited the car and shut the driver's-side door. It didn't close all the way. He opened it again and slammed it this time. I didn't know if I should follow him or give him space. My stomach rumbled and I thought back, mournfully, to the fiesta eggs I could have eaten at breakfast.

I instinctually reached in my pockets, not for my iPhone this time but for money, in case there was a rumpled bill somewhere. They were empty except for a quarter, which reminded me of the Ziploc bag in my backpack. It was embarrassing as hell—as though Renee had dropped me off at summer camp instead of rehab—but desperate times called for desperate measures.

I stepped out of the car and jangled the bag of coins to get Thom's attention. "Truce?"

3

Ariel's Blogspot
May 2010—Not That Into Her

With Brody and Melody's nasty split (anyone else have Mel's "Low Down, Dirty (Cheat)" playing on repeat?!) I thought it was the perfect time to talk about the hee-larious Diego and the Lion's Den taping I went to when I was 9. I was OBSESSED with that show. OB-SESSED. When my parents took me and my older brother on a spring break trip to San Diego, the only thing I cared about was getting tickets.

Stuff I remember:

1. The hype guy for the audience threw so much candy at us that they could've sat onstage reading the

Yellow Pages (remember those) (lol I'm old!) and we would've screamed our sugared heads off.

2. Kelly had a person following her around at all times who was JUST in charge of her hair.

3. J. J. led a prayer off to the side before the cameras started rolling.

4. Tara and Brody were constantly hugging and whispering together. I NEVER saw him smile or interact with Melody. (Anyone else think "LDD(C)" might be about TARA? Like Brody is working his way through the Manchots?) In every interview they would say they were childhood sweethearts, but my scoop is, he was NOT THAT INTO HER back then!

5. Ethan Mallard was ADORABLE with his braces.

6. The taping took FOREVER. I'm talking two hours for a ten-minute skit. Before we could leave—I swear, they TRAPPED us there—we had to fill out a survey about whether we would watch a spin-off of the show, and if so, with which characters. The choices were: Tara as a princess (we were soooo confused by this? but in the episodes that hadn't aired yet, her character was revealed to be a secret princess who had swapped places with her identical cousin so she could "live a normal life"); Ethan as the new junior zookeeper (YES PLEASE haha); or Brody/Diego as

a lion tamer for the circus. I don't think any of these spin-offs came to fruition, but if anyone remembers anything about them, sound off in the comments.

7. The next night, my brother and I saw the actors at a café downtown, all hanging out. We went over for autographs and photos. Everyone was game except one person—the girl who always did the silliest stuff on the show. Tilly? Lily? She is NOT funny in real life. She was like, "Sorry but this is our last night together and we want to finish talking but can we meet you in front of the restaurant in a few minutes" blah blah. The others were happy to sign napkins and take pics right away except for that one girl, who, not kidding, never went on to do anything else. Just goes to show you why: what a bad attitude! If you're not even going to give back to the fans you don't have the right to be on TV.

Inside the Cracker Barrel, we ordered two coffees, two ice waters, and a bucket of fries to share. Thom dipped his in mayonnaise; I went for ketchup. You know, for health reasons. A vegetable.

A TV in the upper corner was halfway through an ad for Kelly's new TV show in which she played a single mom / undercover narc with Chicago PD.

Thom saw me watching and glanced up at it. "Is that . . . ?"

"Yep." I tore my eyes away. "I'm sorry I misled you about the money," I said, head down. "We'll keep track of every expense, save all the receipts, and I'll mail you a check the instant I get home. I'm good for it, I swear."

"That's nice and everything, but the problem is *I* don't have my ATM or credit card, either."

His words hovered in the air, refusing to land, because if they landed I might have to acknowledge what that meant, and how screwed we were.

"Did you leave your wallet at Prevail!?" I asked pleasantly. That wasn't a big deal. "We have time to go back..."

"I have my wallet but I don't have access to my money. My parents are in charge of my finances."

"Why?"

"I asked them to be. I transferred my bank accounts to their names so they could pay for whatever Sammy needed while I was gone."

That seemed extreme to me, but okay. "So we'll stop at a bank and fill out a form and have it revert back to you. Right?"

"It's a local credit union in Greenburgh. All three of us need to be there in person to sign off on it. *Also* my idea." He swallowed. "I didn't trust myself."

"I don't understand."

"And you don't need to. All you need to know is that I don't have credit cards or much cash."

"But that doesn't make any *sense.* None of what you're saying makes sense."

"Online gambling." He sounded impatient. "Poker. Okay? That's—that was my addiction." He took a deep breath, started again. "If I had access to money, I'd have kept losing it."

"Oh."

"Now you know my deep dark secret."

I had no idea what to say, so I went with the first thing that came to mind. "I don't think any less of you," I offered awkwardly.

"You will," he responded. "Give it time."

"I don't—"

"You want to know the worst part? I blamed Sammy for it. 'No sense going to sleep if I'll be up again when he has a nightmare. Gotta kill the time somehow.' As though it was a *little boy's* fault his dad's such a—"

I held my hand up. "Stop. The important thing is you took steps to fix the situation, and you got help. I know I sound cliché, but I also happen to believe what I'm saying, and I want to talk about it more, but right now we have to figure out what we're going to do."

"Yeah. You're right." He took a long pull off his coffee. Dug his fingers roughly through his hair in what I now recognized as a tic when he was upset with himself. Hence the reason it had always, always been messy at Prevail!

"How on earth were you planning to get home?" I asked as gently as I could.

He set his coffee mug down. "My per diems. I worked it out when I first arrived." He borrowed a pen from our waitress and jotted down figures on his napkin.

Expenses

Per diem: 10 bucks a day x 42 days = $420

Woodbury, Minnesota, to Greenburgh, New York = 1,207 miles

Fill up the car 4 times, at $2.60/gallon, with 18.5 gallons/tank = $192

Three nights at a hotel that's not sketchy = $150
Food = $60
Total = $402
Left over = $18

Wow. Eighteen entire dollars for emergencies.

In the blinding light of the diner his eyes were a translucent blue, and I knew I should proceed with caution given the vulnerabilities he'd exposed, but the situation seemed to call for a little tough love.

"Twenty dollars a day for food might not be enough. Even if it was just you. And gas is up to three bucks in most places."

He dismissed me. "It would've worked. I would've been fine."

"The good news is, with me along to help drive, we can shift the columns around, and we only need one night in a hotel."

He pointed at me with a french fry. "This from the person who threw away ten bucks in under a minute."

"It wasn't part of the budget, it was from my quarters. From now on we'll take austerity measures."

"I'm not dumpster diving."

On a separate napkin, I scribbled down new figures.

"Tonight, we'll share a room with twin beds, in a 'non-sketchy' Econolodge or anyplace that takes cash."

"Places that take cash *are* sketchy, and it probably won't have a pool," he pointed out.

We'd officially swapped roles. He had fallen off the cliff's edge and I was holding out a rope for him to grab onto. "You can't go one night without it?"

"Exercise is part of my treatment. And it helps me sleep."

"Do some jumping jacks, *buckaroo*."

Motel 6 = $39/night x 1 night = $39
Gas = $222
Food = $100
Total = $361
Left over = $59

"Boom." I handed him my napkin. "Problem solved. 'Why thank you, Holly, I'm so glad you're along for the trip.' *With* a day to spare before the anniversary."

He scrutinized my napkin. "I guess it's the only plan we've got."

He opened the map app on his phone.

The fry I was eating tumbled out of my mouth as my world shrank to a single directive. *Screen. Screen. Screen.*

"Let's aim for seven more hours today—you can take over for all of it, or part of it, and that should get us to Pennsylvania," he suggested.

"That's far for one day. I figured we'd stop at more of a halfway point."

My eyes remained locked on his phone. *SCREEN.*

"Can I just...? Please?" I gasped, reaching for it again.

Calmly, Thom looked between me and his phone, enjoying the power trip.

"What time is it?" he asked at last.

What did *that* have to do with anything? "Food o'clock," I snapped. "I don't know. Two."

"Okay, then yes. You may have it for fifteen minutes."

Very suspicious turnaround. "Really? Why? Is there no reception, or something?"

"Reception's fine, and middle of the day is perfect."

"Says who? Lisa? The person who 'can't find her ass with both hands'?"

He offered his phone to me, and my sense of unease went up another notch. I had figured he'd say, *Not until we reach the hotel tonight.*

Something else gave me pause: I'd gone three weeks without internet use, my longest stretch since high school. Did I want to give in? How long *could* I go, if I had to?

On the other hand, what if something else changed regarding the time or location of the anniversary? I couldn't be caught unaware again.

"How about last thing before bed?" I suggested. "Make me earn it?"

A lazy smile wrapped around his face. "How would you earn it?"

I blushed. "That's not what I—"

"Middle of the day. Take it or leave it." His confident blustering wasn't enough to convince me.

"Why is that the best time?"

"If you check email last thing before bed, it'll ruin your sleep. You'll be thinking about how to respond, or worse, you'll decide to stay up and answer the damn things, when you're already tired and not thinking straight. Ditto if you check first thing in the morning: You won't be able to concentrate on any other tasks if something in your email, newsfeed, or social media upsets you or requires attention you don't have time to give it. Not to mention if you check in the morning, you'll be pissed off if the emails you sent at midnight haven't been answered, which is absurd because you only sent them six hours ago when the rest of the world was sleeping. The best method is to check once, in the middle of the day when you can respond, so you don't run into either of those problems."

It made sense. Lecture-mode Thom was extremely persuasive, and I was painfully familiar with the pattern he'd described: When I didn't get the email responses I was waiting for or hoping for, I ended up refreshing my inbox every few minutes, because—and this was the killer, the root of it all—it could technically arrive any second; therefore each time it didn't, I grew more anxious and angry. It was a terrible way to live, handcuffed to one's phone and feeling microbursts of rage in minute intervals, all day, every day.

It occurred to me that snail mail came once a day when I was a kid, in the middle of the day no less, and never on Sundays, which freed us to get on with our lives during the in-between spaces. Now there *were* no in-between spaces.

"Think of the places you truly need to go and don't deviate," Thom instructed me before typing in his code to unlock the phone. "That's the main thing: *need*. Not *want*. And remember, the clock is ticking." He set his iPhone's countdown timer to fifteen minutes and slid it to me across the table like it was an envelope filled with cash.

Since he was watching, I pretended to take his advice and opened my email.

Of the 1,728 emails that had accumulated in the past three weeks, 97 percent were spam. It was possible people respected my journey and to prove it resisted emailing while I "recovered," but that seemed unlikely. Almost no one from my day-to-day life knew where I was or why. Mostly my inbox overflowed with urgent messages from the Democrats, as well as a children's charity group I'd donated to a few years back.

I looked up. Thom watched me curiously.

"What?" I said.

"Your eyes are dilated. You look like an anime character."

"Just trying to take it all in," I hedged. Really I was thinking, *This is what I missed? This is what I was so excited about?* "Go ahead and add a minute to your timer to make up for the interruption."

"No can do—"

"Do *not* call me 'buckaroo.'"

"How you spend the fifteen minutes is up to you. Not my fault I'm more interesting than your inbox."

"May I surf in private, please?" I asked, crisp as a Granny Smith apple.

He smiled and walked to the counter for a coffee refill.

I took care of logistics first. Shot off a rapid, typo-filled email to Renee explaining the situation and giving her Thom's number. "Call us once you're Stateside." I signed off, "xoxoxo."

While his back was turned, I headed to Twitter. I didn't usually go there but it felt good delaying my visit to Reddit. I liked to think I'd developed self-control.

Hashtag JJJ trended nationwide. Curious, and not a little ill, I clicked the hashtag and pulled up the top mentions. Sure enough, it was *that* J. J.

My J. J.

He would be on *The Jerry Levine Show* tonight promoting the twenty-fifth anniversary of *Diego and the Lion's Den*. J. J.'s fifty-seven million tweeps papered the web with gifs and memes of J. J. and Jerry (hence the third *J*), who were bros on and off camera.

It would probably be a laugh riot.

Unless, for example, you were me.

Fuck it. I closed out the window and logged in to Reddit.

What a relief to be back on friendly, familiar ground. Adrenaline, and a sense of belonging, coursed through me. *Ahhhh.*

The mods could have closed out my thread for lack of activity, but there it was—pulsing enticingly, right where I left it. Memories from the past few weeks—staying up all hours, guzzling iced coffees, ignoring phone calls, emails, texts, *people*, hitting refresh refresh refresh—engulfed me. The first several times I'd posted, fear and excitement had jolted through my veins. The novelty of speaking about a time long past, a time I'd suppressed and ignored and fought down for so many years, was a joyful rebellion. Now I felt mostly dread.

Should I have stayed at Prevail! and finished the program?

No, I couldn't stay, because then they'd get away with it.

It wasn't enough to have strangers read my Reddit posts and enjoy the behind-the-scenes info, because the intended audience, all five of them, were oblivious as ever, unaware of and incurious about my perspective on our shared history. It was way past time they were confronted with it. With *me*. All five of them in the same room—I'd never get that chance again.

Leaving was the right move.

Still, I couldn't help feeling as though I watched myself from a distance, hovering outside my body. Nothing seemed real; not my actions, not my posts, and not the responses. *There were never enough.*

My existential dread (and its corresponding lack of movement) activated Thom's auto lock. Shit, what was his password?

7269, I typed ("SAMY").

The phone buzzed angrily.

7266, I typed ("SAMM").

Bzzz.

One more chance before it shut me down. If that happened I'd be forced to admit I tried to crack his code.

7263, I typed ("SAME"—that is, Sam-e), not expecting it to work.

But it did.

The implications were delicious.

When Thom fell asleep tonight, I'd have unfettered access for hours. All my revelations and misgivings about Reddit from seconds ago took a swan dive out the window.

Working hard to keep the evil smirk off my face, I opened a new tab and headed to the *Daily Denizen* website. And there it was, confirmation of InstaMom's countdown clock: 2 days, 5 hours, 29 minutes, and 3 seconds until the *Diego and the Lion's Den* reunion in NYC. Mesmerized, I watched the seconds tick down. My stomach dropped with each movement.

"Whatcha readin'?" Thom appeared behind me so suddenly I almost dropped his phone. Can you imagine if I'd broken it?

I covered the screen with my hand. "Nothing."

His wolfish grin came out. "This is your thirty-second warning."

Jesus! Had it already been fourteen and a half minutes? I frantically toggled back to my inbox. Nothing new except for an email I'd missed during my first perusal.

> Hello Holly,
>
> I hope this message finds you well. I'm an assistant editor at Jinx Books, an imprint of PopTV, which is part of YouTube Red. I don't know if

you're familiar with our series *Stars: Behind the Spotlight*, but it's rated #2 in the 18-34-year-old demo, in the category of "online music shows about the 1990s."

Anyway, I'm writing because I've been reading your Reddit AMA with keen interest. Everyone here loves what you have to say and thinks your voice is fabulous. We'd like to make you an offer to publish the entire thread, and we'd ask you to write about 10,000 additional words of never-before-seen information, plus a foreword (perhaps someone from your past could write that? Wink wink). We're a small e-publisher so we can't offer much, but the possibilities for royalties are limitless. Our standard contract is $150 upfront, and $150 once it goes live. Let's talk!

Best,
Diane

I couldn't wrap my head around it. Had I been offered a book deal (. . . of sorts)? Frazzled and confused, I stared at the words until—BEEP BEEP BEEP BEEP.

I nearly jumped out of my skin, and glared at Thom. "That's your alarm? The one the phone comes with?"

"It's alarming," Thom said defensively. "As it should be."

"It sounds like a nuclear reactor's about to blow. 'Core meltdown. Core meltdown. Please evacuate,'" I said in a breathy, AI death-voice.

"How come female robots are always sexy?"

I tried not to smile. (*Sexy, huh?*)

He leaned his hands on his palms and spoke in a gossipy tone. "Where'd you go? What'd you do?"

"I froze up at first. I had no idea what to do."

His normal voice came back, low and sympathetic. "My first time back online, I was so overwhelmed by the amount of work emails I'd missed, it paralyzed me."

"I got a strange email from a publishing company."

"Oh?"

"I should go to rehab more often," I joked. "I went in with no job, and I came out with a book offer."

"A book offer?" he sputtered.

"This small online publisher—I guess they have a show, or something, too, about music and the 'nineties. Anyway, they want to reprint my Reddit thread."

"I'm not sure what that would look like."

"I'm not sure, either." I pulled up the email and showed it to him. He scanned it quickly. "Doesn't fifteen hundred seem a little low?" he asked.

I closed my eyes briefly, regretting the conversation. No matter how many times I'm humiliated, I never get better at it. "Not fifteen hundred. One hundred. And fifty." I paused. "Dollars."

He whistled.

"When I wrote for *Dying* magazine, I made six fifty per article."

"This would be a significant downgrade, then."

"There shouldn't be anything lower than *Dying*, though. This shouldn't even be possible."

"Tell them to screw off."

He was right. Jinx's offer was insulting.

"Besides, don't you want to tell your *own* stories?" Thom asked.

"Yeah, definitely."

That settled it.

And yet. *And yet.*

"Permission to delete?" I asked Thom.

He slid the phone back into my palm. "Granted. But no funny stuff."

"Aye, aye, Captain."

Was it rude to not respond at all? Would a quick "Thanks but no thanks" suffice?

"You're worth so much more than that," Thom said firmly, as though he'd heard my misgivings. "You know that, right?"

He might think that, but the fact remained $150 was the only offer on the table.

I tapped the trash button. Deleted.

That's when we noticed the diner was playing Brody's latest single, "Two Hearts Beating."

"Time to leave," I announced.

I was still hungry.

```
INT. LION'S DEN—DAY

(DIEGO)
Diego does a cartwheel onto the set.

                    DIEGO
    It's time for some fun facts! In
    captivity, panda bears live to be 30
```

years old. They have BIG appetites. Every day they fill up their bellies with 27 *pounds* of bamboo.

(grabs his stomach, moans)

That's a lotta 'boo. I'd rather eat apples and bananas, wouldn't you?

Music cue: Apples and Bananas song.

DIEGO (cont'd)

I like to eat, eat, eat apples and bananas

I like to eat, eat, eat apples and bananas

(Change vowel sound to A)

I like to ate, ate, ate ay-ples and ba-nay-nays

I like to ate, ate, ate ay-ples and ba-nay-nays

(Change vowel sound to E)

I like to eat, eat, eat ee-ples and bee-nee-nees

I like to eat, eat, eat ee-ples and bee-nee-nees

(Change vowel sound to I)

I like to ite, ite, ite i-ples and bi-ni-nis

I like to ite, ite, ite i-ples and bi-ni-nis

4

After Thom filled up the Passat, I approached the driver's side with trepidation.

"How are you at driving stick?" Thom asked. "I probably should've asked you that earlier."

"A bit rusty, but I can do it." Somehow, I didn't think the death trap he called a car was unaccustomed to a dragging clutch, or the exquisite grinding noise that came with it.

"Well, heads up, it doesn't like to shift beyond third gear."

Alarm gripped my body. "It doesn't 'like' to?"

"It's okay, all that means is we can't back up."

"We can't back up," I repeated in a daze.

"I don't see why we'd need to, though."

"What about when we *park*?"

"We'll park on the side of the road and make sure no one parks in front of us. Don't worry about it. Let's focus on getting to Pennsylvania."

When I fastened my seat belt, the click was ominous. "I genuinely think I would be safer without this," I told him, tugging on the wide belt. I'd already conjured up visions of us submerged underwater with no escape, or helplessly waiting to be consumed by a fireball.

To my surprise, he agreed. "I know what you mean, but we can't risk a cop seeing us."

It took two tries to start the car without stalling. The clutch pushed back—the biting point—and I winced with the effort to find the sweet spot. I practiced shifting gears in the gas station / Cracker Barrel lot for another ten minutes until I felt moderately capable.

"You're doing great," Thom encouraged me. "Do you feel okay about this? I can drive a couple more hours if you need me to, or we can find a bigger parking lot and practice more."

"Thanks. I'm okay. I feel like I'm driving a boat."

"You're overlooking its strengths, though."

"It has strengths?"

"The rub strip. The plastic rim around the car. It's held up well."

"You mean the crazy-looking double bumper?"

"*Impervious* to shopping carts."

I laughed. "You're right, that adds at least twenty cents to the Blue Book value."

We exited the lot and tentatively merged onto the freeway, staying to the right until I felt comfortable changing lanes. Which, based on my clenched butt and tense shoulders, might not be for years. It didn't help that the car constantly urged me to drift left; its bias took concentration to deflect, along with everything else I had to think about.

"What car do you drive in San Diego?" Thom asked, settling in and adjusting his seat to give himself more leg room.

"A Camry hybrid."

"Fancy."

"That's me. Total baller."

We passed a billboard advertising Ethan's new film, a remake of *The Thin Man*. He'd be Nick Charles, naturally.

"That was creepy," Thom remarked. "First the TV ad, then the song, then the billboard? It's like they're watching us." In a quieter voice: "No wonder you needed rehab."

I didn't reply, because I was too busy trying to shift into third. Did it have problems *getting* there? Or just going higher? "When do I switch? Now? *Now?*"

"Wait till it hits three thousand RPMs," Thom advised.

I slowly released the clutch while tapping the gas. We jolted violently forward, but it worked.

"Yeah, baby," I shouted. "How about I drive us all the way to New York? Because I don't actually know how to stop."

Three hours later, my adrenaline-fear took its toll. My muscles were stiff and sore but I refused to call it a day considering Thom drove a five-hour shift.

"Can I ask you something personal?" Thom said.

"As opposed to the polite small talk we usually engage in?"

"When guys find out you dated J. J. Randall, do they look at you differently?"

I was pretty sure I knew what he meant, but it was worth verifying. "In what way?"

"Do they become more interested, or less? Like, do they get off on the idea of dating a J. J.–caliber girl? Or does it intimidate them?"

I couldn't shrug because my shoulders were already bunched up around my ears. "I don't know if they 'get off,' but I don't go around telling people."

"Why'd you tell *me*?"

"At the time? To get you to shut up. I thought you'd be stunned silent, and I could eat dinner in peace."

He chuckled. "That backfired."

"Tell me about it. You kept on talking and talking until it turned out you were funny and nice and . . . " I trailed off, embarrassed. *Stop it, Holly. For God's sake, he's not interested.*

"But for real, how's a standard human male supposed to compete with '*People*'s Sexiest Moron'?" Thom asked.

"Oddly enough, I don't make them." I pretended to remember something. "Although, there was that one time when I made, like, four different guys compete in a marathon and a few other categories: Flowers, Chocolates, the Presentation of the Pecs . . . Winner got to date me."

"No cage fights?"

"My insurance wouldn't cover it."

"Bastards."

"Is that why you didn't sleep with me?" There had been something between us; at least, I'd believed there was. "You thought I'd be comparing you with J. J.?"

"No. It was because you looked like you'd been crying."

My breath caught. "Oh."

"Had you been?"

"A little bit, yeah. I'd had an upsetting phone call."

He cleared his throat. "Sorry."

"It's okay."

It was a relief to clear the air, but also painful; a sharp ache in my chest I decided to ignore. And if I couldn't ignore it yet, I would learn how.

Thom reached across the armrest and placed his hand on

mine. His hand was warm and dry, his fingers long and artistic looking. Something inside me settled, like autumn leaves fluttering into a pile. He radiated calm. I wanted to absorb it via skin-to-skin contact.

Then he lifted my hand and placed it on the gearshift.

"Hit the clutch," he said, and when I did, he moved my hand with his and shifted down to second gear. "Our exit's coming up."

The tension rolled off me in waves once I heard the word *exit*. But I hadn't driven nearly as much as he had.

"Are you sure? I can keep going," I offered.

"I think that's enough for today, don't you?"

He kept our hands together, his larger fingers curled over mine.

Without a word, he continued to guide my movements until we'd somehow slowed down and pulled over to the side of the road across from a Motel 6 in Elyria, Ohio. I'd told him I was worried about getting the car into park, and without drawing attention to my fears, or making fun of me for them, he'd helped me accomplish it.

"I know you were hoping to get to Pennsylvania," I said. "Sorry I—"

"I'm exhausted," he deflected smoothly. "It's good we're stopping."

I nodded. I'd clearly reached my limit with the stick and he was letting me off the hook. I remained quiet as the engine shook and gradually fell silent.

Thom asked me to stay in the car while he scoped the place out. Was he looking for prowlers?

When he returned from the front desk he held a set of keys in his hand.

"Wanted to make sure they had rooms on the second floor," he explained. "Most break-ins happen on the first."

Okay, he *was* looking for prowlers.

We hauled our bags out of the trunk and walked up the moderately clean staircase.

The sky had gone pink, but it wasn't late. A cricket orchestra filled the air, backed up by the thrum of passing trucks out on the road.

"You mind if I lie down for a second?" I asked.

"Sure, no problem."

We stowed our bags and I flopped onto the bed closer to the window. I drifted off immediately, my "second" of shut-eye turning into several hours. The last thing I saw was Thom settling into a chair, his long legs crossed at the ankle. He closed his eyes as well, but the fact that he'd chosen the chair instead of the other bed made me feel protected, as though he were keeping watch while I rested.

INT. LION'S DEN

(TARA, J. J., KELLY)
TARA, dressed as Mary Poppins, tucks the injured bird she rescued into the nest they constructed in the previous scene.

TARA

Good night, my little Chirpy. Sleep tight and feel better in the morning.

Music cue: "Stay Awake," from *Mary Poppins*.

TARA

Stay awake, don't rest your head . . .

While Tara sings the lullaby (and/or "our" version), J. J. and KELLY tidy up the den in the background, dancing gently with their brooms (if this mimics the chimney sweeps from *Mary Poppins*, all the better), pushing the bits of nest that didn't make it into a pile.

When I jolted awake, it was dark outside. I groaned. "How long was I out?"

"Don't worry about it," Thom said. "If you're hungry, I saw a Chili's across the street."

"I'm ravenous."

"We'll have to choose between appetizers and drinks, or a main meal."

"Drinks," we said simultaneously, and grinned at each other.

I'd vowed to ignore the way I felt when he was near me. But the way he smiled at me was making that difficult.

5

Expenses for Wednesday, April 22
(starting at $420)

gas fill up ($55.50 x 2) = $111.00
drinks (2 "premium ritas" at 6.99 each = $13.98)
appetizer (1 "triple dipper" to split = $12.99)
tax and tip (because we're not monsters) = $7.44
1 night at Motel 6 ($59.99)

I'd miscalculated by twenty bucks on the motel, but that was okay because we still had:

Money remaining = $214.60

6

As I watched Thom devour the sliders from our Triple Dipper and wipe the mystery sauce off his mouth, it occurred to me that if we lived in Elyria, if this were a normal night in the lives of two Midwesterners after a long day, this dinner would likely be considered a date. I wished, not for the first time, that I'd taken him up on his Mall of America offer. Imagine how much fun we would have had, considering we had managed to have fun in a hospital cafeteria. We'd had fun hanging out at a vending machine at three a.m.

At least things between us were back to normal, or what passed for normal considering how and where we'd met. Somehow after the day's driving and conversation, we weren't defensive or snappish anymore; the awkward phase seemed to have passed.

So why did I want more? Why did I think it was even possible? Come Friday, we'd go our separate ways forever. I should've been content with repairing our friendship.

The trouble was, I had the distinct feeling he *knew* me. That I was known to him in a way I hadn't been known to anyone in a long time. I didn't want to let it go. It was rare and special.

He claimed never to have flirted with me. But what about the casual compliments he inserted throughout our interactions? How certain he was that I was Somebody. How certain he was that I was worth more than a $150 e-book. How certain he was that my days on *Diego* were not, in fact, the most interesting thing about me.

How he refused to haul my "ass" across the country while I looked down at a phone. Was there meaning to be gleaned from his choice of word? Did that suggest he'd noticed it? (Of course, I'd noticed his ass, too. I just hadn't brought it up, yet.)

My inventory of his possible flirting did not provide anything conclusive. He was, apparently, the king of mixed signals.

Or maybe my receiver was broken.

Maybe J. J. had smashed it to bits.

The object of my fascination raised his margarita: "To being halfway home."

We clinked our glasses together.

"I hate to say it, but I'm still hungry," I said, once we'd polished off the Triple Dipper. "I know we prioritized drinks, and I'm not questioning that, but there has to be a way to..."

Our waiter popped over to check on us, so I swiveled in his direction. "Anyone send back their food, and it would otherwise go to waste? Maybe someone had the wrong order, or...?"

"She's joking," Thom interjected quickly.

"No, I'm not. What happens to incorrect orders that don't have anything wrong with them? Are they thrown out? Could we meet you around back later, and..."

"Holly." Thom shot me a look.

"Or pie. Do you give away the day-old pies?"

Thom threw his hands up, defeated. The waiter glanced between us, confused as to whether he'd been given an official request or not. "I could, uh, go check. It's my first week here."

"Thanks," I said sweetly.

A text arrived on Thom's phone.

"Shit," he muttered after silencing it. "Sammy tried to do a FaceTime call an hour ago. I didn't hear it ring."

"Is it too late to call back?"

"Big time, it's almost eleven. It might make me feel less guilty, but it won't do anything for *him* if I called right now."

He tapped his photo album and turned the screen toward me: a school photo of Sammy, who was tall and thin with twig arms, little cowlicks in his hair, Thom's bright-blue eyes, and a teeth-clenched grimace on his face. Despite the forced expression, my heart melted at the sight of him. It felt as though I was seeing Thom as a child. I wondered if Sammy liked to skateboard, too, and if Thom constructed ramps for him in the backyard. The kid was missing one of his baby teeth, the spot where the little fang would be. Why did I find that tooth so endearing in the grown-up version?

The answer came to me fast. *Because it's not picture-perfect. Because it's not ready for its close-up. Because it would never be allowed on TV.*

Thom mistook my staring for judgment.

"He doesn't smile on command," he explained rapidly. "He doesn't see why he should have to, and of course photographers don't get that, so they try to *make* him, which makes everything worse, so..."

"Thom, he's adorable," I assured him.

"He told me once, 'I save my smiles for when I'm really happy or really excited.' "

My heart clenched. He *saved* them. "As a grown woman, I certainly don't know what it's like for strangers to order me to smile."

He chuckled ruefully. "Right. You get it."

"I'll have to remember that line, though, about saving them up. And hey, when he does smile, at least you know it's real."

He cleared his throat. "Yeah."

"Got any videos?" I asked.

A grin leapt onto his face as he scrolled through his options. Once he found the one he was looking for, he pumped the volume and handed me the phone. It was a small thing, him passing it to me, but it meant a lot. About trust. About sharing part of his life with me that he'd been afraid to before. I was touched.

I tapped the play button.

Onscreen, Sammy picked his nose. A hand (Thom's, I assumed) reached into frame and pulled his hand away from his nose.

"Say it again," Thom's voice, amused and eager. "Say what you just said."

Sammy's big blue eyes sparkled. "I shi—I shit a fan." He giggled uncontrollably. "I shit a *fan*!"

"He heard one of my clients, on speakerphone, say 'the shit's about to hit the fan.' I couldn't turn off the speaker in time, and for a week I couldn't get him to stop saying 'I'm going to shit a fan' because that's what he thought he said."

"If I could shit any appliance, it would be a microwave," I said. "No, a blender."

"Air conditioner. For the car."

"Radio."

"I think you're missing the bigger picture. I'd be filthy rich. No overhead, no storage. Just Sammy shitting out household goods."

"He's ridiculously cute."

A cloud passed over Thom's face. "Sometimes. How old's your niece, again? Lacey, right?"

"Close. Lainey. She's ten—about to turn eleven. It's probably good I'm not watching her anymore. That's when girls 'turn.'" I pretended to wipe my brow with relief. "Got out just in time."

The TV above the bar, which I faced from our booth, was turned to the nightly news. The local anchor bantered with his co-host in a way I'd describe as "nearly human" about tonight's *Jerry Levine Show*, which started in ten minutes.

"Don't shit a fan, but J. J.'s on TV in a few minutes," I said in a rush.

"Why would I shit a fan?"

"You called him *People*'s Sexiest Moron."

"Yeah, well..." He looked down. "It's kind of loud in here," he pointed out. "Should we head back to the motel?"

"*You* don't have to watch. I can find a quieter spot." I looked around the Chili's, but if there was a quieter spot, it wasn't evident to me.

"Let's go. No big deal." He acted blasé, but the way he knocked back the rest of his drink suggested fortification.

7

Top 20 Most Crack-tastic TV Episodes of the '90s

Medium Editors

20. *Boy Meets World*, "And Then There Was Shawn." Most of the cast bites it (yes, even Mr. Feeny) in this slasher-flick homage to *Scream* and *I Know What You Did Last Summer*. Murder weapons include pencils and scissors. Jennifer Love Hewitt stops by for a cameo. What more could you ask for?

19. *Days of Our Lives*, "Marlena Is Possessed by the Devil." For several months in 1995 and 1996, mild-mannered perpetual victim Dr. Marlena Evans went through a killer menopause (or was that just my interpretation?) in which the good doctor transformed into a panther, seduced a priest (her former husband John Black), ruined Christmas, and flashed yellow demon eyes whenever other people exited the room.

18. *Diego and the Lion's Den*, "Fairy Tales Come True." Before starring in the WB's *Honeypot* and ABC's upcoming *Narc*, Kelly Hale sang and danced on a children's educational show set at the San Diego Zoo. In the third season—I swear to God this happened—she licked a toad and hallucinated. Some fans believe the rest of the series from that point on takes place entirely in Kelly's mind.

Jerry Levine's shtick—the mood of his entire talk show, really—was that of a fanboy Everyman who was suuuuuuper stoked to meet *everyone on earth*, from a cup-stacking tween to Vin Diesel. He was the anti-Letterman; a sweet younger brother to Jimmy Kimmel. Guests felt safe, which was how he booked all the top stars. They knew he'd make them look good and that his questions wouldn't approach anything resembling insightful.

Back in our room, I flipped on all the lights and located the right TV channel in time to hear the announcer's voice-over: "Tonight's guests are J. J. Randall, followed by the Be-Bop Bunnies!" The audience whooped. The Be-Bop Bunnies—two bunnies who'd been trained to "dance" by jumping sideways, alternating who went over and who went under the other—had gone viral two months ago when some YouTuber recorded them boogying down to "Last Resort" by Papa Roach.

Thom stretched out across his bed, his long legs reaching

nearly to the end of it, and fit his earbuds in. "I'll be on my phone. Holler when the bunnies do their thing."

"How come you get to use your phone?"

"Because I'm cured." He stuck his tongue out.

I had the strongest urge to shut off the TV and find out what it tasted like.

I wiped my mouth, shook off my wanton thoughts, and focused on the program.

The opening monologue provoked zero laughs from me. It wasn't entirely Jerry Levine's fault; I was nervous and twitchy. Although I'd been stalking the *Den* gang online for several weeks, I'd deliberately avoided J. J. Last I heard he was dating the new choreographer of the *Break It Down* dance movies. I hadn't gone looking for details. And then of course there was the phone call last week where he offered me money. Thinking about that made my insides twist.

Years and continents had passed since we last interacted. I'd seen his picture online or in magazines, of course, but I hoped this interview would serve as a warm-up for Friday night, take some of the shock out of it.

The fact that there were only two guests instead of three told me it would be an in-depth interview. (If Jerry had had depth.)

Jerry asked that we give a warm welcome to "Jason. James. Randalllllll!" Screams and general cacophony filled the air. Thom looked up sharply from his phone. I took the hint and lowered the volume.

On TV, a young woman in the first row held up a handmade sign: J. J., YOU'VE BEEN A BAD BOY. GO TO MY ROOM.

I rolled my eyes—it wasn't the first time I'd seen that sign—but the rest of me didn't respond so casually. My stomach clenched and I realized I was holding my breath.

J. J. sauntered out. He wore a bright-orange Supremes tank top, a pair of shredded, stonewashed jeans, striped socks, and red checkerboard Vans. Around his neck he wore not one, not two, but three crosses, and his left arm was covered in ink; I'd held his hand for the first three designs, now lost among the jumble of ones I'd never seen before. A backward trucker hat and barely visible skinny bandanna held his unruly hair back from his face.

Thom stifled a laugh.

"What?" I asked.

"All that streetwear." He sounded affronted. "Does he even ride?"

"Not that I know of."

"I thought celebrities had people who dressed them for these kinds of things."

I nodded vaguely.

The ensemble had obviously been painstakingly crafted in the new spring style. The hair filled with product to make it appear unwashed in the look *Vogue* had called Scuzz Couture, but Thom didn't need that information. Nor did he need to know J. J. had once employed the services of a Swag Coach.

The frenzied patterns, gauche colors, needless layers, $1,000 jeans, overlapping tattoos, and scruffy facial hair made no difference; to me, J. J. would always be as clean-cut as the day I met him. Because I knew his heart. His kindness. His unending patience. The person I'd loved more than half my life was still in there, so quick to blush, so eager to be *good*, his eyes bright and warm and eager, and it made my breath catch.

He and Jerry enacted an elaborate handshake to even louder shrieks from the audience.

“You know they practiced that for weeks,” Thom remarked, with a roll of his eyes.

I ignored him, but I knew he was right.

Once they’d settled in their cushy chairs, Jerry welcomed J. J. to the show and lobbed him a softball question. “You’re from North Carolina originally, right? What are your favorite things they say back home that might get you a funny look in other places?”

J. J. smiled. “If it’s rainin’ real hard, we’d say, ‘The devil’s beatin’ his wife and ran off with his stepdaughter.’ If someone’s a rascally sort o’ character without any prospects, we’d say, ‘He ain’t got a pot to piss in or a window to throw it out of.’ ”

J. J. hadn’t lived in North Carolina since he was a kid, but he still had a slight drawl. Renee and I used to do his banking for him, because there wasn’t an automated phone system on earth that could understand him. When given the choice of “Yes” or “No,” J. J. politely added “sir” or “ma’am” afterward, in full accent.

“Let’s go back, let’s go back…” Jerry sang, in a passable Aretha Franklin impression.

“Let’s go way back, a-way-back when,” J. J. finished.

“You had some good news this week. Your former manager, OffBeat’s former manager, was sentenced for fraud. Twenty years in the slammer! Let’s talk about that for a second.”

“Do we have to?” J. J. replied, deadpan. The crowd laughed heartily, thinking he’d made a joke.

I guaran-fucking-tee you he did not want to talk about it.

That’s when it hit me. The reason he’d called me at rehab: Pam was finally, *finally* going to jail, and he’d wanted to share the news. (“Wait, there’s something else…” he’d said, before I hung up.) He hadn't been checking in on me. He'd been checking in on himself, through me.

J. J. was convinced Pam had ruined his life. His determination to view things that way overflowed like sewage into the rest of his relationships, including ours. Especially ours.

Onstage with Jerry, he succumbed to a micro-expression of annoyance but quickly altered it to a smile. "Sure. What do you want to know?" *Everything's great, nothing to see here, I'm just your average thirty-something Christian pop star enjoying a #blessed existence!*

"You told the *New York Times* back in 2012 that your manager, Pam Oyster, had financially assaulted you guys. What happened there? Walk us through it."

"Yeah. Our first clue should've been that she wasn't even in the music business."

Laughter from the audience, as though he were sharing a silly story from his weekend.

"I'm serious. She had a company that rented party zeppelins. Which, if you don't know, is sort of like a blimp. She'd rent them out for special events, supposedly. We found out later she didn't even have any; just an empty warehouse and a website for investors. And that's where we would rehearse, in the empty warehouse, in like a hundred and ten degrees. But she spent money like a billionaire so we figured she was legit."

"And how'd she find you guys? How'd she put the band together in the first place?"

"Well, two of us—me and Brody Rutherford..." (He paused for screams.) "...were on a kids' TV show together—"

"*Diego and the Lion's Den*," Jerry interrupted. "Which we'll get to in a second because oh-em-gee, classic."

"—and when he joined the group, over in Texas, he called me to audition, too. We wanted to make good music for other kids to dance to, you know?"

I glanced over at Thom, who was watching the TV. When he saw I'd caught him, he returned to scrolling on his phone.

"In hindsight it's obvious," J. J. added, "but at the time, no one would've guessed she was shady. She told us to call her Mom."

"Ugh, super creepy." Jerry shivered.

A still photo of Pam in a prison jumpsuit, handcuffed, flashed on the screen.

"She was finally sentenced last week," Jerry explained. "After how many years of litigation? Ten? Fifteen?"

"Something like that." (Trust me. He knew *precisely*.) J. J. raised a mock glass to Pam. "Cheers, Pammy."

Scattered laughs came and went; perhaps they'd finally caught on to the fact that J. J. might be bitter about the past.

Join the club, Jay.

Jerry swiftly changed topics. "So, the PBS kids' show, *Diego and the Lion's Den*, is having its twenty-fifth anniversary this Friday at Rockefeller Centerrrrrr." From his seat, he made a quick raise-the-roof motion. "And guess who's hosting the after-party?"

Successfully rerouted, the audience slid onto this new path with relief, and offered up cheers and screams.

"It's time for a commercial break but when we come back, I have a super-awesome clip from the show. If you were a kid in the 'nineties you do *not* want to miss it."

Thom's earbuds were on the bedspread now.

"I never understood what happened with the manager," he told me. "Who was she? How did she get away with it?"

I muted the TV and we faced each other, cross-legged, from our respective beds.

"From my seventeen-year-old perspective, Pam seemed weird but benign; she sort of faded into the wallpaper. You most definitely did *not* think *international con artist*."

"Ah."

"J. J., Brody, and the rest of the band performed in Europe nonstop for years. Pam paid for everything—flights, hotels, meals, clothes, rehearsal, demos. She even paid for *me* to fly out and visit J. J. in London."

(If we go to hell it'll be worth it.)

"She told the boys that once she recouped the money she'd invested in them, they'd all get paid," I explained. "They expected half a mil each, easy. On the day of reckoning, they had the number-one single and video in Britain. But the check was for ten grand each, for years and years of work.

"It turned out their contracts were completely bogus. She'd put herself in them to get paid five different ways. First, as a member of the band—I know, it's absurd, a fifty-year-old woman in a boy band—but also as a producer, manager, booking agent, and songwriter."

"Holy shit. What'd the judge say?"

"The judge agreed she couldn't possibly pay herself as a member of the band, but otherwise the contract was technically legal. The trial took forever because she fled the country and they had to extradite her. What nailed her in the end was the zeppelin Ponzi scheme."

"It's back on." Thom nodded toward the TV and picked up his phone. However, he didn't put his earbuds back in.

Onscreen, to my surprise, a familiar tune poured through the speakers and I automatically mouthed the words:

What would you do
If you could live at the zoo?
Roar like a lion
Stretch like a giraffe
Jump like a kang-a-rooooo
Join us! Join us!
We live at the zoo
You can visit us too
Join us! Come join us!
Our days are filled with derring-do

The final part of the show's theme song showed each cast member popping their head out from a different section of the titular lion's den to shout his or her name.

Brody! J. J.! Mel-o-dee!
Holly! Ethan! Tara and Kel-ly!

Back to the late-night studio, the camera swung over to Jerry's empty desk as he jumped up behind it to shout, "Jerry!" then turned to reveal an empty couch as J. J. leapt out: "J. J.! Again!"

The audience lost it.

"*Lion's Den* Roll Call. I just fulfilled a lifelong dream," Jerry said, breathing hard. Once he and J. J. were settled in their seats, he asked, "What was it like, being on TV when you were, what, eleven? Twelve?"

"Oh my goodness, it was like summer camp." (That's what *I* used to say.) "Free trips to SeaWorld. Joyrides in stolen golf carts. Running around the beach at Hotel Del in the middle of the night. Talent shows. Mixtapes. Remember those? Crushes on our tutors. All that good stuff."

Don't forget promises to always be there for each other.

The execution of which turned out to be pretty lopsided.

"I need to ask you some things about the show, because looking back, it doesn't make a whole lot of sense."

J .J. pretended to play dumb. "It was basically a documentary, so I have no idea what you mean."

I grinned despite myself.

"Why did you live in a lion's den?" Jerry asked. "Isn't that a lawsuit waiting to happen?"

"No, it was safe, the lion was never there. In the first episode you find out he was getting a new habitat. So we were able to chill there."

"For five years?"

J. J. laughed. "It was for little kids."

"Hey, I watched it until I was like, twelve." He coughed. "Mostly for Kelly."

"But only for Kelly, right?" J. J. said at the same moment, and everyone laughed.

"Next problem: Did they ever go to school? How did they learn anything?"

"They learned at the zoo."

"Only about zoo stuff!"

"What do you want from me?" J. J. said.

"These are pretty thin answers, I gotta say. Was it true Tara was secretly twenty-seven when she auditioned for the show?"

J. J. laughed. "No, man, she was ten like the rest of us. She always sounded like that. Even at four foot nine, in braids, she was a belter."

"Last question, then we'll show the clip. There's a fan theory from a while back that got resurrected this week, about the time Kelly licked a toad in season three and went on a drug trip."

J. J. threw his hands up in pretend-frustration. "What are you even talking about? Are you sure you aren't the one tripping?"

"I'm just saying, it would explain *a lot*..."

"Does the guy from *Blue's Clues* get interrogated like this?"

I guffawed. He and Lainey used to watch it on DVD, and he was right: That show made *no* sense.

"That was pretty funny," Thom conceded.

"Roll the clip," directed J. J., circling his finger in the air.

"Hey, that's my line. Ahem. I have a clip from the show," Jerry announced. "And it's not any clip. It's the blooper reel from the first episode."

J. J. covered his face in mock-horror. "How'd you even find that?"

I knew what it would show, because you don't forget a train wreck of that size. We were supposed to ad-lib the opening segment. For most of us, it was our first time on camera.

The blooper scene fired up.

"People! We are live in five! Four! Three! Two!" (Mr. Studdard, off camera.)

Kelly was only half made up. She looked like the villain in a Batman comic.

On tape days she gelled her epic curly hair back into a bun that slowly unfurled as the day wore on. Due to the Studdards' insistence on producing the show themselves, no one had hired a script supervisor or continuity editor, so close-ups of Kelly within the same scene were jarring. She'd go from long hair to short hair and back like a subliminal message. In their Retro Flashback Summaries, *Television Without Mercy* once referred to season one as "seizure-inducing."

Kelly, Tara, Brody, J. J., and I ran onto the set.

Watching from two and a half decades removed, I inhaled sharply, practically feeling the cold air of the soundstage hit my skin. The thermostat was kept at fifty-eight degrees because the audience members, lights, and constant physical activity—singing and dancing, mainly—heated the place up. The chill kept us focused, too; after three hours of tutoring and five hours of rehearsals every day, we needed the cold blast to reenergize us for the live audience. By the time we shot the studio segments in the late afternoon / early evening, we were exhausted, but the adrenaline rush from performing kept us bouncing and bopping.

The main set piece was the Lion's Den itself: a smooth, fiberglass-coated "mountain" that composed the lion's living area. The boys used to jump from peak to peak until the health insurance company forbade it. The enclosure had a large open space with a tan camouflage dance floor, as well as a roofed section, bed-size cubbies embedded in the main structure where we allegedly slept (on hay and straw, for some reason), and a picnic table where we ate. It was rare for the scripts to include eating, but for one of the Christmas episodes we baked pies, "and with a parent's help, you can follow along at home. *Yum.*"

"Rolling," said Mr. Studdard once the five of us had gathered in a lump in the middle of the set. But his ear mike had malfunctioned and no one heard him.

"What a cock-up this is," Tara sighed, smoothing her hair.

J. J. turned beet red.

Brody hissed, "You can't say that. You can't say that word."

"What, *cock-up*?"

"Stop saying it!"

"In the theater, they would've—"

"You guys," Kelly said through clenched teeth, "the TVs are rolling. The TVs are rolling."

" 'The TVs are rolling'?" Tara repeated, perplexed.

"The cameras, she means the cameras," Brody shouted.

"The telly's not *rolling*." Tara giggled hysterically. Even our professional stage actress fell prey to nerves.

"Get it together," Kelly pleaded out the side of her mouth.

J. J. froze and stared directly into the camera. He didn't utter a peep for the rest of the opening segment.

The others talked vaguely and loudly about the agreed-upon ad-libs regarding "the band's demo" and "waiting to hit it big" despite "living at the San Diego Zoo," until mercifully...

Kelly performed an old drill team routine from school, minus the team.

Brody tossed her a wooden walking stick. She caught it effortlessly and used it as a baton. While the rest of us watched, she performed a military march, a solo Rockette kick line, and a few twirls without music or sound.

When she finished, I stepped forward to provide the edutainment aspect of the scene: "Did you know the California sea lion is the fastest of all the sea lions and that males can weigh up to seven hundred seventy pounds?" I squawked.

"Noooo," said Kelly.

"Oh my God, pause it," Thom begged. His eyes shone with delight. He even threw in a toddler-esque handclap.

"It's not a DVR," I said.

He pointed at the TV with glee. "That's you, though, isn't it?"

I blushed. "Uh, yeah."

Onscreen, Tara reemerged from behind Brody, her human shield, and tried to draw out the California sea lion sequence with me, asking me questions about their eating habits and vocalization barks, but Brody was acting like the main character in *Memento*; he couldn't seem to remember anything that had happened in the previous thirty seconds, so his way of coping was to repeat Tara's questions after they'd already been addressed.

The three of us attempted to steer the conversation in opposing directions until J. J. boldly stepped forward.

And that's how we found out he couldn't just sing.

He could motherfucking dance.

No wonder Jerry chose that particular blooper. It showcased his ol'-buddy-ol'-pal in the most flattering light. The current studio audience went nuts for it.

The clip ended.

"You had some serious moves," Jerry said. "Give it up for baby J. J."

J. J. smiled modestly, looking a bit dazed. "Wow. Lots of memories."

"Got a favorite one?"

"Yeah. How close we all were, getting to play pretend all day, how every day was something new. I actually lived with one of my castmates because my parents had to get back to work. Her parents became my legal guardians so I could stay on the show."

Jerry about popped a forehead vein from the sheer *Teen Bop* Excitement of it all. "'*Her*'? Who was it? Kelly? Please let it be Kelly, please let it be Kelly..." He crossed both sets of fingers and held them aloft.

"No, it wasn't her."

"Oh man...we've got to break for a commercial, but when we come back maybe we can find out who the mystery girl is."

Ad break.

I studiously avoided Thom's gaze.

"It's you, isn't it?" he deduced. "You're the one he lived with." His voice sounded flat, but then again, everyone on earth's voice sounded flat when contrasted with Jerry Levine's.

I nodded. "His parents ran the youth group at a megachurch in North Carolina and couldn't take all those months off. But the *real* reason was they had second thoughts after arriving in California and decided they didn't want J. J. to be on TV. They wanted him to live a life serving God and didn't think the two were compatible. I saw how heartbroken J. J. was, so I begged my parents to step in, just for a little while so he could tape the show. We thought it would last a few months, tops."

"And his parents agreed?"

"Well, no. Until J. J. told them they could have every dollar he made for the church, even the stuff that was supposed to go into a trust fund by state law."

Thom looked appalled. "Jesus."

"Exactly."

The years he spent living at my parents' house in San Diego were wonderful. It was the only time of my life I'd go back to and relive without changing a single thing. So much of our relationship to come was about the distance between us. It was hard to remember we lived under the same roof for *years*. Hard because it hurt to think about, and hard because it felt like a fantasy; but it was real, it happened, and no one could take it away from us. There'd been so many paths ahead of us, so many choices. Back then, it felt as though the future was vast, and friendly, and receptive to any possibility, when in fact my best parts had already happened, and only J. J.'s future was wide open.

"When they come back from commercial, he won't say my name, though. Just wait. He'll change the subject. He's never mentioned me by name to the press. Not once."

"Why the hell not?"

His anger startled me. I always forgot that while the story was old news to me, something I'd lived with since adolescence, it sounded strange to everyone else.

"He was protecting me from hate mail," I explained. "Nobody wanted to imagine the cute boys from OffBeat dating anyone. They weren't allowed to have girlfriends because it would alienate their fans. That's what Pam always said."

"But Brody and Melody dated," Thom pointed out. "And no one was bothered by that. That was, like, tabloid ecstasy."

"That was okay because they were equally famous and she was the band's opening act. That *helped* the band; constant free publicity. But it wasn't real."

"Are you kidding me?"

"I'm really not."

His knowledge of pop culture had been thrown out of alignment. "But...but...Brody and Melody were, like, a super couple. And that's not a word I use lightly. Or ever."

I shrugged. "That's what you were meant to think."

Once again, he noticed the program's return before I did. "Show's back on."

I hesitated to turn up the volume. I would rather have talked more with Thom.

When I didn't move right away, Thom pumped the volume in time to hear J. J. confess, "She was my first girlfriend. My first kiss. My first love, Holly Danner. And we tried to make it work for years, under the radar."

I felt a detonation in my gut. It spread through my limbs. Why on earth did he wait till now, when we hadn't spoken in five years, to talk about me to the press? How could he do something like that without discussing it with me first?

The answer hit me like a pile of bricks.

He'd done it because he was mad.

It had thrown him for a loop when he showed up in San Diego and I wasn't there, waiting for him. In the past I'd stood by him, argued for him, taken him back over and over, because the main, unspoken agreement between us was that I was supposed to wait for him, and then I was supposed to fold at a moment's notice, whenever and wherever he asked. That's how it worked for so many years; why would this time be any different?

Yet it had been. When he sauntered back to our old stomping grounds, I was gone, and all he could do was ask Renee for my phone number. And then when he reached out, I hung up on him. I'd flipped the script, and he couldn't handle it.

J. J. leaned in toward Jerry as though he were sharing a heartbreaking story with a friend instead of millions of viewers.

"And now she won't talk to me," J. J. pouted.

"Awwww," fretted the audience.

"She won't even pick up the phone."

They booed me! Assholes!

I flailed at Thom. "See? He's getting them on his side. Who would hang up on J. J.? She must be AN UNGRATEFUL BITCH."

"Wow. He didn't say *that*..."

"Oh, come on. That was obviously the implication." I shut the TV off with a decisive click.

"Are you okay?" Thom asked.

I flexed my fingers in his direction. "Phone, please? I need to correct some shit on Reddit."

"He cheated on you, didn't he? I'm not judging you, I'm judging him."

"No. He really didn't."

"Come on. He was in a *boy band, traveling the world*."

"He could barely get past the guilt of having sex with *me*. Why would he cheat with a stranger?"

"He barely had sex with you?" Thom lowered his voice. "J. J. Randall's gay?"

"No, he's born again. And again. And again."

"Wait, didn't he get a DUI?"

I jerked my chin in a manner that could be construed as a nod.

"Was it church wine?" Thom goaded me. "Or was that between confessions?"

"He's evangelical, not Catholic. And after the whole debacle with his manager ripping them off, he became a..." I closed my eyes briefly. "A Christian stoner."

Thom tried to stifle a laugh, and failed. Badly. "Wait, what?"

"You know, 'God gave us this plant' and 'God helps those who help themselves' and 'Behold, I have given you every herb-bearing seed.'"

Thom's eyes practically twinkled. "No."

"Oh yes."

"But having sex with you was verboten?"

"No, I already told you, we had sex. Just... in bouts."

"I don't know what that means."

"It means whenever we reunited we hit it like jackrabbits but then he'd leave on tour again or to promote an album and while he was away he'd convince himself we shouldn't have done those things outside the bonds of marriage."

"Easy fix," Thom snapped. "Marry you."

"That was a whole other can of worms. Notice the lack of crosses on my person?"

"Atheist?"

"Agnostic. You?"

"I definitely see the value of churches, having a community to lean on, but dogma is a tough sell for me."

"I think it would have been easier if I was a nonbeliever. Then he could have walked away. But knowing there was a chance I'd come around, any moment, any day, probably kept us together past the expiration date."

Thinking back, it probably tortured him as much as his back-and-forth about sex tortured me. Our hopes that the other person would change inevitably turned to resentment.

"His faith inspired Renee's, though, and I'll always be grateful for that," I said.

Thom squinted at me. "Are you sure he's not gay?"

"How many times do I have to say it? He's not gay, Brody is." I clamped a hand over my mouth.

Thom's had fallen open.

"You didn't hear that from me," I insisted. "I never said that."

"So Melody wasn't just a fake girlfriend?" he whispered back. "She was a full-on beard?"

I nodded mutely.

"I would never say anything," Thom assured me. "And anyway, it's his business, not mine."

"It should have been Tara who faux-dated him," I remarked. I couldn't stop myself; talking with him was natural and easy, and I'd been starved for conversation about this particular topic for years. J. J. and I used to discuss it but we both found it hard to accept. I thought Brody should come out, and J. J. thought he shouldn't do anything. He never said "love the sinner, hate the sin" or anything like that—and he did love Brody—but I think he was still hoping Brody might turn out to be bi instead.

"Why Tara?" Thom leaned against the headboard with his hands behind his head, the way he used to sit at Prevail!, like he was settling in for a spell.

"They were close for a long time. But she didn't want any part of it. Until..." I hesitated, out of habit.

"You're the one who brought it up," Thom teased me. "Let the record state I have not been hounding you for information on Brody Rutherford's fake love life—"

"Shh, okay." I moved onto Thom's bed and he pulled his legs in so I'd have more room. I kept my voice low. "Melody's contract with Brody was about to fizzle out, and she wanted to date other people for real, so they agreed to 'break up' and say he'd cheated on her."

"Better to be an asshole to women than loving toward men," Thom paraphrased. "This just in: I hate everyone."

"Mel's team had written 'Low Down, Dirty (Cheat),' so it was perfect timing. It debuted at number one and helped Brody score an audition as a bad boy in one of the *Fast & Furious* derivatives."

Thom looked a bit ill. "Win-win, I guess."

"But back to Tara. She saw how much publicity he and Mel got for being a couple, how that could've been her, and I think she regretted turning him down. She and Brody came up with a long-term plan. Years one, two, and three, they'd plant items in the press and let the public wonder who he cheated on Melody with."

"Ugh, I remember that," Thom said. "Wasn't it a sketch on *SNL*, too?"

I nodded. "Year four, they'd float the possibility it was Tara and see how people reacted."

"How *did* people react?"

"Mixed, which was the point. Countless opinion pieces. Year five, they'd confirm it all in time for the release of Manchot's greatest hits, and play up the love-triangle / girl-fight angle. Year six, which is coming up now I think, is where it gets psycho—"

"Stop, I can't take any more," Thom begged.

"Sorry. Meet my 'friends,' for whom nothing is real and everything is calculated."

"But not you and J. J.," he floated.

"No," I said softly. "That was as real as it gets."

It was after midnight. Ten hours since I'd last been online, and so much had happened since then.

"Phone, please?" I opened my hand and waggled my fingers at Thom. "This can count for tomorrow's session, I swear. But I have to see what people are saying about J. J.'s interview."

"Nope. This would, in fact, be the worst time for you to go online."

"You get that you're not really my sober companion, right?"

"It was literally the only condition of my driving you to New York. And considering you've reneged on every other promise you made . . . " His tone was light, not serious, so I responded in kind.

"What are you, a lawyer now?"

"Secondly..." Thom intoned pompously.

"Stop pontificating. Give it to me," I interrupted, and moved closer to him on the bed.

He looked startled and held the phone behind his back. I tried to grab it.

He scrambled toward the headboard and I pursued him. I managed to get my fingers around the phone. His hand covered mine, warm and firm, like it had on the stick shift earlier today.

"What are you doing?" he asked.

Electric sparks flew between us. Around us. Under us. Over us.

I pulled and pulled and manage to dislodge it from his grasp. I whooped in triumph.

He wrapped one strong arm around my waist from behind and lifted me up, then reached around with his other hand and stole the phone back.

I turned in his arms. Our faces were inches apart.

He moved closer.

I stared at his lips. My entire body hummed in anticipation. Sure, I'd kissed him at Prevail!, but that was in service of getting his clothes off before either of us could think straight. This time, it would count. I would make sure of it.

But the knee-buckling kiss I longed for never came.

Instead, he let go of me, and I nearly toppled over. The hesitant smile on his face slowly morphed into a smug one.

"What?" I asked.

"Go ahead," he replied casually, handing me the phone and leaning against the headboard again, all stretched out on the bed like a jungle cat.

"Really?"

"Sure."

I remained standing above him, like a tower, but more like the Leaning Tower of Pisa; I swayed from how off balance he'd made me when he removed his arms from around my body. I moved with as much dignity as I could muster—which wasn't much—over to my own twin bed. It was like walking on a trampoline.

Mirroring his pose, I lay on my back and held the phone aloft.

"After those huge beds at Prevail!, this is an adjustment," Thom said.

"They're an obscenity."

I swiped my finger across his phone and filled in the password, vaguely curious how Thom knew that I knew it.

Bzz.

I swallowed, tried again. SAM-E, same as before.

Bzz.

I ground my teeth. Looked over at Thom on the opposite bed.

"Something wrong?" he asked innocently.

"You changed it, didn't you?"

"I have no idea what you're talking about." His grin widened.

"Oh, shut up."

"Do I need to sleep with it under my pillow, or are you going to behave tonight?"

In response, I chucked the phone at his bed. It bounced once on the mattress before he retrieved it.

I didn't want to behave. I wanted his arms around me again.

According to Thom, the reason he didn't have sex with me

before was because I'd been crying. Did that mean if I'd been cheerful, we would've gone at it full tilt?

Another thought hit me, unbidden: What if we *had* done it, and the sex was bad, and *then* we'd been forced on this road trip together? That would've made things more awkward than they already were. I should be relieved, I decided. It was a good thing he'd turned me down.

Please. Who was I kidding.

I *knew* it wouldn't have been bad sex.

A moment later, the lights were out and the room was dark. I lay under the sheets, listened to Thom breathe, and stared at the ceiling, unable to stop smiling.

I think he knew it, too.

8

INT. LION'S DEN—DAY

(ETHAN, J. J., DIEGO, KELLY, TARA, HOLLY)
Ethan, wearing a bear costume (minus the head), sits at the picnic table, surrounded by party streamers, banners, balloons, etc.

ETHAN

Fun fact: When bears wake up from hibernation, they don't sleep for the next three months. They haven't eaten in forever, so they spend all day and night looking for food. It's a non-stop party! If they live near humans, they'll even eat garbage.

(puts on the bear head, walks to the front door and opens it)

Hey guys, come on in!

Music cue: generic party music in the b.g. (no lyrics). The PARTY BEARS enter (J. J., DIEGO, KELLY, TARA), dressed up as different bears (panda, brown bear, koala bear, and black bear, respectively), wearing party hats, carrying gifts, amped up. They set their items down and begin to dance. HOLLY staggers in, dragging four garbage bags behind her.

HOLLY

Sorry I'm late! I brought the chow!

She tosses full garbage bags into the room and everyone cheers. The bears dive in, ripping open the garbage and stuffing their faces.

J. J.

I call dibs on the banana peels!

Audience laughter.

At six a.m. on the dot, Thom's horrible alarming-alarm bleated from the floor where it was plugged in. He moaned and rolled toward it, leaning over the mattress and sliding his thumb across the screen. His gym shorts got tugged down slightly in the process and I enjoyed the view of his sharp hip bone. I remained quiet, pretending to sleep, but sneaking a few looks over to see what he would do next. Sure enough, he broke his own rule and went online, his forefinger scrolling here and there, before tossing the phone back on the carpet.

While he used the bathroom, I sprang out of bed and dove

for the phone. To his credit, he hadn't been checking email, he'd been checking FaceTime, probably to see if he'd missed any other calls from home. I tapped settings and tried to change the auto lock to an hour instead of two minutes, but that in itself required use of the password.

Thinking fast, I tapped the YouTube app and played the first thing that came up so as to thwart the auto lock from kicking in. I muted the video and slid the phone under the bed.

Oh-so-nonchalantly, I joined him in the bathroom to brush my teeth.

We stood side by side, lather-rinse-repeating, domestic and comfortable. We looked like an ad for toothpaste and suburban calm.

"It's still early—all right with you if I go for a swim before we head out?" Thom asked over a foamy mouthful. Our eyes met in the mirror.

Thinking about the phone primed and ready for me under the bed, I nodded. "Sure, yes, absolutely," I said, still brushing. It came out like this: "Sir, wes, asso-woot-lee."

In unison, we spat, drank water, and wiped our mouths with face towels.

"You speak Toothbrush," he said.

"Certain dialects," I replied. "Crest, Colgate. I'm hopeless at Aquafresh."

He laughed and the sound made my heart sing. "Why don't you sleep in a bit more while I hit the pool?"

"Sounds good."

The instant the door, closed behind him, I dropped to the floor and threw myself under the bed where his phone continued playing whatever video I'd clicked to keep his auto lock from deploying.

When I saw what it was, I yelped, which caused me to bang my head on the under-frame of the bed.

Thom, you dirty dog. It was a pimple popping video. He'd been watching it last night during *The Jerry Levine Show.* That's why it was the first thing to come up when I opened YouTube.

I opened a new browser and scrolled through Thom's bookmarked sites. Was it weird I was semi-hoping for porn links? Not a lot of them—just one or two that might give me a glimpse into his turn-ons. But there was nothing like that saved. He probably deleted them before handing his phone to Lisa. At least, that's what I would've done if Renee hadn't offered to hold on to it for me.

The only bookmarks were for job sites, résumé builders, some game apps for children, his son's school calendar, and a TED Talk from three years ago.

What do we have here?

The TED Talk was Thom's! I obviously hit play.

Wearing a formfitting suit and old-school Vans with thick rubber soles, his dirty-blond hair gelled high and his sleeves rolled up, Thom was a skater boi who wouldn't look out of place on the cover of *Fortune* magazine. He addressed a modest crowd for his speech, and expounded upon a theme from Malcolm Gladwell's *Freakonomics*, which posited that when communities painted over graffiti and fixed broken windows, crime dropped in those areas. It was a psychological response—when residents and local police groups proved they *cared*, and that neglect and crime wouldn't be tolerated, it changed the perception of the location for the people who lived there, and they saw its value, too. As a result, they treated it better.

Thom's addition to the theory was that when you built

kids their own place—like a large, sound, well-lit skate park designed by someone familiar with the sport and its subculture—delinquency plummeted. "Give them a space that's theirs," Thom explained, "and they'll shower it with pride. They'll even volunteer a few hours a week to keep it in good condition.

"Let me give you an example. I grew up in Youngstown, Ohio. In the late nineteen nineties and early two thousands, huge swaths of Ohio got swept up in the opioid crisis, including my hometown. I watched kids I grew up with—pretty much everyone I knew—have it affect them in some way. I got my high from skateboarding. The kid I hung out with the most, though, broke his elbow—separated the tendon from the bone—and that was pretty much it for him. He was prescribed Oxycontin, with no intention of misusing it, but the withdrawals were brutal, and..." He trailed off. "I was always interested in what could have been done differently there. What would it have taken? A community center, a functioning city council, a place to go? A skateboard park with better safety measures in place?

"There's a sense of adventure when kids seek out their own place; it comes from the thrill that you might get caught. Critics might say the skate parks take that element away, in a sense, but they also provide something better: a sense of community. I like to think they do, anyway, and the evidence backs it up."

Thom's expertise shone through as he unveiled charts depicting the success he'd had all over the eastern seaboard ("I always took Sammy with me, or I made sure I got back before bedtime so I could read him a story"). He and his company had transformed neighborhoods and earned the respect of local businesses and families. He also wrote out specific steps community leaders could take to enhance opportunities for underserved youth by speaking to their passions in a manner that was neither condescending nor restrictive.

His speech was so compelling, I was ready to hire him to build a skate park in Balboa Park in San Diego.

He was a seasoned pro.

Fiercely intelligent.

Changing people's lives.

Making a difference.

I shut off his phone and lay on the carpeted floor in the darkened room, stunned, not moving.

I believed him, now; he'd told me the truth.

He hadn't been flirting with me.

Why would he have?

He was way, way out of my league.

His phone rang, the bright rectangle of light cutting into the darkness, the ring of FaceTime filling the quiet room. Using the bare minimum of movement, I rolled my body over to see who it was.

Sammy.

I leapt into action. I couldn't let my private pity party ruin Thom's chance to see his little boy. If it were Lainey calling, I'd have wanted him to do the same for me.

I accepted the call and waved into the camera. Onscreen, a rectangle of my face popped up. "Hi, you've reached Thom's phone," I said, as cheerfully as I could muster.

A confused pause. "Where's my dad?" Sammy tilted his head as though trying to look behind me.

"I'm going to find him for you."

Sam looked a little different from his photo—he'd recently

had a haircut, and there was a bit of food on his face—strawberry jam?—but his messy hair and lanky frame were pure, miniature Thom, a fact I found incredibly bittersweet right now.

I searched for my room key, unbolted the door and stepped into the hallway in my pajamas and socks, still chatting to him.

"I might lose you in the elevator, but don't hang up. I know he wants to talk to you. He's at the swimming pool. Okay?"

"Okay," Sammy said. "Who are you?"

"I'm Holly. We both needed to get to New York, so we're carpooling."

As predicted, we couldn't hear each other in the elevator, and his image froze on a serious expression, but once I made it to the first floor, he sprang back to life.

"Where are you?"

"We're in Elyria, about five hundred miles outside New York. So he'll be home late tonight, I should think."

"Oh."

"What's your favorite TV show?" I asked, darting down the hall toward what I believed was the pool.

"Um, I like *MythBusters*. It's kind of cool."

" 'Kind of cool,' huh? But what's your *favorite*? What do you watch when you're home sick and you get to watch whatever you want all day?" The way he smiled, a bit shyly, like he had a secret, made me think I was onto something, and my heart clenched.

"*PJ Masks*. I know it's, like, for little kids, but I still like it," he said matter-of-factly.

"I love *PJ Masks*! Who's your favorite bad guy? Mine's Luna Girl."

"I like Night Ninja and the Ninjalinos."

I pushed the doors open for the pool, inhaled the chlorine smell and damp air, and scanned the room. No Thom. *Maybe he was underwater holding his breath? For, like, a long time?* I walked closer and peered into the depths of the water. No Thom. Crap crap crap. Was he in the bathroom? Locker room? He'd be crushed if he missed the call…

Sam's grandmother—Thom's mother—entered the frame, all bobbed gray hair, bifocals, and curious eyes. She leaned in close to the camera and I could see up her nostrils for a moment. "Who are you talking to, Sam-Sam?"

"This woman who picked up Dad's phone."

Sammy turned his back to me so he could talk to her. Through his T-shirt, his shoulder blades were so sharp, it made my breath hitch in my throat. Lainey was the same way at that age, even up until two or three years ago, the blades like the nubs of angel wings trying to grow. That's what I'd always thought, anyway.

I waved. "Hi. Hello. Thom's here somewhere, I'm trying to find him, I'm going to circle back up to the room."

"How do you know Thom?" his mother asked. "He didn't mention he'd be traveling with anyone." She was probably wondering if she'd caught her son with a hitchhiker, a hooker, or both. At least I wore a respectable ensemble. My pink-and-gray polka-dot flannel outfit covered me from head to toe.

"I'm a friend from…" I had no idea if they'd used euphemisms for Prevail! or been upfront with Sam. "The health…provider…location. He's kindly giving me a lift. We're not staying in the same room." It was one of the dumbest lies I'd ever told. Obviously we were staying in the same room if I'd picked up his phone.

I retraced my steps, grateful for frozen screen images when

I entered the elevator again. Any follow-up questions they had about my existence would have to wait.

I entered the hallway to our room again, praying he was behind the door, but when I used my keycard and called out to him, there was no reply. There was, however, the sound of the shower running.

Shit.

"He's not there," Sammy told his grandma. His voice was one part resigned, one part jaded. As though he'd predicted this very thing, and had been vindicated.

"We'll try him again tonight," she replied smoothly.

"No, wait!" I knocked loudly on the bathroom door. No response. I jiggled the knob. Locked. I knocked louder. I would not be the reason he missed his son today. I would not be the reason for Sam's disappointment.

"Yeah?" came a muffled voice. "Kinda busy here."

"It's Sam. For you."

The door opened a crack and a dripping wet arm reached for the phone.

"Sorry," I told the arm, "I was trying to track you down, but..." I turned to the phone again. "Bye, nice to meet you."

"Bye. Nice to meet you, too," Sam parroted, waving.

"Hey, Sammy Bear," Thom said enthusiastically. He sounded like a morning show host, caffeinated and strained, like a switch had been flipped, or his battery had been replaced.

Sam's demeanor instantly changed. He stared back, eyes infuriated. "Not Sammy anymore. *Just* Sam. I told you that."

I placed the phone in Thom's hand and scurried away to give them privacy.

"Yeah, okay, I'm going to..." Thom swallowed and closed the door.

I rapidly dressed and packed my bag. Five minutes later, Thom exited the bathroom, fully dressed as well. His face looked ashen, rather than pink from the steam of the shower.

"Everything okay?" I asked carefully.

He slumped onto his bed. "'Just Sam' wasn't feeling the conversation."

"For what it's worth he was very polite when I talked with him."

"That's how I tried to raise him."

"From what I saw you've done a great job."

"You should've seen us six weeks ago. He couldn't get enough of me. Now everything I do annoys him. He's *eight*, it's not like he's a teenager, and I don't know how to fix it. If it *can* be fixed. I don't think he trusts me anymore. And I don't even blame him."

I sat beside Thom on the edge of the mattress. His skin radiated warmth, and his hair remained damp from the shower.

"I've never introduced him to a girl before," he said. "I always date on the down low. Not that I date much."

The women of upstate New York clearly didn't know a good thing when they saw it.

"Well, I introduced myself, so that doesn't count, and I definitely wouldn't have if I'd—"

"He liked you. Said you 'seemed cool.'"

"I can think of no higher praise. But don't sell yourself short. I watched your TED Talk. It was really, really good."

"Yeah?" He looked shyly pleased. It perfectly mirrored his son's expression when he'd talked about *PJ Masks*.

His relaxed expression tightened. "Wait, when did you see my TED Talk?"

"Um..."

It occurred to him I must've broken the internet rule and his eyes widened. "You sneaky little... You've been bad."

His voice pricked my nerves in a way that could only be described as anticipatory. "What are you going to do about it?"

"You get *no* screentime today."

His command did things to my insides, but my irritation overrode it. "You're treating me like a child. I did not agree to that. Besides, I didn't go to my usual site. I *cross-pollinated.* I had a chance to check Reddit *and* the *Daily Denizen*, but I didn't. That's got to count for something."

"Do you even know what cross-pollination is?" He folded his arms and waited for me to tighten my own noose.

"Maybe."

"I don't know if I should tell you. That's for graduates of Prevail! only."

"Just tell me."

"I don't know if you're ready for it."

"Thom!"

"If you take a tour of someone else's obsession, it will seem silly, thus puncturing the importance of our own obsessions when we imagine them viewed through others' eyes. It's a way of inserting objectivity and distance into our behavior."

"Did Lisa say all that?"

"It's my interpretation."

Damn, he was good. He could sell milk to a cow.

"If we're going to be all judgmental," I groused, "how do you explain *this*?"

I dramatically raised his phone and opened it to the YouTube video of pimple popping.

The only indication I'd surprised him was that one of his

eyebrows lifted. I wondered if Sammy could do that move. It had taken Lainey half her life to learn how to wink.

"She said it was relaxing, so I thought I'd try it out," he answered matter-of-factly.

"She said it was relaxing until she became addicted."

He shrugged. "We all have our crosses to bear."

"And was it? Relaxing?"

"No, it was fucking gross. The production values were terrible."

I snorted. "Shocker."

"The camera kept zooming in and out of focus, and there was always one zit over to the side that was ripe for popping that the doctor—or whoever, I got the feeling most of them aren't doctors—ignored, or didn't see. So the whole video becomes about hoping they'll get the *one* I had my eye on, and when they don't... Opposite of relaxing."

"Thanks for those visuals. I'm so hungry for breakfast now."

He stood, slid his phone in his back pocket. (*Lucky phone*, I thought idly.) "No time to eat."

We conducted a quick room check and picked up our bags. "I should at least raid the continental breakfast," I said.

"Okay, I'll go check us out."

9

In what would turn out to be a mistake, I insisted on driving the first shift.

Thom fed me pieces of toast and spoonfuls of yogurt while I drove. Normally I wouldn't have been impressed by the paltry food selection Motel 6 had on offer, but I was so hungry it tasted like a Thanksgiving feast.

The way he brought the toast to my lips made me self-conscious. Did I have crumbs on my lips? And what did he think of said lips? If I didn't know better, I'd think we were a couple. A nauseatingly cute couple.

We're saying goodbye in a few hours, I reminded myself. *Your crush is not only unreciprocated, it's pointless.*

He wiped a smattering of bread crumbs off his hands. "What's on your mind? Besides that, of course." (We were passing another one of Kelly's "Single Mom Cop Show" billboards. Gotta promote the Chicago-set TV program in the heartland, even though it's filmed in Canada.)

"Can I ask you something personal?" I said.

He finished chewing the last of his toast. "Okay."

"How come you chose internet rehab instead of Gamblers Anonymous?"

"Two reasons. First, it was free. Second, it was free."

"How can you be sure the treatment's going to work?"

"I don't think anyone can. I never sought out real-life poker, though; my problem was strictly online, which definitely exacerbated the situation. It didn't feel real; it was like playing a video game, which meant my money got swallowed up before I comprehended it, before I could see that it corresponded to a real bank account with real money in it. It seemed harmless. Pixels and pictures on a screen."

"You were scammed, you mean?"

"No, I knew what I was doing, but I didn't *let* myself know. You know what I mean? It was all about the endorphin rush I'd get when my phone or my desktop 'won' a round. It's the same spike of excitement you feel when a new email comes in, or you see a new response to your Reddit posts."

I'd felt those exact spikes at the Cracker Barrel yesterday, yet the high was brief, and didn't correspond to the level of anticipation I'd ascribed to it the previous three weeks.

"It's the same with gambling," Thom continued. "You're rewarded at random intervals. You might go days without winning, and then, *bam*, win six in a row. It happens enough to keep you hooked, and since it's random, there's no incentive to stop. In the next round, you *could* make all your money back. You really could. It's not likely, but it's possible." He cleared his throat, and I wondered if he was remembering a rewarding or terrible experience at his computer. Either way, he seemed ready to drop the subject. "Lisa referred me to a local GA group that meets every week in Greenburgh, so I'll check it out once I get home."

"Sounds like a plan," I chirped. Overconfident in my stick-shift abilities, I didn't slow down enough switching gears. Incensed, the Passat made a noise like broken glass dragged through gravel.

Thom winced at the sound.

"Sorry, sorry," I said.

"It's okay, take your time."

I concentrated on driving for the next forty-five minutes.

Perhaps sensing I'd regained my equilibrium, Thom started to talk, right when I said, "About when we get there..."

"Go ahead," he said.

"No, you."

Nauseatingly cute couple again.

I forged ahead. "I'll have a whole day and night to kill before the anniversary on Friday. I might be able to crash at a friend's place, but I'm not sure."

"We'll figure something out. Whether it's finding you a room in the city, getting you to a friend's, or...of course, you could, uh, crash at my place. In the guest room, obviously. Until you needed to go." He sounded nervous, the way he did before he asked me to hang out at Mall of America.

I took my eyes off the road for a split second. His clear blue eyes offered a calming solace. All I had to do was fall into them and float, dreamily, to shore.

"I won't leave you stranded," he promised.

I was dead certain he wouldn't. Thom was reliable. Thom was safe. (If I hadn't felt safe with him, I never would have gotten in his car in the first place. Still, it was nice to know he had my back.)

I tapped the brake and shifted gears again, a big improvement on my earlier attempts. It should have been a seamless transition (or as seamless as his POS car allowed), but the horrid screech returned, catching us off guard and menacing our ears.

That's when the engine died.

10

INT. LION'S DEN—DAY
(MELODY, HOLLY)

MELODY

Fun fact: Did you know crocodiles can't chew? It's true! Once their jaws clamp down, they can't lift up again, so they have to spin their bodies around to rip off smaller chunks and swallow them whole.

HOLLY, wearing Croc shoes, with a stuffed animal in her mouth, spins in a circle to demonstrate, thrashing her "prey" to and fro and growling. Cue: AUDIENCE LAUGHTER.

MELODY

(cheerful)

Same thing goes in a fight. The best way for one croc to kill another is to

```
    clamp down with its jaws on the other
    croc's face, piercing through its brain
    and eyes.

Song cue: "Never Smile at a Crocodile" (Melody
on vocals, Holly tap-dancing).
```

It took the tow truck an hour to reach us, and another twenty minutes for the mechanic to drive back and ferry us to his repair shop in Harrisburg. At least we'd crossed the border into Pennsylvania a while back.

The mechanic wore a long-sleeved shirt and Wranglers over his boots. A patch with his name stitched on it—BENJAMIN—completed the ensemble. He tried to keep his voice free of judgment but it was pretty effing obvious he couldn't believe how old our car was.

"Engine failure" was the official diagnosis. "You see this a lot with the older Passats," he said, jotting words on his clipboard. "Most likely caused by an oil sludge."

"See?" I muttered childishly. "It wasn't my fault."

Thom had been silently seething ever since we'd pushed the car over to the side of the highway and called for help. The ride to Ben's shop had only increased his frustration.

"I never should have let you drive."

"'Let me'?" I repeated, enraged.

"What if we'd gotten pulled over? You don't even have your license on you."

Ah. True. I decided shutting up was my best move.

"You'll need a new engine—" said Ben.

"Not an option," Thom interrupted.

"At the very least, I need to clean it and replace a few parts, but to be honest, from where I'm standing, the car's not worth the parts."

"Yeah, okay," Thom replied gruffly, swiping a hand through his hair. "But that doesn't exactly help us."

"I'd offer to buy it from you, but it's not eligible for the Cash for Clunkers program."

Something about that combination of words, and the fact they'd been used by a business owner in an actual sentence about our fate struck me as comical.

"Did you hear that?" I shrieked at Thom. "He said it's not up to the standards of a Clunker." I laughed like a lunatic. Confused by my contradictory, potent emotions, tears of mirth *and* anger filled my eyes. I was light-headed from lack of food, and *Clunker* had become the only word I ever wanted to see, use, or hear for the rest of my life. It was clearly the most perfect word ever invented. It captured the sadness of its subject as well as the sound it made when it fell to pieces. I was so grateful to whoever made up that word that I couldn't stop talking even if I'd wanted to. "It's not Clunker material," I sputtered helplessly. "The *Clunkers* won't allow it in their *club*."

Ben faced Thom. "Is she okay?"

"This is how she always is," Thom said.

"Oh, nice," I snapped.

"Get it together," he added through clenched teeth. It was exactly what Kelly had said in the blooper reel from the first day on set.

I no longer saw the guy I'd shared secrets with, the guy I

admired, who understood and challenged me in ways I hadn't known I was missing.

I saw a stranger preventing me from what I needed to do and where I needed to go. The whole reason I'd gone on the ridiculous road trip was to bust up the anniversary, and I'd lost sight of that, and it was Thom's fault for having such an absurd, ancient CLUNKER of a car.

I glared at the Passat and flung my arm in its direction. "Why is this your car? *Why?*"

He didn't answer, which angered me further, so I got in his face. "Seriously. Why would this be anyone's car? You have a good job, you're obviously smart, so what the actual fuck?"

"I sold my Mercedes to pay off my debts, okay?" he bellowed. "Are you happy now? I stole from Sammy's 529 to fund my gambling, and until I pay him back, until I put every goddamn cent back in his college account where it belongs, I'm living like a pauper and my car was the first thing to go. So to answer your question, it's a piece of shit because *I'm* a piece of shit!"

I knew I should argue, tell him it wasn't true and he had so much to be proud of, at work and with his kid, but I didn't have it in me right then. All of this was for nothing. If I was going to miss the anniversary anyway, I should've stayed at Prevail! and tried to have a normal existence again, whatever that meant.

"So what'll it be?" Ben said. "The tow's on me if you decide to fix the car, but otherwise I'm going to need seventy-five."

"Seventy-five just to walk away from it? Can we at least set it on fire first?" I moaned.

"What'll it cost to clean out the sludge and get the other parts you need?" Thom said.

He thought for a moment. "Seventy-five."

Of course. "Either way he needs seventy-five. Give him the money," I told Thom.

"Then we only have twenty-six left," Thom exploded. "That's barely enough for half a tank of gas!"

"Then we better hope he can fix it!"

"I'll throw in gas," Ben offered, probably to shut us up.

A cord in Thom's neck twitched as he reluctantly handed Ben the cash. "Fill it all the way up."

Ben nodded. "I'll get started on the paperwork." He walked away quickly, to escape our spat before we got any more of it on him.

I angled my head so I could see Thom's watch. Even his watch annoyed me right now. *Who wears a watch?*

"It's noon," I said. "Can I go online, 'Daddy'?"

He shot me a withering look. "Fine."

He tapped the code and handed the phone over.

"Aren't you going to set the timer?" I asked.

"Fuck it. I'm going on a walk," he said tonelessly.

"Good idea. Maybe some exercise will make you feel better."

He didn't reply. His face remained blank, which upset me more than his earlier despair. I could see him shutting down right before my eyes.

He left and I sat on the curb outside the repair shop and refreshed the *Daily Denizen*'s countdown clock.

1 day

8 hours

7 minutes, 26 seconds

We weren't completely out of the running yet. Maybe Ben would surprise us and pull off a miracle.

Next up, Twitter. At least #JJJ was no longer trending.

However, something else was, and it took me a moment to understand what it meant.

#PickupthephoneHolly

I clicked on the phrase and entered a house of horrors. He'd tattled on national television last night, claiming I wouldn't take his calls. Played the part of a poor, jilted lover left out in the cold.

Somehow, he'd spun my "hanging up on him once" into "Holly should be publicly shamed for not following the protocols of interacting with famous people."

#PickupthephoneHolly

Some of the tweets included gifs of J. J. in the *Break It Down* movies crying into a pay phone, or his face hovering over a nuclear explosion. Yet another involved a speech bubble drawn above J. J.'s head: "Surprise, BeatOffs! Not gay!"

There were thousands of mentions, and even links to articles purporting to "introduce me" to "the world."

"Who the Hell Is Holly Danner?" TMZ demanded to know.

As if in response, a *People* magazine headline read, "The Girl Next Door Who Captured J. J. Randall's Heart." They chose a blurry photo from their archives, me at Brody's twenty-seventh birthday party at Soho House, the same batch of WireImages Lisa had shown me in her cramped office. In the picture, I raised a glass of champagne, my mouth wide with laughter. The champagne had spilled and dribbled on my shirt. *Girl next door, my ass,* the image seemed to say. *Next door to a liquor store, maybe.*

At least I looked happy in the photo. I'd been nannying for over a year by then, and the party provided a much-needed break from diapers and spit-up.

Star magazine pondered, "Childhood Sweethearts No More?"

Us Weekly took it a salacious step further with "The Girl

Who Broke His Heart," a misleading statement paired with a photo from my senior year in high school in which I rehearsed for the school play as Diana in *Lend Me a Tenor*. Diana's sort of a sexy role, and I'd been proud of my teen-self for doing it justice. I got to wear my hair in a Lauren Bacall style and a low-cut dress with a slit up the thigh. In the photo, *as the character*, I kissed another character, because that was what happened in the play. *Us Weekly* clearly intended to imply I'd cheated on J. J. all those years ago.

I asked myself something many a celebrity has likely pondered: Why was there always someone with a yearbook handy, willing to scan it at a moment's notice?

The hate directed at me in the comments section was astounding. All the things I'd been insulated from in the '90s, especially pre-internet, rushed out at full speed. A geyser of mean.

ewwwww

Howl-y is like if a horse had a baby with the clown from american horror story

she thirsty AF. Run, JJ!

would not bang

Yikes! Jay-jay darling you can do so much better

For the first time I understood, on a visceral level, why it had been a good idea to keep me a secret.

J. J. *had* been protecting me.

I'd accepted it intellectually at the time. I'd understood in the abstract that it wasn't healthy to court the press or invite them into my life. I'd seen the damage paparazzi could cause, read the fabricated articles speculating on my friends' personal lives, and naively felt left out of their shared experience of running from the cameras.

But today, five years since J. J. and I broke up for the final time, and twenty-five years since I'd first been on TV, a shudder of relief rolled through me regarding what might have been, and I sent a prayer up to the heavens. Thank God no one knew about me back then. Thank God I had been left alone.

Thom's hand appeared and playfully covered the screen.

"Come to put a stop to my fun?" I asked.

"Is that what your expression means?"

"I'm trending on Twitter." I pivoted the phone screen so he could look. "Hashtag PickupthephoneHolly."

"How do you know you're the Holly?"

"Look at this one: 'What an ungrateful bitch.' What did I tell you? Word for word." I felt strangely pleased.

"Congratulations. You predicted the internet's misogyny."

"Some group calling themselves J-fenders have decided to hold a candlelight vigil on his behalf. Until I pick up the phone, I guess. You'll be waiting a long time, J-fenders. Don't burn down the house."

After reading insults about myself for five minutes, numbness spread over me. I'd been removed from the world, peeled off like a scab and thrown away. The only thing I knew for sure was this Holly Danner chick seemed like a grotesque waste of skin.

Why did anyone think social media would improve humanity? How could anyone handle that kind of treatment for years on end? Day, after day, after day?

I popped over to my inbox, where emails from twenty or so entertainment publications, blogs, and gossip rags waited for me, requesting interviews. They probably thought I'd leap at the chance to cast off the shackles of obscurity.

Instead I scrolled until I found an email from my sister, time-stamped yesterday afternoon.

> We're taking the red-eye home tonight. I can't believe you left rehab! YOU MUST TELL ME EVERYTHING. I'll FedEx your purse to you—where do I send it? Love, Renee and Lainey

I handed the phone to Thom. "Could you type in your address, please? My sister needs to know where to send my stuff. If it's okay with you, I mean."

"Sure, no problem." He dutifully followed my request.

"Thanks."

We both seemed to be overcompensating for our earlier fight by treating each other with kid gloves.

"What's all this stuff?" he asked, referring to the influx of interview requests.

"Everyone wants a piece of J. J.'s piece."

"Make 'em wait," he suggested. "You'll be giving those reporters a great story tomorrow night. Let the mystery about you build. Better they're clamoring for you and curious about you."

If there's one thing I'm good at, it's keeping a low profile.

"That's a good point."

"I occasionally have them."

"You think we can still get there before eight o'clock tomorrow?" I asked tentatively.

"We don't have far to go. Three hours' drive, four tops. If the car cooperates."

"Bus tickets?"

He shook his head. "The closest station is fifteen miles away.

We don't have enough cash to get to the station *and* pay for tickets."

"Train?"

"Even worse."

"So waiting on Ben is our only choice?"

"Looks like it."

There *was* another choice, but I wasn't going to be the one to bring it up. It had to be Thom. I'd give him a few hours, and if he didn't say it by then, I would. But I owed him time to come around on his own.

We went inside the shop, found Ben, confirmed that he had Thom's number and would call us with updates, and walked across the street to a charming little restaurant. It seemed silly to starve ourselves after the morning we'd had.

The place reminded me of Café Aurelie, my parents' restaurant in San Diego. There were two outside tables and a small newsstand carrying local publications as well as the *New York Times* and *Washington Post*. Like Aurelie, this place was small, with four tables inside and a countertop where people could stand. The tables were all different shapes, sizes, and styles, from smooth mahogany wood to colorful plastic mosaics, giving the café a homey, curated vibe.

Thick, fresh, lopsided scones sat in the display case. The lunch special, written on a chalkboard with calligraphic flair, was a pomegranate, goat cheese, and arugula sandwich. The cheese was sourced from an Amish goat farm in Fleetwood, Pennsylvania. My mouth filled with saliva and my stomach grumbled. The community message board had several tear-away phone numbers advertising a pet sitter, a computer expert, and a children's swim class, as well as a flyer for an amateur stand-up comedy show tonight at a local bar.

Wistfully, I thought it would be fun to go.

Expenses for Thursday, April 23 (starting at $214.60)

gas fill up ($55.50)
engine failure (part + labor + gas) = 75.00
coffee and sandwiches = 18.36
money remaining = $8.86

I grabbed a new napkin and wrote:

Options:

1. Hitchhike
2. Steal a car
3. Steal a bus
4. Steal a train
5. Put down roots here and form a new life

I slid it over to Thom, hoping to make him laugh, but all he gave me was a haunted smile. His eyes were hollow, his demeanor that of a puppet whose strings had been cut. His confidence had disappeared, as though it had never been there to begin with.

"Before I sold my car I had a Mercedes Convertible Roadster," Thom said.

"What color was it?"

"Silver. And I kept it that way."

"What did it smell like?"

"Like money," he joked.

"How did people look at you when you pulled up in it?"

"Like they wanted to kill me or have my babies."

I smiled. He was loosening up, so I went in for the kill: "Did you hear Jon Hamm's voice narrating your every move?"

"Yeah, but that's how my life always is." He did an impression of the Mercedes ads, his voice low and luxurious like Hamm's. "'The Cheerios are on their last sawdust crumbles. Thom has a precious three and a half seconds to think of an alternative before Sammy Bear loses his mind and wakes the neighbors.'"

Our sandwiches and drinks arrived on a tray and we divvied them up in silence.

We'd about finished eating when Thom wiped his mouth and said, "What's the biggest lie you ever told Lainey?" His blue eyes were intense, probing.

"I once had to pretend the Marriott Courtyard water park in Anaheim was Disneyland. For two days."

"Why?"

"I won a family pack of tickets to Disneyland on the radio, so Renee and I decided to take Lainey for her fourth birthday. But when we arrived, we found out the tickets had expired a month earlier. It had taken us *that* long to save up for the other stuff, like the hotel room and money for food and toys. So there we were, on our way out the door, but we couldn't take another step. Two day-passes for three people would have set us back seven hundred bucks. And here's Lainey with her Minnie Mouse doll staring up at us wondering what's happening and why we aren't leaving the hotel. I led her toward the exit and I veered left at the last second, outside to the hotel water park. It had a bunch of waterslides and pools, so it was exciting anyway, just not Disney-level exciting. I put on a whole act. 'Guess what! Surprise! We're already here! We get to live at Disneyland, and sleep here and eat here, too!' "

"And she bought it?"

"Keep in mind she'd never been to Disney, so she didn't know what to expect. Renee was looking at me like I'd gone off the rails. We returned to the room after the 'tour' and plopped Lainey in front of the Disney Channel. She'd never seen *that* before, either, so I told her that *only* at Disneyland did they show nothing-but-Disney TV shows and movies, and while she sat there, Renee and I had a summit in the bathroom and plotted out what we were going to do, and how it would work."

"How did it work?"

"It involved Renee sobbing a lot in private, and me spending eight hours a day at the water park outside our room with Lainey, never leaving hotel grounds, and limiting her interaction with other children, who at any moment might blow the lid off the whole thing. 'She went on the teacups today? No, honey, that's not a ride. She's confused. She meant she and her mommy drank tea. Would you like to do that, too? Have some tea up in the room, our own little tea party, with teacups? Yay!' It also involved me pretending to be different Disney characters, using cheap hair dye, and knocking on the door to play. To this day, Lainey thinks we took her and that the photos accidentally got deleted."

"That's incredible." Thom raised his coffee. "To the power of memory."

I clinked his mug with mine. "Or lack thereof."

He nodded vacantly, so I turned the question around. "What's the biggest lie you ever told Sammy?"

He pinned me with his gaze.

"That his mother was coming back."

All the air left the café, and I finally found the courage to ask what I'd been wondering since I learned there wasn't a Mrs. Thom.

"Why isn't Sammy's mom in the picture?"

He traced the rim of his coffee mug. "We weren't together long. She didn't want a baby, she was planning on a closed adoption, and I agreed at first, but then he was born, and..." Thom's eyes misted up in wonder. "His hand was so tiny. It took all his fingers to grasp one of mine, and I didn't want him to ever let go. I couldn't imagine a day without him in it, now that I'd met him. And God, his eyes. He looked at me with such trust, and I wanted to live up to whatever it was he saw in me. She was in and out of our lives for a while, but when he turned three she split for good. Some people aren't cut out for parenting."

He didn't need to tell me that was when Sammy's night terrors started.

"When you realize you're all somebody's got in this world, that the whole thing's on you, there's no partner, no teammate, no backup... it's terrifying," he admitted.

"You're a great dad."

He averted his eyes. "I don't know. Sometimes I wonder. He's not officially on the spectrum, but... for a long time, one wrong move on my part was a disaster."

I'd seen plenty of kids—boys in particular—with similar behavior. I gave Thom my entire attention. "Sensory issues, that sort of thing?"

"Everything was too much. The sun was always too bright, but he couldn't bear the way hats or sunglasses felt against his face. And his clothing was too textured, or too rough. I had to cut off every tag right at the edge, and wash new T-shirts and jeans twenty times to soften them up, and he couldn't tolerate drawstrings or adjustable waists but he's such a skinny little dude finding pants to fit him was impossible. Eventually I figured out I could go to thrift stores where the clothes were already worn down. Even if sometimes he looked unkempt or uncared for, I knew it was for the best. And his socks—Jesus—they couldn't be wrinkled, or pulled above the ankle, because that meant they might not line up perfectly with each other. He'd spend ten minutes 'fixing it' so we'd never get out the door. There were so many things to remember, so many rituals, and if I forgot one, he'd scream like he was on fire."

"I'm so sorry."

"All I could do was wrap him in a bear hug and hold him quietly until he calmed down."

Sammy Bear.

"That must be tiring."

"I hate complaining about it, because he doesn't do it on purpose. And he's gotten better than he used to be." He shook his head, and laughed a bit ruefully. "What if I show up tonight and my parents say, 'Everything was fine, Sammy's so easy, we have no idea what you're talking about.' It's not that I want the time they spent with him to be hard, but I want them to understand what I go through, see it firsthand. Because if he isn't that way with them, if he's only that with me, that means *I'm* the problem."

"You aren't," I assured him. "Kids are the way they are, and all we can do is love them. Which you've done. Which you're continuing to do."

I slowly reached across the table, giving him time to move his hand. When he didn't, I held it, lightly, in mine. We stayed like that for a few minutes, enjoying our closeness and the comfort that a simple touch could provide.

"Speaking of my parents, I guess we better do this, huh?" he asked.

I should've known it wouldn't take long for him to reach my same conclusion, that we needed their help. He was practical and pragmatic.

I was surprised when Thom put them on speakerphone, but maybe I shouldn't have been. We'd invited each another into our lives in countless ways since we'd met. Considering how wary he was of introducing new people (new women) to his son, I felt a spark of pride that he'd brought me into the fold.

His parents answered on the third ring.

"Hi, Thom, we just got back from dropping Sammy off at camp. He's excited to get his outdoor cooking badge."

My heart swelled. They did *Scouts*. I wondered if Thom was involved. He'd be a great leader for the boys.

Thom swallowed. I wished, cowardly, that they weren't on speakerphone. But I couldn't get up and walk out, either. He was correct to include me.

"Hi, Mr. and Mrs. Parker. Holly again." I did a little wave, which was pointless since we weren't FaceTiming and they couldn't see me.

"Hi, Holly. Nice to hear you again." (The Mom.)

"What time do you think you'll be getting back tonight?" (The Dad.)

"That's what we're calling about," Thom said, mussing up his hair with tense fingers. He hated this; and because of that, I hated it, too.

"The car broke down, actually, so we're going to need a ride," he explained.

A pause. "How far out did you say you were? We'll need to swing by camp and pick up Sammy first. He'll be disappointed to miss it, but…"

"You know what, we don't have to plan this yet," I blurted out.

Thom gave me a look like, *What are you doing?* but kept his trap shut.

"We're still waiting to hear if the mechanic has the parts. I have an appointment tomorrow night in the city I can't miss, but let's wait and see what happens in a few hours. Don't cut his campout short. Can we give you a call first thing in the morning?"

"Okay, we'll wait to hear from you," Thom's dad said slowly.

Thom stared at me.

"'Thanks, love you,'" I whispered, as a prompt.

"Thanks, love you," he repeated, addressing his parents but looking at me.

I ended the call before he could stop me.

"Why yank Sammy from the campout unless we have to? They can drive up tomorrow, it doesn't have to be tonight."

"But we don't have anywhere to stay. We're down to eight dollars. What are we going to do?" But his mood seemed lighter, which told me it was the right thing to do.

"Guess we'll have to pull an all-nighter, see what the town of…where are we again?"

"Harrisburg."

"…Harrisburg has to offer."

"You know what's funny? I've been to this town before. I built a skate park north of here about ten years ago."

I smacked my hands on the table with excitement. "Let's go see it. Will you show it to me?"

11

"Dropping," yelled a voice. Wheels hit the pavement hard, amid a rumble of teenagers.

"*Sick*," another voice called.

Freed from school for the afternoon, the teenagers of Harrisburg slid and turned and scraped their wheels with abandon against the concrete. No matter how many times the horse threw them, they got back on, started over, and tried again.

Thom and I settled our comparatively creaky bones in the bleacher section to watch. The walk there had taken nearly two hours and we were beyond beat.

"How'd you go about building this place?" I asked. My forehead and the spot between my breasts were damp with sweat.

Thom watched his protégés with rapt interest. "There was an abandoned school the local kids used for their hangout, the parking lot mostly, where they could use the railings and ramps, and when it got torn down they had no place to skate. I got a call from the city council, who had recreational funds to spend before the fiscal year ended, and they wanted ideas. I sold them on the skate park eventually, but it took a few weeks. They were worried it would become a locus of drug dealing, or the kids would get injured and sue the city. I took care of that with some lawyer-approved plaques stating the rules they'd agreed upon."

When I squinted, the skate park looked fantastical, otherworldly, as if the crested waves of an ocean had frozen in peaks at their greatest height; a winter wonderland of snowdrifts and smooth surfaces. The endless combinations of danger and surprise called out to anyone possessed of wheels to coast along the beautiful, alien landscape.

A short, skinny kid slid up, balancing low on his board, out of nowhere. He sported what I thought of as the quintessential skater haircut: long and parted in the middle.

His fierce, skeptical expression suggested he was about to confront us. Indeed, the first words out of his mouth were an accusation. "Hey, Pedos, where's your wheels?"

"'Pedos'?" I repeated, astonished.

"It means—"

"I know what it means." I served up my sternest, most no-nonsense "adult voice." "Do you know who this is?"

His eyes darted between me and Thom. "No."

"He *built* this place. He is your god."

Another kid, older and taller, with thick dark hair, swooped over and executed a "stop" motion, lifting his board into his hand and jumping onto the first rung of the bleachers. The landing reverberated up the rest of the steps, making them vibrate.

"What's going on?" he asked.

"What do you mean, he built it?" the first kid asked me.

"He designed it, and created it, and now it exists. For you guys."

"Really?" The second boy, the one with dark hair, looked impressed.

"Really. His name's Thom Parker."

"Hey, guys." Thom nodded.

The second boy puffed out his chest. "I'm Braden. I'm in charge of the place Tuesdays and Thursdays."

"Good looking out, man."

"How come we have to wear helmets?" the first kid wanted to know, gesturing toward a plaque. "It's a shit rule."

"Don't be a turd," Braden chastised him. "And don't say 'shit,' there's kids here today."

He jerked his chin to one of the less intimidating sections of the skate park, where some boys who looked about a year younger than Braden practiced.

I looked over at the plaque Braden had pointed to. One warned skateboarders, in-line skaters, and BMX bikers that they used the park at their own risk, and that by using it they agreed not to hold the city responsible for any injuries. Another stated the rules:

1. NO PROFANITY, NO GRAFFITI, NO ALCOHOL, TOBACCO, OR DRUGS

2. KNOW YOUR ABILITIES

3. HELMET AND PADDING REQUIRED

A third was a platitude: YOU DON'T STOP SKATING BECAUSE YOU GROW OLD. YOU GROW OLD BECAUSE YOU STOP SKATING.

I tried to imagine Thom as he might have been ten years ago, when he built the park. Before Sammy. Before online gambling. He would have been twenty-six. Already a successful businessman and consultant, meeting with politicians and local governments and convincing them they've got trouble—

right here in River City. Only, unlike Harold Hill, Thom's presentations were sincere. Who needed Seventy-Six Trombones when you could have a skate park? Warmth blossomed inside my heart, the way it had when I'd watched his TED Talk. Nobody knew who he was. He'd never sell out Madison Square Garden or adorn some teenager's bedroom wall or be interviewed by James Corden. But this town was a better place because of him. The kids who lived here and used his park had better day-to-day lives because of him.

Meanwhile, at twenty-six, I'd been changing Lainey's diapers and waiting for J. J. to call. Most of my twenties was spent waiting for J. J. to call.

The "shit"-talking skeptic peeled off from us and slammed his board down with a running start, hopping on it in a motion that suggested catching a train that had already left the station. He couldn't resist looking back to see if Thom was watching.

There was something fearless and romantic about skateboarding. These kids launched themselves into the air; one wrong move and they'd fall onto thick, solid, man-made concrete, breaking one or more of their bones. *Each and every time.* And before they could register what they'd accomplished, upon landing they had to crouch and weave and prepare for the next obstacle. The danger, speed, and freedom seemed like a rush.

"This place delivers, dawg," Braden said. "Thanks. How'd you lay it out?"

"When I'm sketching the design, I always base a portion of it on Burnside. The vibe, the style, the architecture. Pay my respects that way."

"You skate?" Braden asked Thom.

"Yes," I replied.

"Not anymore," Thom said at the same time.

"He does, though," I insisted. "And he's good, too. Why do you think it's such a gnarly park?"

Braden and Thom shared a look, aghast.

"No one says 'gnarly,'" Thom laughed.

"No one," Braden agreed.

"If you're not going to show me any tricks, I'll have to try it myself." I stood and stretched. My calves ached from the long walk, and I was pretty sure I'd gotten blisters on both my heels, but I wasn't going to miss the opportunity to ride on a Thom-created ramp. I gestured to Braden's board. "May I?"

"What are you doing?" Thom said, amused.

Braden smiled devilishly and handed me his board. "Don't kill yourself," he said.

Neon tape was plastered across the surface of the top in two stripes, indicating foot position, perhaps? I had no idea and didn't want to ask.

"I shall sit," I declared primly, toting the board with me to the top of the quarter-pipe.

"Careful, we caked it," Braden called after me.

I didn't know what that meant, but I soon found out. The ledge was extremely slippery and my flats nearly flew skyward as I walked up, Braden's board tucked under my arm. *Iced it* would be a better term, I thought.

Nothing was going to stop me, though. I sat on Braden's death-wheels, knees squished up toward my chin, and gripped the sides of his board with my fingers. I slid down the quarter-pipe shouting "Wheeeee!" the whole time.

I reached the bottom, flushed and exhilarated, and pumped my fist in the air. Braden and Thom cackled at me.

"Dude. Just—no," Braden said.

"Sweet moves, huh? Huh?" I ask, egging them on. "Top that."

Once a clown, always a clown. If I had a chance to make someone laugh, even and especially at my own expense, by God I'd take it.

I handed the board back to Braden, unfazed by the stares and whispers that rose around me. In fact, I reveled in them.

"I'm so sorry she sledded on you," Braden cooed to his board. "It will never happen again, I promise."

Thom stood and shrugged out of his blazer.

"Let me show you how it's done."

12

I held my breath each time Thom's borrowed board cracked against the pavement, but he stuck every landing.

Eventually I relaxed, and I realized how peaceful it was, watching him. Just like when I'd watched him swimming. When his body was in motion, sleek and unburdened, he was a different person. Set free from the difficulties and rewards of raising a possibly-on-the-spectrum child all by himself.

The *Daily Denizen* countdown clock in my head took on a new meaning. Instead of indicating how much time I had until the anniversary special, it told me how much time I had left with Thom. I wished I could reset it, give us more time. A month. A week. *A day.*

I was knocked out of my thoughts when Thom attempted something I later learned was called an invert. He'd twisted his body 180 degrees in the air, like a handstand, except supporting himself by only one hand, on the coping of a ramp. I wanted a photo to capture the moment. Then his arm buckled and he fell, skidding down the ramp without his board, which flew out sideways and followed his body at a reckless clip, gaining speed. He curled away from it, groaning as it sailed overhead and clattered to the ground far away.

Now I remembered why grown adult males shouldn't skate. I raced over, dodging errant skaters, and crouched beside him. "Are you okay?"

"I'll live," Thom mumbled, cradling his arm like a bird with a bent wing.

"I'm so sorry," I cried. "I should've stopped you."

"Why? Most fun I've had in months."

"That's the adrenaline talking. I shouldn't have made you come here."

"Are you kidding? I'm glad you did." He reached for me with his good arm. "I haven't done that in five years."

Not since the mom left. Not since Sammy's night terrors started.

He'd been trapped, all that time, under a mountain of obligations. Even good obligations could be exhausting, could take things from you that you might never get back. But today, for a little while, he flew.

"I *needed* this." He gripped my hand, laughed through the pain. "Even if it fucking stings."

We held hands and I knew better than to read into it. He was in pain, that was all. But my heart skipped all the same. His fingers were dry, smooth, and warm, and I wanted the moment to last.

"Besides," Thom said quietly. "Old habits die hard."

I smiled. "Riding with your brahs?"

"No. Showing off for a pretty girl."

I swallowed. He looked at me with such adoration I almost couldn't breathe. I told myself, again, it was the injury and he wasn't thinking straight. After all, he'd *thanked me* for giving him swellbow.

Braden returned from the park office with an Ace bandage and a bottle of Tylenol. "We're out of ice packs, but I can take you to CVS."

"Do you know Tony Hawk?" one of the girls asked as we shuffled toward Braden's car. I was relieved by its relative newness. By which I meant it was produced within the last twenty years. Even a college student (his bumper sticker read PENN STATE HARRISBURG) had a better car than us. Inside was another story; endless empty cans of Jolt soda and wrinkled comic books decorated the floors and seats.

"I've never personally met him but I've worked with his foundation," Thom replied. He would've gotten trapped answering questions all day, and probably enjoyed it, if Braden and I hadn't forced him inside the backseat, where he'd be able to rest his elbow on the armrest between seats. I joined him on the opposite side and Braden transformed into a tour guide and chauffeur as he drove us through town.

During a lull in the conversation, Braden turned on a local punk station, which gave me and Thom a chance to speak privately.

"How many skate parks have you built?" I asked.

"Twenty so far. About two per year."

"And how many kids use them, do you think?"

"Several thousand each, I guess, over the years."

"So you've changed the lives of twenty thousand kids for the better. Probably more, so we'll say *at least* twenty thousand kids. Do you think a 'piece of shit' would be capable of that?"

He cleared his throat, but didn't answer right away. When

he did, his eyes looked moist, but that could also be from the physical pain. “Is that why you brought me here?”

“Nah,” I joked. “Mostly I wanted to see your sweet moves.”

We smiled at each other. Bopping his head to Bad Religion, Braden yanked the wheel and pulled into a CVS parking lot.

“You know what I miss about parenting?” I said, traversing the junk food aisle once we’d procured the necessary supplies for his arm. “The snacks.”

He got a dreamy look in his eye. “Puffs.”

“Kix.”

“Yes! Animal crackers.”

“*Goldfish* crackers.”

“Fruit roll-ups.”

“Jammy sammies.”

“Nilla Wafers, *ohmygod*.”

“I used to feed those to Lainey to make her smell good.”

It was nice being around someone who got all my parenting references.

Braden caught us shouting children’s foods at each other. “You guys, uh, hungry or something?”

“Holly. Holly!” Thom was practically jumping up and down. “Look what they have!”

And there they were, sent from heaven above: Original Flavor Tato Skins.

“Gimme.” I snatched them off the shelf. “Wait, can we afford these?”

Braden looked extremely confused.

“We’re a bit short on cash,” I admitted vaguely to him.

Thom did the calculations. “I think you deserve them. Go for it.”

Expenses for Thursday, April 23
(starting at $8.86)

Ice pack = $6.49
Tato Skins (Original Flavor) = $1.59
Total Remaining = $0.78

In line at the checkout, my eyes fell on a tabloid.

My castmates were on the cover because of course they were. It wasn't a group photo but a slapdash collage of each person's face cut-and-pasted from their archives. Cheapest cover ever.

"REUNION" screeched the headline. "Test your knowledge! Since 1998... Who's got the highest net worth? Who was supposed to star in a spin-off? Who almost left showbiz FOREVER? Who joined a food cult? Who's been to rehab?"

(*Who hasn't been?* I thought. *Including me.*)

And my personal favorite, "WHO GAINED WEIGHT?"

I snorted. If we hadn't gained weight since childhood, we'd be *dead.*

But beneath my eye-rolling, I allowed myself to fantasize about an alternative time line.

One where my face had been included on the cover, because maybe *Fowl Play* hadn't dumped me and I'd gone on to headline my own sitcom. A time line in which seeing myself at convenience stores was a regular occurrence, in which I was recognized in public, with a team to dress me—never the same outfit twice—and a team to do my hair and makeup, even for a Starbucks run. Especially for a Starbucks run.

It could have been my life with or without *Fowl Play*; as the events from last night proved, being "J. J.'s girl" was enough of an "accomplishment" to put me in the public eye, to make me (in)famous all on its own.

With J. J.'s admission last night, that alternative time line had come back into play, running parallel to my real life. Electric currents of nauseous excitement shot through my belly. I'd be seeing him in less than thirty hours. He seemed interested in reconnecting, or at least reminding me what we'd had, willing to go on the record about our past, pull me into the spotlight with him. Why would he have done that if not as an invitation? *All this could be yours,* his actions seemed to say. *All you have to do is step through the door.*

"Where should I drop you guys?" Braden asked once we were settled back in his car.

That was an excellent question. We were officially broke.

No money for food.

No money for a place to stay tonight.

My vagabond adventure idea, to pull an all-nighter and see where the evening took us, was no longer feasible. Not only were we both sore from the long walk to the skate park, but Thom needed a comfortable place to rest tonight so his elbow could heal.

"Our car's in the shop, let me call and see if it's ready," Thom replied. "If it's fixed you could take us there."

He called and had a brief conversation with Ben. Thom's side of it consisting entirely of the word "Uh-huh."

"Well?" I asked, after the seventh "uh-huh" concluded with Thom hanging up. My leg jiggled impatiently.

"His buddy the next town over *does* have the part...but he can't go over there until tonight, after his shop closes."

"No," I lamented.

"He knows we're in a time crunch so he's willing to open early tomorrow."

Thom and I fell silent.

If we picked up the car first thing, and the tank was full as Ben promised, we'd have all day to drive 250 miles and get to New York City by eight p.m., which was obviously doable, even if we got stuck in Friday-afternoon traffic. My spirits lifted, so much so I envisioned an answer to our most pressing problem.

"What's the nicest hotel around here?" I asked Braden.

"I dunno, the Best Western?"

I bit my lip. "Maybe even nicer?"

"Um...Oh! The Hilton. That's nice."

"Perfect. Take us there, please."

Thom leaned over to whisper in my ear, his stubble tickling my cheek. "What are you up to?"

If I tilted to the right, we'd be kissing. It would be so easy to tilt to the right, and I wanted to, but not in the backseat of a college student's car.

"I might do some strange things in the next hour," I whispered back, putting a few inches of distance between us. "But it's all in service to the plan."

Ten minutes later, our twenty-year-old chauffeur dropped us outside the entrance to the Hilton. We thanked him profusely, and he and Thom shook hands.

The lobby of the hotel was bright and clean and fresh looking, all midcentury-modern furniture, crystal-vase flower displays, and warm lighting.

“Sit tight while I get changed,” I instructed Thom.

In the ladies’ room I transformed myself into someone who might passably be a guest at the Hilton. This involved a flick of mascara, a swipe of lip gloss, ditching my ponytail, and changing into fresh, sexy-but-businesslike clothes. I’d brought the two aforementioned items of makeup, a pencil skirt, and silk top to Prevail! in case there was a graduation dinner at the end. (Years ago, Melody told me some facilities held a dry dance. I’d wanted to be prepared.)

“Hello.” Thom sat up straight when I returned.

I shook my hair out. “Hi.”

He swallowed. Opened his mouth to say something, and shut it again.

“Is this whole getup part of the plan?” he asked a moment later, gesturing at my outfit with his hands.

“Yes. I’m so glad you asked. We’re going to *Remington Steele* them. Operation *Remington Steele* is a go.”

“Pierce Brosnan, right? I think my mom watched it.”

“Everyone’s mom watched it. In the year of our Lord nineteen hundred and eighty-six, *Remington Steele* starred Pierce Brosnan and Stephanie, uh, Somebody in which Stephanie Somebody opens a PI company, but no one will take her seriously unless they think she has a male boss. So she makes one up.”

“Do I get to be your boss?” He rubbed his hands together devilishly.

“Nope. We’re going to pretend we both work for Melody Briar and get ourselves a free room.”

“I don’t follow.”

“That’s okay, I think I can handle this mission.”

“You *think* you can? Why would they give Melody’s

employees a free room? They know she's rich and can pay for them."

"Please. Rich people get free things all the time. The moment you can afford anything on earth, no one asks you to. At the height of her *Honeypot* fame, Kelly took me and Renee to a nightclub opening in San Francisco, and we all got free MacBooks and a Frederick's of Hollywood bra. I still use mine."

"The MacBook or the bra?" His grin was mischievous. He wore it well.

"Both. I might even be wearing it *right now*," I said teasingly.

"Should I get cleaned up, too?"

"That's okay, you've got that whole rugged businessman look. Maybe hide the ice pack. Chill in the lobby or something. Oh. Phone, please."

Understandably suspicious, he kept his phone to himself. "I'll handle the tech."

"Go to WireImages and search Melody Briar, premiere of *The Fantasticks*."

"What am I looking for?"

"You'll know it when you see it."

Within twenty seconds he hit the jackpot. "Melody Briar and 'publicist'? But it's you."

The photo he'd found was of Melody with her arm around me outside the Snapple Theater Center in NYC. The caption read "Melody Briar and publicist attend opening night of Tara Osgood's *The Fantasticks*."

Unlike my former friends, I didn't have to change my look every six months to avoid getting dinged by the *Style Don'ts*—and in fact, oh my God, was I wearing the same skirt today that I'd worn in the photo? Yes, yes I was. I looked identical to the me of five years ago. Which honestly was unsettling.

"If the photo editors couldn't crop me out, they had to identify me and usually they got it wrong. Some of my nicknames over the years have been 'mystery woman,' 'anonymous woman,' 'former castmate,' 'original castmate,' 'unknown companion,' 'personal assistant,' and my new all-time favorite, '...and publicist.'

It had irked me at the time, to be identified as someone who worked for her, but today it was all the inspiration I needed. "May I?"

"Godspeed." He slipped me his phone. I changed the alarm tone to something jaunty and set the timer for one minute. I shook my hair out again and strutted to the front desk. *You are Melody's publicist*, I asserted to myself. *And...go.*

"May I help you?" asked the stout older man stationed there, his green eyes peering at me from behind horn-rimmed glasses. I guessed he was in his fifties.

"Yes, hello, has my luggage arrived yet? From the airport? It got lost in transit but they said they'd send it over as soon as possible."

"I haven't seen any bags arrive—"

"Ugh, typical—"

"But let me check. Name?" he asked.

"I spoke with your manager a few days ago and she said she'd be happy to comp me a night's stay as we make our decision about Melody's accommodations."

"Melody...?"

I peered around and lowered my voice. "Melody Briar. Were you the person I spoke to? No, pretty sure it was a woman. Anyway, I'm part of her advance team, in the publicity office."

I patted my pockets, dug through my purse. "My business cards are in my suitcase, sorry. Holly Danner. Shoot, that means the hotel *contract's* in there, too—"

My phone "rang" and I hastily "answered" it.

"What?" I asked impatiently. "They won't have the bags until tomorrow? Are you serious? Okay, fine... Yes, I'm checking in now—I'll let you know—yes, you can tell her there are flowers in the lobby. Okay. Okay, I have to go." I set my phone down and turned back to the clerk. "Sorry about that. Anyway, I have to personally—*personally*—check out each hotel and make sure it fits what she's looking for prior to booking it. It's for her upcoming stadium tour, shh."

I don't care who you are, what kind of music you listen to, or whether you personally loathe Melody and her brand of pop; if someone shows up at your place of business and suggests the imminent arrival of Melody Briar, even if it's months from now, you're going to damn sure want to nail that down.

In other words, the guy at the front desk had a choice. Go along with my comped room and, for the price of a single night's stay, save his boss thousands of dollars in marketing money when Melody Briar showed up later and Instagrammed a selfie in her room, instantly rebranding the Harrisburg Hilton as sexy and fun to her millions of followers; or turn me down and risk losing Melody's cachet to a competitor.

A female desk clerk nearby had been listening to us, her mouth ever-so-slightly open, watching to see what her colleague would do. Maybe I should've approached her instead.

I had hoped glasses guy would have acquiesced at this point—but maybe he was too far from Hollywood to understand how the game worked.

"Could you show me a room and I'll text her some pics?" I prompted, marching toward the elevator. "What's your name, by the way?"

He raced to catch up with me.

"Mark."

I held back a laugh. Yes, he was.

"We'd be happy to show you a room—" he began.

"How about the penthouse?" In for a penny, in for a pound.

As I passed Thom I brusquely snapped my fingers at him. His brow furrowed but he stood, trying to look like he wasn't cradling his sore elbow.

"My assistant," I explained to the desk clerk.

The three of us entered the elevator.

"The penthouse is currently booked, but we can give you a tour of the conference rooms, swimming pool, spa, gym, and—"

"A suite's fine. I'd like to get settled first, and then I'll have a look around."

I babbled intermittently as we rode the elevator, as though if I stopped talking for even a second the ruse would unfold and reveal itself. When the doors opened on the third floor and Mark exited, I stayed right where I was.

"She prefers a view."

Surprised, he sheepishly pivoted and hit the button for floor eight.

I nodded sharply.

Thom turned away to hide his expression.

We arrived at the room on the eighth floor, and Mark used his universal keycard to let us in.

"I thought Melody was doing a Vegas residency," he said.

"My neighbor's wife and daughter saw her last month. Said it cost an arm and a leg."

I regarded him coolly. "Her performances are legendary."

"Is the residency ending?"

"Yes, it's wrapping up soon," I lied. "But she hasn't announced the stadium tour yet, so if it leaks to the press, we'll know where to look."

He seemed alarmed. "I should have my manager oversee this. You said you spoke with her last week?"

I obviously didn't like the sound of that. The fewer people we interacted with the better. I did my best to brush it off.

"Sure," I said. "Whatever you need to do."

"Why don't you look around, and I'll send down for your room keys and a key to the tenth-floor lounge."

He stepped into the hallway, propped the door open with his foot, and made a call.

I pretended to do whatever it was an advance team member might do, like coast my palm along the bed's thick, soft comforter, open the blinds to see the view, turn the faucets on and off in the cavernous bathroom, pick up the landline, and check out the mini fridge.

It was the most expensive hotel room I'd been in since dating J. J., and I was determined to give it to Thom. It was the least I could do after partially causing his car to break down.

The desk clerk shot me a smile while waiting for his boss to pick up. I smiled back, but not too wide. I was trying to look carefree with a side of expectant impatience.

It was do-or-die time.

Abruptly, he turned his back to us and spoke in low tones I couldn't make out.

Thom gripped my hand.

"There's no way this is going to work. We're going to get arrested," he whispered.

"Worst-case scenario, I'll pretend I mixed it up with a different hotel," I assured him, equally quiet. "They can't arrest us for being confused."

Having a backup plan seemed to calm him. "The Hilton *Garden* in *East* Harrisburg," Thom said. "We can pretend we—" Then he paled. "What if it's not there anymore?"

I squeezed his hand. "No, that's good. That's perfect."

After what felt like an hour, the clerk faced us again, looking pleased. "I couldn't get ahold of her—she's in a meeting—but her assistant signed off on it, so, on behalf of the entire staff, thank you for choosing the Hilton. We'd like to send up complimentary room service, too. How's one of everything? That way you can give a full report to Melody."

I forced down my giddiness. "Sure. Thanks for your help, Mark. Ring us if the luggage miraculously comes early?"

After he left and I closed the door, Thom and I were silent, mutually petrified that if we whooped it up too soon, the whole thing would crash down around us.

Eventually, he broke into a grin. "You *Remington Steeled* them."

"God Bless America for suckling at the teat of fame."

He threw his head back and laughed. We high-fived with his good arm, and he moved to the center of the room and slowly spun in a circle.

"This place kicks ass. And you got us room service! You're amazing."

"Aww, shucks. That's the Tylenol talkin'. Cool if I take a shower? Or did you want first dibs?"

"By all means. Go for it."

I undressed inside the bathroom and took the time to appreciate the intricately folded towels, handcrafted soaps, and mini bottles of rose-infused shampoo. Once the water heated up, I stepped inside the shower. I was light-headed from hunger, but with room service on the way, I'd be able to hold out fine. The steam opened the pores on my face, cleansing me and soothing me after the stress and activities of the day. There was a sweetness to the air, a sweetness to my situation right then, no matter how bizarre it all was.

I unwrapped a complimentary razor and shaved my underarms, legs, and bikini line. I told myself it was because I wanted to feel attractive and confident for the anniversary tomorrow, and I might not have time to prep later.

But it was also to show Thom another side of me. A softer side. (Literally.)

Then I remembered what he'd said at the skate park. How as a kid he couldn't resist showing off for a "pretty girl." He'd thought I was pretty, before ever seeing me with makeup or a nice outfit or shaved legs.

I savored every second of the shower, lathering my hair, closing my eyes, and allowing more happy laughter to bubble forth. We'd gotten away with it!

I toweled off, re-dressed, and entered the main room.

"All yours, Thom." I squeezed out my wet hair and piled it into a bun.

"Think I'll soak my arm in the tub." Thom moved into the bathroom and called back, "Any instructions I should know about?" Before I could answer, his voice rose even higher. "Seriously?"

"What's up?" I joined him in the bathroom, where he held up a bag.

"They have Epsom salts. Are you freaking kidding me? Just sitting around for whoever needs them. I owe you."

I left to give him privacy, and a second later the bath jets fired up with a loud whoosh.

I allowed myself another measure of pride. I'd done this for him. Silly old Holly Danner, taking care of her man.

A man, I corrected myself. *Not belonging to me.*

Half an hour later, refreshed, and wearing different clothes, Thom found me slumped deep in the armchair, zoned out in front of a game show on TV and biting one of my nails. I couldn't help noticing the close shave he'd given himself after his bath. He was disarmingly handsome. I bet he smelled fantastic, too. He toweled off his hair, then balled up the towel and threw it back into the bathroom. I wanted to run my hands through the damp strands, lightly scratch his scalp with my nails.

Breathe him in.

Kiss him into next week.

My gaze fell to his fresh shave again. What would he do if I reached out and tested its smoothness with my fingertips, or caressed it with the back of my knuckles? His skin was slightly pink and looked achingly soft.

We stared at each other for a charged beat.

Anything could have happened.

"That's twice today you've given me exactly what I needed," Thom said. "Thank you."

His smile was genuine as he bridged the distance between us to give me a hug.

My entire body relaxed into his. For a moment, every burden I'd been carrying was lifted as though I'd been transported to the beginning of the year, before I knew about the anniversary, back when my biggest issues were turning in freelance articles on time and planning movie marathons with Lainey.

I was right; he smelled amazing. I inhaled the subtle vanilla spice of his neck and wondered how his warm, damp skin would taste.

"Tell me, Holly Danner. What is it that *you* need?" he murmured into my ear.

A knock at the door cut through the sensual fog.

Room service.

I silently cursed the timing, but we were both starving—in more ways than one—and man cannot live on Original Flavor Tato Skins alone. Thom thanked the delivery person (was it my imagination, or did he sound a bit sarcastic?) and used his good arm to steer the overflowing tray into the room.

The TV suddenly went loud with voices; the game show had finished, and the next program had started, an entertainment news show.

The lead story was me.

13

My first kiss with J. J. was supposed to be during Spin the Bottle. It was a double-shoot day, and we'd broken for lunch while a fresh audience took their seats and the warm-up comedian excited them with trivia games and candy flung into the crowd. Brody wanted to liven things up backstage, so he chugged a bottle of Coke and sacrificed it to the game.

When it was J. J.'s turn and the bottle landed on me, he refused to participate. He took off before he'd kissed me or anyone else. Tears instantly filled my eyes; eventually I felt Kelly's hand on my back. We'd have to redo my makeup before we filmed the second half of the show.

Now I'd been deemed unkissable in front of every important person in my life. J. J. was my best friend, the person I hung out with 24/7 and who lived with me six months out of the year, but maybe he never thought about me like that. Maybe he didn't see me that way, or want to be with me. I'd been fantasizing that we'd get married when we were eighteen. (At the time, it seemed like the ideal age for marriage; it didn't occur to me we wouldn't be able to legally clink champagne glasses at our own reception.)

But when I caught up with him in the darkened corridor of the soundstage, he was as tearful as I was. He told me he wanted our first kiss to be "just for us," not anyone else, not anyone watching.

And then he cupped my face gently with his palms, stared deeply into my eyes, and kissed me.

Even our first kiss, which should've been playful, easy, and fun, had been tinged with pain. At the time, I loved that about it. About us. That we were *fraught*.

Five years later, the ballad "Just 4 Us" debuted. It was OffBeat's least successful single, peaking at 99 on the top 100 before disappearing forever. I was happy it tanked because that kept it more private, the way it was meant to be.

(Also, it wasn't a very good song.)

14

The *ShowBiz Tonight* hosts, one male and one female, weighed in on the topic du jour, which meant reliving the clip from last night's *Jerry Levine Show* wherein J. J. gushed, "She was my first girlfriend. My first kiss. My first love."

The male host's hair was at least six inches high. The female looked as though she'd been configured in a lab. Pert nose, heart-shaped face, blond hair so white it glowed, a tiny cleft chin. In a nod to the season, they both wore Easter-egg-pastel outfits: a pink-and-lavender-striped tie for him, a Peep-yellow blazer and matching skirt for her. Her skin was a deep golden tan, making her teeth compete with her hair for "most blinding."

I had to fixate on their appearances in order to process the fact that *complete strangers were talking about me.*

At least with Reddit, where users were anonymous, I could control the conversation by ignoring questions I didn't like. This chatter couldn't be stopped.

Tall-Hair Man attempted to set the scene. A shot of OffBeat's final album cover—the guys all held different-colored balloons that matched their respective hoodies—

accompanied his voice-over as the camera zoomed in on J. J.'s face. "For those who don't remember, J. J. was 'the quiet one,' 'the thoughtful one,' 'the shy one.'"

"The stoned Christian one," Thom added.

I shot him a faux-stern look, but inside I was cracking up. Inside, I was pleased to be watching it with him, someone who knew the truth.

"Famously single," the blindingly blond female cohost added, "always yearning to find that special girl. Brody was with Melody, of course, and then her bandmate Tara…"

"Quite the controversy at the time."

"It sure was! Alan was the playboy who had a new girl on his arm each week, and Bryan married and fathered six children once the band broke up. But J. J. was the hopeless romantic. Although currently linked to Jenae Billings, who choreographs the *Break It Down* movies, he was rarely photographed during OffBeat's multiplatinum tour some eight years ago. He wasn't a partier and avoided most social scenes. Now we know why! He did have someone. A childhood sweetheart."

A news ticker popped up next to a still photo from my high school yearbook. As though it were newsworthy. "The Cute One's Cute One?" read the text.

"Who keeps giving them yearbooks?" I cried.

"And it sounds like he's still pining for her," Tall-Hair Man said slimily. "Twenty-five years is a long time to be on and off with someone."

"It sure is," his counterpart replied.

"How come there's never *truly* a 'bad boy'?" Thom wondered. It felt like he was deliberately interrupting the hosts. "'The ex-con.' 'The car thief.'"

"Are you questioning the bona fides of Donnie Wahlberg?"

"Ever since Paul McCartney, aren't they *all* 'the cute one'? There's never been a boy band with ugly boys. Never."

"And there's never been a female solo artist who wasn't glammed up."

"True."

We focused back on the TV.

"Her castmates are all household names, but how has Holly Danner been spending her time since the show's cancellation twenty years ago?"

"Masturbation," I shouted at the screen.

Apparently, *ShowBiz Tonight*'s crack research team had managed to dredge up information on my life.

"Looks like she was . . . " Tall-Hair Man consulted his notes. ". . . er, *almost* in *Fowl Play*, and then became a low-level copywriter whose work has appeared in a variety of national and local publications."

"Nice," nodded his cohost, clearly lying. "Good for her." The expression on her face betrayed her true feelings: *Why are we talking about this woman?*

"Barely human, she roams from town to town, eking out an existence that would destroy most people," Thom intoned.

"I've always relied on the kindness of strangers," I added in my best *Streetcar* drawl.

"Should we turn it off?" Thom said.

"The question on everyone's mind is: Will she be at the anniversary tomorrow, and will there be a romantic reunion between her and J. J.? He seemed to be sending her a message on *The Jerry Levine Show* last night," the blond woman said, looking slightly intrigued by the possibility. Pretending to, at least. "Let's check in with social media and see what people are saying."

"Must we?" I moaned.

"A poll on Twitter wants to know, 'What should J. J. and Holly's couple-name be?'"

A graphic popped up. Twelve percent had voted for "Hay-hay"...

"'Hay-hay'?" I repeated. "Like the chicken in *Moana*?"

...with 88 percent for "Jolly."

"Look: 'Jolly,'" Thom said tonelessly. "Nickname achievement unlocked, I guess."

He swallowed and studied his arm, gently flexing it and avoiding my gaze. The spark from our near-kiss had gone out. I wanted to make him smile again but I also felt an undeniable satisfaction from the TV program, from the public finally giving me something. *You exist*, they said. *I always did*, I reminded myself. But now millions of people knew it. Did it make me more real somehow? Or was it all pointless bullshit? Even now my own words, my entire side of the story, were nowhere to be found. Words were my refuge, my only source of power, and I hadn't gotten a single one in.

If the public had been invested in us as a couple years ago, would J. J. and I have stayed together? Succumbed to lovey-dovey pretenses, no matter what had gone on behind the scenes?

The memory of our last fight still made my stomach clench, as though deflecting a punch.

I tuned back in to hear the woman say, "Calls to her reps went unanswered as of airtime."

"That's because I don't have any. Fools!" I cackled, and glanced at Thom for his reaction. He remained closed off, eyes averted.

"We caught up with Ethan Mallard an hour ago to see if he had the inside scoop."

Cut to: Ethan sauntering through Logan Airport in Boston, in skinny jeans and an ironic "grandpa"-type cardigan that fell to his knees. He was annoyed at being pursued. "Yeah, I don't know if she's coming. We haven't spoken in years."

Gee, Ethan, you think my chances of attending might have gone up if you'd INVITED ME? It's okay, it's okay. The truth will come out tomorrow.

"The event is sold out, but I hear scalpers on StubHub still have a few left in the five-figure price range."

"It's a hot ticket, all right."

"All proceeds will go to GirlsWrite, a mentorship program for middle school and high school girls who have a passion for writing."

A feminist Ethan Mallard meme generated in my head: Hey girl. I may be immersing myself in Betty Friedan and bell hooks, but I still make time to help underserved young women learn to write.

"I've reached my threshold," I announced.

Thom instantly killed the TV. "Was it weird seeing yourself talked about like that?"

He always knew what to say.

Damn. I'm going to miss that.

"I'm not sure," I said. "It doesn't seem real."

Was that how it had been for the others all these years? Not quite real? How did anyone live that way? Years of mean-spirited speculation, delivered with a Joker's grin by strangers feigning "concern." Constant scrutiny and unsolicited opinions on your every waking movement, starting at age sixteen. Before the internet it was, I imagine, *slightly* easier to handle. But most of them hit it big in the late '90s, at the exact moment the internet rose up to devour us all. The trajectories of the two phenomena were intertwined.

Until today, I'd observed their level of fame close-up, nearby, or offstage, but never as a participant.

My parents' house in San Diego was their refuge, their secret retreat, where Renee and I would always greet them with warmth, companionship, and zero judgment. The only place they felt free. The only place they could relax, be themselves, and talk about their problems without worrying the information might leak to the press. They could stay for a weekend, a week, or a month, however long they needed.

But once they'd achieved a measure of calm, the strength to get back out there, my friendship was disposable to them.

I was disposable.

Until the next crisis hit.

So, five years ago, I'd put a stop to it.

Regardless of what we were, or weren't, to each other now, I always figured when push came to shove they'd stand up for me. That if they collectively agreed to a televised anniversary they'd have both the power and the desire to say, *Let's reach out to Holly*. I'd never needed to be front and center—I didn't even like it—but I should have been a part of it. I should have been *asked*. It was an ensemble show, and we had been equals, once.

"I'm not a fan of your nickname. The Cute One's Cute One? It makes you sound like a kitten. It's diminutive," Thom said.

"That's the best thing a woman in show business can be. Tiny. Not quite there. Size Zero."

"You're being acknowledged now, though. Wasn't that the endgame?"

"No," I insisted. "The endgame is seeing them face-to-face. Making them see what they did to me."

"What'd they do to you?"

I fell quiet for a while, contemplating the right way to phrase it.

"They used me up."

15

Room service was delectable and extravagant: As promised, we received samples of every item.

"I feel like we're picking out food for our wedding," I quipped awkwardly. All I could think about was our earlier conversation. The caress of his warm breath on my ear.

Tell me, Holly Danner. What is it that you need?

What would I have said?

Nothing. I would have shown him.

Was it possible to steer things in that direction again, or had we lost the moment forever?

We ate like ravenous beasts. We crouched on the floor, hunched over the little plates, as though guarding our food from other predators, trying to scarf it down before the vultures arrived.

I think we sensed we were eating on borrowed time.

We'd managed to choke back two-thirds of the food when a knock at the door sounded, louder and angrier than last time.

Thom and I stared at each other, paralyzed.

"We already have our room service," I yelled to whomever was behind the door. "Thanks."

An authoritative woman's voice: "This isn't room service. Please open the door."

Crap.

"Um, we're not decent..." (Oh God, was she picturing us naked, smearing ourselves with the sample menu?) "Could you come back later?"

"I'm afraid not. Please open the door, or I'll have to use my own key," the woman answered. Her voice was quiet but no-nonsense.

She didn't want to cause a scene for her legitimate guests; maybe I could use that to our advantage?

I guess we weren't fast enough reaching her because the door handle turned and a curly-haired, middle-aged woman in a peach-colored pantsuit strode in. She was flanked by two well-dressed security guards and a younger woman I remembered from the lobby—the other desk clerk who'd kept eyeing me and Thom. I'd figured her for an eavesdropping Melody fan, and maybe she was, but she'd also been onto us, possibly from the jump. I sent a thank-you to the God of Grifters that we hadn't approached *her* when we'd arrived or we might not have gotten as far as we had. No shower, no food.

"I'm the manager, and you need to leave. If you come quietly, hotel security will stay a respectful distance behind you, but if you don't, you'll need to be escorted physically, okay?"

Shaking, I nodded and set about gathering my items as swiftly as possible. It didn't take long because I hadn't unpacked yet. I'd do whatever they asked; couldn't risk the security guys grabbing Thom by the elbow and worsening his injury.

"How did you know?" Thom asked her. He looked pale. I was thrown by his question—who cared how they knew? We needed to go quietly, right now.

"I looked you up," said the younger woman proudly. She stepped into the room like an amateur detective, eager to display her go-getter genius. "Melody's office is closed for the night but I left a message and an after-hours person rang back just now saying they've never heard of you and that Melody isn't planning any stadium tours," Veronica Mars finished tartly.

"Please don't press charges," I begged. "We'll leave. We're leaving right now and we won't cause a fuss. We just ran out of cash. Long story. If you want to take down our names, or hold something for collateral, I'll call you with my credit card number the moment we arrive in New York tomorrow. We ran into some bad luck, and..."

"I won't press charges because I don't want the bad publicity," the older woman, the manager, replied.

We all moved down the hallway now, and as promised, the security guards kept a respectful distance.

"But you do know her, don't you?" the manager pressed. "We found a picture of you two together online. Unless that was Photoshopped or manipulated somehow?"

I ducked my head, ashamed. "No, ma'am. It wasn't Photoshopped."

I sounded like J. J. *Yes, sir. No, ma'am.*

The manager lowered her voice. "Send me some autographed photos for my daughters and we'll drop the whole thing. You don't need to pay for your...activities."

Maybe she *did* think we'd had sex?

On our perp ride down to the lobby, my heart pounded,

even though I knew how lucky we were to have escaped unscathed.

"I'm so sorry," I whispered to Thom when we reached the front exit.

"It was still the most fantastic thing I've ever seen," he said. "And my arm feels a lot better after the bath."

It was true that we looked and smelled delicious.

We looked like we were still guests here.

We looked like we were headed for a night on the town.

Which was how we ended up on a party limo with a group of bachelorette girls, on their way to a comedy club.

16

In the parking lot out front, eight women in cocktail dresses stood next to a white stretch Lincoln Town Car, gabbing and laughing as they downed plastic chalices of champagne. Penis necklaces adorned their necks, with paper tiaras tucked into their elaborate hairdos. A petite redhead was the first to finish knocking back her bubbly, and when she walked to the garbage can to toss it out, she saw me and Thom loitering.

Scratch that: She saw *Thom*. And she liked what she saw.

"Whatcha up to?" she singsonged, twirling a strand of curly red hair around her finger and gazing at Thom with an enviable pair of green eyes.

"Uh, me?"

She pointed flirtatiously at him. "Yes, you."

Thom smiled tentatively back.

It was clear he was our ticket in.

Into what, exactly, I wasn't sure, but anything was better than our current situation. A new plan formed and I decided to go with it.

"My friend and I were about to head out to dinner," I said,

placing a subtle emphasis on *friend* and hoping they'd assess him as eligible. "How about you? Which one's the bride?"

"The bride is upstairs praying to the porcelain god. Her cousin doesn't drink..." (Here, the redhead rolled her eyes and I did my best "smh" right back at her—ingratiating myself as best I could.) "...so she's staying behind, too. She told us to continue to the club, but we have two extra seats now." She pretended to have a lightbulb moment. "I know: You guys should totally come!"

This was once again addressed to Thom, who had the good sense to pretend he wasn't sure. (First rule of scamming: Never look eager.) "Oh, I'd hate to crash your girls' night," he said modestly.

"No, I insist. The more the merrier." The redhead held out her hand. "I'm Becky Lynn."

Once we'd shaken hands and introduced ourselves, she clapped, as if that settled it.

"But isn't it ladies only?" Thom asked. His eyes darted to her penis necklace and back up.

What was wrong with him? It occurred to me he might not have a strategy. He might really be trying to get out of going.

"I think it sounds fun. We can have dinner anytime," I assured him loudly, with a jovial slap on the back.

"Yeah, come on, live a little." Becky Lynn turned and yelled to her cohorts, "Hey, everyone, I filled our slots."

The seven other women gave a collective "wooo!" and raised their glasses to us.

"She'd like you to fill *her* slot," I murmured to Thom as we climbed inside the stretch. I'd hoped to stay together, but he was swiftly commandeered into a different seat by two other partygoers, who placed him in the middle and covered his legs from either side with both of theirs. He shot me a helpless look and I pressed my lips together to keep from laughing, trying to convey with my eyes that I had a plan.

Ten minutes later, we arrived at a comedy club, where the line wound out the door and around the side of the building. Since our group had prepaid for tables, we were swept inside and escorted to our seats in the reserved section.

"Isn't this better than some stuffy old dinner?" Becky Lynn placed her hand on Thom's arm and ordered pomegranate margaritas for the group. Thom and I thanked the women for letting us tag along.

Once everyone was seated, I leaned in close to him. "Here's the game plan. Look around at each of the women, and pick one."

"'Pick one'?"

"Pick one to flirt with. If you hit it off, maybe she'll invite us back to the room and we can crash there tonight."

"You want me to hook up with one of them?"

My whole body stiffened. "No!" The others looked over and I lowered my voice. "Pretend you might. Let her know that an after-party at the hotel *with everyone* would be nice. Say you want to pay your respects to the bride or whatever, up in the penthouse. Then hopefully everyone will fall into a drunken sleep and we can take the couch or the chair or the floor. They think we're guests at the hotel already, so they won't be suspicious. Maybe we can even pretend we lost our key or we can't remember our room number. Whatever it takes to find a place to crash."

"Then I better get some condoms from the men's room," Thom said, launching himself from the table.

"No," I yelled again. "I mean," I covered, "it won't get that far."

"Won't they crucify me for coming with one girl but trying to leave with another?"

"I've been establishing that we're friends and I'll keep emphasizing it while you go in for the kill."

"What are you guys talking about?" Becky Lynn asked, plopping down between us. "Lovers' spat?"

I laughed a hearty laugh. "I could *never*. He's like a brother to me."

Thom frowned. He didn't like that. But I didn't like the idea of him buying condoms for use with other women, so there.

"Can we come home with you after?" Thom asked Becky Lynn. "I mean, not 'home' but to the hotel with you?"

My eyes bugged out and I pinched his leg under the table. Either he had no game, or he was trying to make a point. All signs indicated sabotage.

"Both of you?" Becky Lynn said, confused.

"Uh, yes?"

"Naughty, naughty. But I'm not into kinky stuff."

"You misunderstood—I don't mean a threesome." He pointed to me. "She'll just watch."

My face turned hot. "What? He's kidding!"

"You're so funny," Becky Lynn said.

The MC wandered over. "Which one of you is performing?"

Becky Lynn sipped her drink and said, "It was supposed to be Juleen the bride, but she's sick and couldn't make it."

"Do you have a backup?" the MC asked.

No one wanted to do it. They'd come to drink and laugh and watch the bride-to-be try stand-up. It was never going to be one of *them* up there.

Becky Lynn tried to lift Thom's hand as a volunteer. "He's hilarious, he should do it."

Thom shook his head vehemently.

The MC laid out the prizes to entice us. "First place is two hundred dollars, second place is one hundred, third place is fifty."

My hand shot up. "I'll do it."

"Sign here, here, and here," the MC said, shoving a clipboard in my hands. It was a standard disclaimer saying they could film me and use it for promotional purposes if they wanted. "You're up first," he added.

Oh God. What was I even going to say?

Then I remembered.

I *had* a nightclub act, courtesy of Thom. The beginnings of one, anyway.

"Wish me luck."

He gently tugged on my hand. "You don't have to do this."

"If I place we'll have enough money for a hotel room tonight," I said through clenched teeth.

He nodded, eyes narrowed. "Destroy them."

I took the stage and tested the mike. "My name is Holly Danner, how you all doing tonight?"

Some people weren't aware the contest had started, so the MC joined me onstage.

"Hey everybody, put your hands together for Holly Danner from San Diego, our first competitor tonight."

The bachelorettes cheered. The lights dimmed.

A spotlight landed on my face, and my pulse quickened. I thought back to my "share day" at Prevail! and knew I at least had an opening line. After that, I'd have to improvise.

"Something weird happened to me when I was a kid. I was on a TV show, and afterward, everyone on it became famous except for me. Odds are you've seen my elbow in a photograph. Yep. Anyone read the tabloids at the grocery store?"

Becky Lynn and our new friends said, "Woooo!" but the rest of the crowd remained silent.

"Okay, I call bullshit right now because ALL OF YOU read the tabloids at the grocery store."

Scattered laughter, not just from my group this time.

"It's okay, it's not like you buy them. It's not like you take them *home*. But you've seen them. So that means you've met me before and didn't know it. Well, you've met my elbow. I've been cropped out of more photographs than you can count. 'Cause anytime I've stood next to Melody Briar, Ethan Mallard, Brody Rutherford, Tara Osgood, or Kelly Hale, there's suddenly no room for me in the picture."

(Once again, I'd left J. J. out of the lineup. Force of habit, I guess.)

The audience took in what I'd said, and hushed conversations filled the club. I gave them another few seconds (probably abhorrent in the comedy world) to register who/what I was, then plunged ahead.

"When they can't crop me out they have to identify me somehow, but editors at magazines are on tight deadlines and don't always have time to find out who's next to a celebrity. They're household names.

"As you may have noticed, I am not a household name. I'm, like, a crawl-space name. An under-the-porch name. A stairwell name. Remember how Harry Potter's aunt and uncle made him live under the stairs in that shitty little room? That's the type of place where they know my name, that's where I'm famous."

A few appreciative claps.

"But you know, I get it. The other kids on the show, they all had something, you know? A specific talent. Most of them could do at least two things well, and learned how to cover up the third thing so it looked good, too. That's what the industry calls a triple threat. When you can sing, dance, and act.

"I was *not* a triple threat. I was, like, a mild warning. A Road Hump sign. Talent Up Ahead. No, wait, go back, you missed it... Nope, too far. Wait, turn around again...

"There! There it is; her.

"This was my talent. Are you ready? Can you handle this? I'm not sure you can handle this."

I plunged into a vigorous tap dance. My rhythm wasn't particularly tight but the crowd loved it so I milked the moment until the applause died down.

"Turns out there wasn't a huge market for tap-dancing in the 'nineties. Who knew? Unless you were Savion Glover, then you could tap-dance all you want.

"Last guy I dated, he loved it. *Loved it.* When I told him who I was and what I used to do, he got really quiet. The next day, he said he had an acting job for me. Awesome, right? Guess what it was."

"Porn," yelled a hearty dude, followed by scattered laughs.

"Close," I said.

"Take it all off!" the same dude yelled.

Thom stood and scanned the crowd in the dark. "What did you say?"

I couldn't see Thom's expression in the dark of the club, but his posture was unmistakably alpha. Tall, commanding, confident.

"Lighten up. It's a comedy show."

"Stop interrupting her," Thom ordered.

"She told us to guess."

"And you did, and now you're done."

Thom stared daggers at him and eventually sat. Becky Lynn whispered something in Thom's ear, but he didn't reply. I was touched, but he better not have ruined my set.

I shook out my hair and continued. There couldn't have been more than a minute to go. I wanted to time it right, like a stinger. (A stinger was TV-speak for a quick joke after the credits rolled. It was a reward to the audience for watching every last bit.)

"The acting job he lined up for me was not porn. No, they were clear about that. It would be me tap-dancing. Naked."

The audience reacted with laughter and groans.

"Well, first I'd be in pasties and a G-string. It was at a super-classy joint in LA, maybe you've heard of it? Jumbo's Clown Room. They billed the show as 'TV Kids Gone Bad!' It was ten look-alikes, you know, professional impersonators, like you see in Vegas sometimes. They had, let's see, Urkel, the Olsen twins, Melissa Joan Hart, Vicki—the robot girl from *Small Wonder*—Punky Brewster, all these look-alikes pretending to be Child Stars All Grown Up and Ready to... Fff—rolic."

More laughter and claps.

"Except *I* wouldn't be an impersonator. I would just be me."

Audience cringed.

"So insulting, right? I broke up with him, of course."

(Beat.)

"*After* I did the show. A girl's got to eat, you know?"

Cheers and laughter rang out, and a bell rang, releasing me to saunter offstage to a standing ovation when I bowed. It felt good, but I couldn't tell if it was because the set was worthy of one, or because I happened to be the first performer. Still, I'd done my best on zero notice, and the laughter had been gratifying.

If I didn't place, maybe another club around here was holding a lucrative contest we could enter. I bet we'd rule at bar trivia.

I slipped into my seat next to Thom and refastened my hair into a ponytail.

"You were amazing," he said, wrapping his good arm around my shoulders in a half hug.

I leaned in close to him.

"Was any of that stuff true?" he whispered.

"Part of it. I didn't do the burlesque show, but I *was* asked."

"Asshole."

"You know what they say: 'Tragedy plus time equals comedy.' I could use some air, though," I told him. "Come with?"

"Yeah, let's sit outside until they announce the winners."

There was a courtyard out back for smokers, so we propped the door open and sat on the outdoor couch by the firepit, which displayed evidence of its usual occupants: Cigarette burns dotted the cushions, and the ashtray perched on the armrest nearest me smelled like burnt toast. I wrinkled my nose and placed it on the ground away from us. Of course, if I thought we could get away with it, I'd have slept out there happily for the night. It was peaceful, a little chilly, and the stars shone brightly in the sky above us. In California the air quality and light pollution made it difficult to see them, but here in the Northeast, Orion's Belt was visible.

The next performer started up, but based on the muffled, light applause, he wasn't receiving the same loud reactions I had.

"Does stuff like that happen to you a lot?" Thom asked. "People trying to exploit you?"

His good arm stretched behind me along the back of the

couch. His nearness, the warmth emanating from his body, had become so familiar to me. It hurt to think that with each passing second, we were closer and closer to leaving each other behind.

"Sometimes. Not quite that rudely." I shrugged. I didn't know what else to say.

Thom did, though. And since we were running out of time to have conversations like this, I welcomed the opportunity.

"After the show tomorrow," he began.

"Assuming we make it in time..."

"Assuming we make it in time, come stay at my place, okay? I don't want you to have to worry about where you're going to go. We'll make up the extra bed, you can sleep all day if you want, whatever's comfortable."

"Are you sure?"

"Positive." He cleared his throat. "Can I ask you something?"

I smiled. "Probably?"

"If he didn't cheat on you, and he's straight as an arrow, why did you and J. J. break up? Did you grow apart, or...?"

"You really want to know?"

"Yeah, I do." He looked at me intently, and it was strange to realize I hadn't told him this yet, because it seemed like we talked about everything. Yet we never ran out of topics.

I took a deep breath.

Lainey was five, I explained, learning to swing dance by standing on J. J.'s feet as he guided her around the kitchen.

Watching them gave me déjà vu. I was transported back to J. J. teaching me the jitterbug at my parents' house when we were thirteen. The Studdards had begun editing me out of dance numbers when the moves proved too complicated (my dancing skills began and ended with tap), but J. J. refused to let that happen again.

It was difficult to find a place to practice, though. Having noticed our hand-holding and stolen kisses, my parents implemented a new rule: First, there was to be "no closing of the door" when we hung out in each other's bedrooms, and then it escalated to "no more hanging out in each other's bedrooms, period." It was too dark in the yard to see clearly at night, so he taught me the dance routines in the hallway. My elbows would bang into the walls when he spun me. His patience knew no bounds; he practiced as long as I needed, whenever I needed it. When it came time to film the segments, I was so accustomed to dancing in the cramped hallway, my movements were squashed and odd. But at least they put me back on camera.

Two decades later I watched him guide Lainey the way he used to guide me. "Move your feet like this...and twirl, and dip...together, apart, you got it. You did it!"

Lainey jumped up for a high five and J. J., looking sweaty, missed her hand.

Not to be silly. Not to make her laugh.

Because he was high.

Again.

"Can I talk to you outside for a sec?" I asked sweetly.

He swiveled to face me, eyes red. Could he have been more obvious?

"Oh no, am I in twubble?" he asked once we were outside in my sister's backyard. Lainey colored in the kitchen, and Renee was upstairs if she needed anything.

I sat on the patio, and J. J. followed suit.

"I can't have you coming around when you're like this, Jay.

You know I don't mind if you smoke every once in a while, but this is different. This is all the time."

He laughed. "Well, you know why I'm like this, don't you?"

I was so tired of talking about the lawsuit I could barely stand it, but if he needed to rehash it one more time, I could try. "I know you're having a tough time about Pam," I began.

"Not Pam." He pointed at me, a sneer lighting up his face. "You."

"Me?"

"You."

He stood, which proved difficult. "You, you, you," he repeated.

"What about me?"

He held his arms out wide and spun in a circle. "None of this would have happened. None of it. Why didn't you leave me alone? Why didn't your *fucking family* leave me alone?"

(I stiffened, my eyes automatically shooting to the kitchen, hoping Lainey couldn't hear. He never said the f-word, as far as I knew, and I knew him better than anyone.)

"What? My 'fucking family' helped you," I hissed back. "You begged us to take you in. You were devastated when your parents threatened to pull the plug."

He rolled his eyes. "I was a kid. I didn't know what was good for me. I needed guidance, I needed perspective."

"Every year my mom and dad said to us, 'The moment this stops being fun, you tell us and you can stop.' You know they did. They'd have hired a team of lawyers if they'd needed to, they'd have gotten us out of it, all we had to do was ask."

I may as well never have spoken.

"If you'd left me alone, let me go back to North Carolina like I was supposed to, like my parents wanted," he said, "I wouldn't have gotten emancipated, I wouldn't have let Pammy screw me over. I could've lived a Godly life, like they wanted for me. Like I should've been doing. I could've *known* Him, I could've found a purpose in Him, something *real*, not this secular *bullshit*. I chose the world, instead of Him, and I'll be paying for it the rest of my life."

Tears of frustration filled his eyes. He stared at me and I didn't dare look away. I was pinned in place, and it was painful, so painful to see him like that.

"I don't feel Him anymore," he whispered, the ultimate confession. The worst confession, because it was the only one that couldn't be forgiven. "I don't feel His presence anymore. I've been trying to get it back, and I can't."

I moved to hug him, but he shook his head and pulled away. His face was blotchy and although he whispered, the words cracked in my ears like thunder. "I wish I'd never met you. You separated me from God."

Outside the comedy club, I held my breath and looked at my hands, curled in my lap.

"Hey," Thom said softly.

I risked a glance, fearful of what I'd see in his eyes. (Horror. Agreement.)

But the look he gave me could only be described as tender.

"I believe Eleanor Roosevelt said it best, and I'm paraphrasing here, but 'No one can separate you from God without your permission.'"

Tears pulled at the edges of my eyes. I'd never told anyone

what J. J. said to me that day; not even Renee. I hadn't wanted it to affect her own faith, since it was helping her combat her depression. But by telling another person about it, and seeing the words through a five-year lens, it dawned on me how far-fetched and manipulative it sounded. My family hadn't done anything wrong. They'd provided a home and a second family to a preternaturally talented eleven-year-old boy who had wanted to see what the world had to offer beyond Charlotte, North Carolina; an eleven-year-old boy who was apoplectic when his parents interrupted rehearsal to inform him they were yanking him from the show.

We'd loved him like our own. He'd been my brother. My best friend. My boyfriend. My lover. My everything another person could be.

Which, in retrospect, was one of the problems. There was no room for anyone or anything else, except, eventually, my niece. I'd had few friends; fewer dates. I'd chased him, emotionally and physically, for as long as I could remember. And now he regretted every moment of knowing me. By wishing me out of his life, he may as well have wished me dead.

"There was a time, once before, when we didn't speak for two years," I admitted. "And when we got back together, it was like nothing had happened, like we were never apart. Once the show ended, we never lived with each other again. We were never in the same city for long, so every visit was a reunion of sorts anyway. The breakups had more time in between, but otherwise there wasn't much difference between being 'on' and being 'off.' But I think... he represented home to me for so long, it didn't matter if he was on the other side of the world, because you can always go home."

He nodded, the brightness in his eyes dimming slightly.

"What about you?" I asked. "Do you ever miss Sammy's mother?"

"We weren't a good fit," he said carefully. "But I'll never consider Sammy to be a mistake, and I'll always be grateful to her for giving him to me."

I cuddled against him, tucked under his arm. We looked up at the stars and he said quietly, "Thanks for telling me."

Becky Lynn from our party group leaned her face out, her red curls bouncing. "They're announcing the winners, you guys!"

I'd been so immersed in our conversation I'd nearly forgotten about the contest.

Once we were back inside, my eyes slowly adjusted to the darkness. The seven other competitors and I were led onstage, and the MC strolled the line while the audience indicated their enthusiasm via applause for each candidate.

When the applause-o-meter was calculated, I was declared the second-place winner, with a prize of $100. Suck it, Hilton. I tapped out a dance of joy and grabbed the envelope with a flourish. I flew off the stage double-time, looking for Thom. I didn't see him, so I turned into the darkened hallway, the one we'd used to get outside.

A low voice: "Hey."

I bumped into Thom's chest. He slid his good hand to the back of my neck, leaned down, and kissed me.

His lips were soft but firm, and he tasted tart and sweet from the pomegranate margaritas we'd all had, but his steady movements proved he was sober and in control. The fact that it was a deliberate choice on his part made me feel strong and weak at the same time. The way his hand trailed lightly down my back, like stones skipping across a lake, sent delicious shudders through my body.

"You're so out of my league," I murmured against his lips.

He kissed me again and again, cupping my chin delicately in his hand. When our eyes met, he said forcefully, "Are you kidding? I'm crazy about you. Why do you think I let you come with me to New York?"

His tongue stroked mine in a way that had me delirious for more. We made out with abandon, pausing every few seconds to whisper our affection, as though we were in a race to say nicer and nicer things to each other.

"The way you cut through everyone's BS—how you got on Lisa's nerves—I loved it—and the work you do, not to mention you're gorgeous, and—"

"I knew you were special the moment I met you. Your sense of humor, your kindness—"

"My lack of shame?" I added drily.

"Yes!" Kiss. "All of it!" Kiss. "Every time a new person came to group, I'd say, 'Pretend it's your nightclub act.' They all acted like I was nuts. You're the only one who went up there and *put on a nightclub act*."

"And look at us now, rolling in cash." I pinched the envelope between my fingers and rubbed them back and forth.

"I love how brilliant and quick you are, like I'll never keep up but I want to keep trying anyway," he said.

"I love how confident you are, even when you're totally wrong."

He grinned sheepishly.

"But especially when you're right," I added.

Moving as one, we glided farther into the darkened hall.

"You want to know one of my secrets?" Thom whispered in my ear.

"Yeah."

"When you came on to me at Prevail!, in your room?"

"Yeah?"

"I couldn't even go swimming after. And I really wanted to go swimming."

"Is that so?" I had to admit, it did my pride good to hear.

"That." Kiss. "Is." Kiss. "So."

"What was it that got to you?" I asked.

"When you suggested we do it against the wall to keep the door shut."

"Then we'll have to try that out as soon as possible," I suggested.

Thom's hand made its way under my shirt to caress my skin. My stomach fluttered at the sensation. We needed to get out of there. He kissed me with such complete assurance despite his clipped wing that I couldn't even imagine how amazing it would feel if he had the use of both arms right now. He felt damn good already. And somehow, the whole thing worked for us; with his injured arm at his side, the kiss perfectly encapsulated what I'd learned about him on the trip.

That he's full of swagger but also guarded; that he doesn't let anything stop him from going after what he wants, even if it might be difficult; that he's both self-possessed and vulnerable, and not afraid to show it. At least, he wasn't afraid to show it to *me*, which made me see myself, briefly, the way he did: special.

"This," I managed to gasp when we broke apart for air.

"Hmm?" He kissed the shell of my ear, down my jaw, under my chin, and to my favorite spot, the side of my neck. Sensing how much I liked it, he lingered there, as I tried to suppress the appreciative sounds I yearned to make.

"At the hotel, you asked me what I needed. It was this." I

succumbed to the noise I'd been holding in, a sigh mixed with a whimper.

"*Only* this?" he teased.

"It's a good start, anyway..."

I gazed into his eyes, which were heavy-lidded with desire.

"We have a place to stay," he remarked, tucking a strand of hair behind my ear.

"We have a place to..." I whispered the last part in his ear.

He nodded and swallowed. "About that condom..."

"Yes, please."

He kissed my neck once more, the spot that sent me into overdrive, and it took all my willpower to push him away. "Hurry, hurry."

The idea of him buying a condom to use with someone else had sent my blood boiling earlier. But I hadn't envisioned *we'd* be the ones using it. I couldn't stop smiling as Thom swiveled toward the men's room. I gripped his shirt and pulled him back so I could plant another kiss on his lips.

My entire body smiled. I moved to the bar, hips swishing, hair a mess, skirt disheveled, and lipstick smeared. The night could not have gone better, particularly if you remembered how it started: committing fraud at the Hilton. Now I was about to crack open a $100 bill and find a place to be alone with Thom.

17

"Hey, Becky Lynn, wait up. Want another 'rita? On me?" After tax and tip, that would set me back $20 but it seemed a steal considering what she'd inadvertently done for us.

She raised her eyebrows. "You're paying? Sure."

While the bartender finished up with another member of our group, she remarked, "I thought you said you and Thom were just friends."

I blushed, wondering how much of our PDA she saw. "Uh...we are. That's been building for a while, I think."

She beamed. "You gave in to your feelings at a bachelorette party! The bride will love it, knowing she played matchmaker."

I placed Becky Lynn's order and ripped open the prize envelope with my thumb.

Inside was a gift card.

To Lowe's, the home goods store.

For $100.

"What the rancid fucking shit is this?" I sputtered.

Becky Lynn looked shocked by my language. She recovered quickly, though. Swift as a hummingbird, she grabbed her cocktail off the bar and began drinking before it could be rescinded.

I turned the gift card over in my hand, livid. The MC was chatting with the first-place winner when I stormed over and demanded an explanation.

"I laid out the prizes clear as day before the contest. You must not have been paying attention," he said, unconcerned. "Everyone else understood what they were."

"I can't use this. Will you cash it out for me?"

"Does it look like you're in a Lowe's?" he replied. He and the first-place winner chortled.

A warm, calming hand rested on the small of my back. Thom had returned, triumphant, the condom(s) presumably stowed away.

"Everything cool?" he asked.

"No, the prize was a *gift card.*" I slammed the offending plastic rectangle against his chest. My teeth were so clenched I feared they would shatter.

"Can you cash it out?" Thom asked.

" 'That's what she said,' " the MC quipped. "But really, that's actually what she said."

"Can you cash it out or not?" Thom snapped.

"If the store's open they might do it for you, but I don't know for sure."

Becky Lynn looked up from her iPhone's map. "There's one near here, but it's closing in fifteen."

Why wouldn't this day end? All I wanted was a clean hotel and soft sheets and a firm mattress and Thom, Thom, Thom.

After a brief confab with her cohorts, Becky Lynn said, "We have the limo till one a.m."

"To the limo," Thom ordered in grim determination.

18

INT. LION'S DEN—DAY

(KELLY, HOLLY, TARA, DIEGO (O.S.))
The girls sit on the picnic table, legs dangling down. Each wears an outfit with fake "cheetah" print on it—tan with black polka dots—as they paint their nails and chat.

TARA

Fun fact: Cheetahs are the fastest animals in the world.

KELLY

On land, that is.

TARA

They can reach speeds up to 110 kilometers, or 70 miles, in just three seconds!

HOLLY

That's as fast as a car.

(beat)

Or me, if someone's got s'mores cooking.

AUDIENCE LAUGHTER.

DIEGO (O.S.)

Hey girls! The s'mores are ready!

HOLLY hops off the table and moves her arms and legs back and forth, running in place as if gaining speed (FX: smoke from her legs), then runs straight through the plywood set, leaving a Holly-size hole behind.

TARA

Bollocks.

KELLY

I hope she leaves some for us!

We made it to Lowe's one minute before closing. The manager was undoubtedly perplexed by the group of intoxicated, happy women in semi-formal dresses who spilled out of the bus like a clown car, but he wasn't quick enough to lock the doors. We made our descent and he allowed it, but all the cash registers were dark. Also, he locked the door behind us, which made me worry we'd entered a horror film scenario until I realized it was to keep out additional after-hours customers.

We scattered like cockroaches.

"Find the cheapest item possible," I called out. "Whoever finds the cheapest thing wins."

"We may as well find something useful," Thom argued. "Sammy could use a new flashlight."

"Are you really going shopping right now?"

"Maybe. What are *you* going to do about it?" He pushed me up against a sample refrigerator and all the heat and dizziness from the bar returned to us full force.

We kissed like mad until an irritated voice said, "Please find what you need in a timely manner and I'll ring you up at customer service. The regular checkouts are locked."

We jumped apart and Thom apologized. "Sorry, man. We got this gift card, but what we need is the money."

"We're not an ATM. The money can only be spent in-store."

"What if we buy something for twenty or thirty bucks?" he said reasonably. "Could you slip us the rest?"

"The money can only be spent in-store."

"Find what we need, got it," he agreed.

I couldn't believe what I was hearing. "No, this is ridiculous."

Thom beckoned me to a "private" aisle. "Let's buy something and then immediately return it for cash."

"Whoever finds the most expensive thing wins," I shouted to whomever was listening. Judging by the silence that greeted us, I'd guess no one.

Two minutes later we approached the checkout with a mailbox ($97.85, including tax). After he rang it up and swiped the gift card, I announced, "Oops, wrong color, sorry, we need to return it but since you're closing we'll take cash, please, thanks so much."

The employee regarded us for a moment. I felt certain he would give in, if only to get rid of us.

He swiped the card again and typed on his keyboard. "You'll get store credit for next time."

"Oh come on!" I sensed a Cash-for-Clunkers-type hysteria approaching me on the horizon and I refused to give in to it. (*Was that only today?*)

"We're out of options," Thom said through clenched teeth. "The car is about to leave, and we have no place to stay."

"I'm aware of our predicament."

"We need to accept that it's time to buy camping gear."

"Oh my God." I took a deep breath, tried to align my brain with the reality of our situation. "Okay. Okay."

I nodded rhythmically, over and over, as if each movement would further convince myself of the facts. Then I smacked my hands together. "Let's do this."

"Where's the camping gear?" Thom asked our robotic friend.

19

The Coleman Flatiron 3-Person Instant Dome Tent was not, in fact, instant.

First we had to wait for the Lowe's clerk to lock up and leave the vicinity, which seemed to take abnormally long. Then we had to carry our heavy gear, as well as our duffel bag and backpack, to the back of the shopping plaza property into the "corporate woods" (scattered trees and parking lots) where we hopefully wouldn't be seen or heard by patrol cars or other passersby on the main road. Then we spent the better part of an hour setting up our sleeping space. By the time we finished, we agreed sex was no longer in the cards. Neither of us wanted a public indecency arrest to go along with our narrow escape earlier, and our accommodations weren't the most comfortable. Still, we had a roof over our heads, and for one night, that was enough.

We crawled inside the tent, unzipped our sleeping bag, and spread it out like a blanket. We hadn't been able to afford two of them. He crawled to me and we lay next to each other, his arms wrapped around my waist, his face resting on my belly. I played with his hair, stroking my nails lightly through it.

He swiveled his face so he could look up at me. "I'm sorry we're not at the Hilton," he said. "Or some other hotel." Beat. "Or indoors."

I smiled back. "That's okay. Rain check, this time tomorrow?" I gave him a chaste kiss so as not to set the fire blazing again.

This time tomorrow we'd be at Thom's house in upstate New York. This time tomorrow I'd be sharing his bed. The thought kept me warm and toasty.

"Deal." We kissed once more. Then we shook hands. Then he kissed my hands, the back and front and each knuckle and each fingertip.

I cuddled closer so I could nestle my head under his chin. It was strangely peaceful out there. Silent except for the crickets, and the occasional rumble of car wheels in the distance. Most importantly, I was with Thom, and we'd confessed our feelings to each other, which made that tent the most perfect spot on earth right now.

I'd never been a camper, but I could be a great one, if Thom were with me. I could do *anything* if Thom were with me.

The tent was warm from the heat of our bodies by then, so we unzipped one of the "window" panels and breathed in the dark, cold air.

Something I think is underrated in men: how soft their skin can be. I like a hard belly and tight abs as much as the next girl, but what gets my heart racing is when you're coasting your hands over a guy's chest—Thom had the perfect amount of chest hair, by the way—and you encounter a strip of skin amid all that solid manliness that's like silk. At the apex of

Thom's hip, angled down toward his thigh, was a strip of skin so smooth I want to run my tongue along it.

So I did. He goose-bumped instantly and I liked that, too.

"We had an agreement," he murmured, fisting my hair in his hands and raising my head up. "And you are dangerously close to breaking it."

"You're right." I shimmied up his body to safer territory. "What's this?" I asked, tracing a tattooed image on his biceps. It was a small cartoon drawing of a fish leaping against the current, followed by a smaller, identical fish. It was clearly a parent and child.

"Salmon swimming upstream. I got it when Sammy's mom left. Because salmon shouldn't be able to swim upstream. It's impossible. But they do it anyway."

I kissed both images and rested my head on his chest. A second later I felt the rumble of his laugh. "I thought *you* were going to be *my* pillow."

"Nope," I yawned. "Good night."

20

Are you shocked, given the chaotic events of the night before, that we overslept?

21

Thom's phone rang, permeating our sleep fog.

I nudged him, getting progressively more violent, until he rolled over and startled himself awake. I didn't want to know what time it was. The fact that daylight surrounded our tent was answer enough.

A moment later, Thom pushed the phone into my hand. "It's for you," he slurred, and rolled back over to sleep.

"Hello?"

"Holly, hey," Renee said. "Where are you?" Her voice lowered, as though she were worried Thom could hear. "Was that Thom? He sounded cute."

"Hey, welcome back. We're in Pennsylvania, in the woods behind a Lowe's. Long story."

"I look forward to hearing it."

"And I want to hear all about Belgium. How was Lainey's birthday?" A lump filled my throat but I managed to make my voice sound normal. Bright, even. The first birthday I hadn't helped to plan. The first birthday I hadn't been around for. The first of many to come.

"That's a long story, too." Muffled voices in the background. "Just a second, Laine, I'm talking to her—okay, *okay*... Uh, someone wants to talk to you."

"Molly," yelled a voice.

It was her old nickname for me, one she hadn't used in years. The lump expanded in my throat. Tears filled my eyes and I tried my best to hide them by sniffing them back in.

"Sir Laines-a-lot! Did you buy me anything from abroad?" I expanded the last word so it came out "abrawwwwd."

"Yes, some chocolates. They're a bit squished, but I kept them safe."

"We can't keep her long, she's on someone else's phone," Renee said. To me, she added, "We got in the night before last, and I already FedExed your stuff. But listen, you had a ton of messages on the home line. I'll text you the names and numbers and you can get back to them when you have a chance. I can't believe you left rehab to drive to New York! I haven't told Mom and Dad yet. They still think you're meditating all day or something."

"Thanks for keeping it quiet. I'll be on the anniversary special tonight if you guys want to watch."

"Mmm," she said noncommittally.

With thousands of miles between us, and Thom's phone as a shield, I found the wherewithal to ask something I'd been wondering about for a while. "How come you're not angry with them?"

Silence. Then: "It would be like being angry at a good memory."

"What do you mean?"

"Well, there are people you meet when you're young, right, and as you get older, you realize that if you met them *now*, you never would have become friends. You're too different. So the fact that you met them early enough to be friends at all makes it even more special."

"You're being way too enlightened about this."

"I also pretend they died."

My almost-tears become a bark of laughter. "Renee!"

"What? I do. They kind of *did*."

"You know they used us. For years and years."

"Didn't we use them, too?"

"No," I retorted.

"Think about it. Wasn't it fun when they would visit, and we were the only people who knew where they were, and what they were up to? Wasn't it fun sneaking them out of the house in hats and scarves and pretending they were our cousins from out of town who suffered from 'sun weakness'?"

"You're really not mad at them? Not even Kelly?"

"If I give them any thought, it's usually *What an unfortunate outfit* at the checkout line. Although, whenever I'm at an airport, like yesterday, I think about the time we picked up Kelly before the second season. Remember?"

After the first season of *Diego and the Lion's Den* ended in 1993 and everyone flew back to their home states for the summer, Renee and I received a package in the mail, in a thick, twelve-by-fourteen padded envelope from Muncie, Indiana. It was a flat stack of folded clothing from a store called Units that had taken the Midwest by storm. Renee and I had nearly peed ourselves when Kelly described it to us; for her part, she couldn't believe we'd never heard of it. According to Kelly, the Units store at the Muncie Mall had no changing rooms, aisles, hangers, or *mirrors*. It was nothing but white shelving built into a wall, piled high with one-size-fits-all rectangles of fabric in solid colors. The fabric could be worn in any capacity the wearer wished. Mini skirts and tube tops were indistinguishable; slouchy dresses, tunics, and pullover sweaters oddly similar; belts and head wraps interchangeable. You were supposed to layer the "units" in endless varieties of personal style yet the only possible outcome screamed "futuristic drapery."

They were, in a word, and to an item, hideous. Especially the neon-pink and -orange ones that Kelly had been sure to send us.

So naturally, when we picked her up at the airport that fall to shoot season two, we wore every Units item she'd sent us—all ten of them—one on top of the other. It was enough to send us into fits of shrieking every time we caught sight of ourselves walking past a mirror or reflective window in the airport. In those days you could walk right up to the gate and greet your people as they disembarked from the plane.

Passengers trickled out.

"Quick, Holly, take off the belt-thing..." Renee whispered, half pushing me.

"What? Why?"

"Hurry, just, like, step out of it or lift it over your head. I'm going to conjoin us..."

"Oh my God," I giggled.

Once I'd wriggled free of one of my top layers, Renee snatched the neon-green band from my hand, looped it over her head, and pulled it down over mine. It got twisted and stuck, serving as a strapless "over-bra" for her and a neck brace for me.

A shout: Kelly had spotted us.

We hobbled toward her, a laughing, two-headed monster.

She hugged us, then unzipped her carry-on and removed *another* Unit, which she proceeded to configure to make us a *three*-headed monster. We tripped and giggled and knocked into things all the way down to baggage claim.

"It sucks she wasn't there for you after Lainey was born," I pointed out. I knew I was pushing on a bruise by bringing it up, but I needed *something* from Renee. Proof that my feelings were valid, that the hurt I'd been tending to these past two months deserved its own garden.

Renee got quiet. "Yeah, it does. But what I remember most about that time is that you *were* there for me. Anyway, your purse and phone and all that stuff is on its way, and don't forget to check your texts. Call me after the show. Good luck!"

We said goodbye, and I lifted Thom's sleep-weighted hand.

"You have a bunch of missed calls, all from the same number. It's probably Ben. Put in your password and let's find out if the car's—" The digital clock read ten fifty-six. "Oh my God, it's eleven. How is it eleven?"

"I don't know," Thom protested, shielding his eyes from the light.

I paced in the tent, throwing my hands up at random intervals. "How can it be eleven right now?"

"I set the alarm for six."

"Let me see." He unlocked the phone, tapped his clock app, and groaned. "I set it for six *p.m.*"

"No."

"Yes. I'm so sorry."

I flopped down beside him. He was shirtless, with mussy hair—mussed by me—and part of me wanted to wrap my arms around him and go back to sleep and forget about the world and everyone in it. Because last night... had been perfect. Perfectly us, at least, which was why I loved it so much.

But the *Daily Denizen* countdown clock chugged along, ticking down the seconds. I didn't need to pull it up online to know what it said:

9 hours

21 minutes

We were still in the wrong *state*.

I was considering hyperventilating and wondering whether being in a tent would make it worse when Thom's phone rang again. He hit answer and speaker in rapid succession so I could hear, too.

"Hello?" He rubbed his eyes.

"Hi, it's Ben over at Harrisburg Motors. I've been trying to reach you guys all morning."

I knew it. Dammit!

Thom and I exchanged worried looks. "Is the engine fixed?" Thom asked.

"I got the part, and I tested it several times, and it doesn't work. I'm sorry, guys."

"Thanks anyway," Thom said before hanging up.

"What are we going to do?" I asked.

"Let me call my parents." We kissed like it was a promise.

Thom stepped outside the tent as I packed our bags. By the time he finished the call, I'd torn down the tent.

"It's too late for my parents to come get us—they won't make it in time for the return trip to get us there by eight."

"Shit. Shit. Shit." I snapped my fingers, remembering. "Your groupie, Braden. Call him."

"I don't have his—"

"We got his number when he dropped us off. Hurry, hurry."

He hit the call button and I stood next to him so we could both talk.

"Braden, hey, it's Thom, we met yesterday?"

"Sure man, what's up?"

"We need a ride to the train station," I said. "And money for tickets."

Silence on the other end. "How much?"

"A hundred bucks. Do you like camping?"

22

An hour later, Braden had come to our rescue, and he was willing to speed, although that may have had more to do with the fact that he was late for Econ 101 than wanting to be a hero. Nevertheless, he was happy to accept the camping gear as payment, and handed us five well-used $20 bills for our train tickets.

When Braden pulled up to the station, we shouted our thanks, and he barely waited for us to exit before he hit the gas.

The train rumbled into view, so we raced inside. We shoved our wrinkled, compromised, sad twenties through the ticket window to the cashier.

"You're short five dollars," she said.

"No, it should be exactly right, we calculated it—"

"After taxes, you're five dollars short."

"That's all we have," I said. "Please."

"Ma'am," said the ticket taker. "You have to let the next person come up. There's an ATM outside. If you hurry, you can still make it."

The train had arrived. A rush of movement whirled around

us as passengers stood from their benches and moved to the door.

The next train wouldn't be here for three hours.

"Oh, come on," I groaned, to no one in particular.

"Next!"

"Wonderful," I muttered to Thom as we reconvened in the corner. "I've been ma'am'd and ATM'd and we're totally screwed." I lowered my voice and glanced around for eavesdroppers. "Should we hop on anyway, and hope the guy forgets to check our tickets?"

"While I've often fantasized about the hobo life, it's only twelve thirty," he pointed out. "If we catch the three thirty, we'll get there by six, with two hours to spare."

"How do we get tickets for the three thirty? We're still five short."

"Easy. Go forth and busk." He sat on a vacated bench, propped his arms behind his head, and stretched his legs out. "Chop, chop."

"Mmm, no."

He grinned. "Your call. I'll be waiting right here, silently rooting for you." He closed his eyes.

I wanted to wipe the smirk off his face. The easiest way was through a kiss. A bitey one.

"Ow," he complained, touching his lip. "Here, I'll get you started."

He found a pen in his bag, and wrote thickly on an abandoned newspaper sheet: YOUTUBE STAR NEEDS TO GET TO NEW YORK!

It was the most asshole thing I'd ever done.

Sensing the ticket-taker would not approve my own version of an ATM, I moved my "show" outside the station to the parking lot. I flipped Thom's Yankees cap upside down and set it on the ground to hold coins. Unfortunately, Friday-afternoon traffic to New York was not as robust as the morning commute would have been, so there was a lot of downtime before the next passengers trickled in from the park 'n' ride.

Having pegged my latent tap-dancing skills as the most pathetic and therefore the most pity-inducing, I danced my heart out while intermittently singing a medley of '90s songs. Maybe some fellow thirty-somethings would pay me for the nostalgia. Plus, it was on-brand for me.

"Don't Go Chasing Waterfalls," "Here's Where the Story Ends," "Hey Jealousy," "Creep," and "Wonderwall" got me up to four smackers.

One more dollar and we'd be set. Tired and hungry, I shuffled back inside the station on aching feet and handed Thom the fruits of my labor.

He stood, stretched, and rotated his neck. "Guess it's up to me."

"Gee, thanks for participating," I responded sarcastically. "By all means..."

He flipped my newspaper sign over and scrawled across it in deep dark pen: PAY ME TO STOP.

He stood on the bench, held the sign aloft like Lloyd Dobler with his stereo in *Say Anything*, took a deep breath, and...orated. I didn't know if he was truly tone deaf, or pretending, but barely a verse into his half-shouted / half-"sung" version of "Bye Bye Miss American Pie," we received the final dollar we required and nine beyond it, courtesy of an irritated Mr. Moneybags, whose crumpled-up tenner chucked at Thom's face caused cheers to break out from everyone in the waiting area. Including the ticket-taker.

Thom bowed, stretched out the bill, lifted it to the light as though making sure it wasn't counterfeit, and kissed it.

"Four measly bucks for an hour of tap-dancing," I said. "No one appreciates the arts anymore."

"At least they appreciate peace and quiet."

We kissed and boarded the train, holding hands.

Hoarse, relieved, and safe at last, we flung our weary bodies across from each other by one of the large window seats.

I wanted to crawl into his lap and stay there forever, but we'd reached the limit of goodwill from the people around us.

Safe, legally seated on the train, headed in the right direction, with an estimated travel time of two hours and forty-five minutes, I predicted we'd reach Grand Central Station at six thirty p.m. No more planning, no more worries.

We made it.

We're almost there.

"While you were singing for your supper, Renee sent about twenty texts," Thom said. "You have some phone calls to return."

I clicked on the first number, which had a San Diego area code and looked vaguely familiar. I'd just registered who it belonged to when a gruff voice answered, "All-Star Management, Geoffrey speaking."

It was the direct line of my former talent rep. I hadn't even had this number when I was a *client*, just the number for the front desk.

"Hi, it's Holly Danner returning your call."

"Danner! In all the years we worked together, why didn't you tell me you were a master at self-promotion? We could've capitalized on this years ago. But no matter," he backtracked, perhaps sensing insulting me was not the way to go. "No time like the present. The anniversary, the sudden interest in you, the timing couldn't be more perfect. We've got four offers right now."

"Four offers on what?" My pulse jumped and my palms turned cold and sweaty. Every phone call I ever had with Geoffrey made me feel this way. I didn't like it. The gut-churning sensation of money being offered and yanked away; the unrelenting knowledge my life could change in an instant, but more likely it would not. More likely it would continue indefinitely while my self-worth got chipped away.

It had been a decade since we'd spoken, but the old anxiety fell on me like an illness.

Geoffrey didn't answer right away. I realized later it was because he felt insecure about his ability to handle what had occurred.

"I know my expertise is mostly for above-the-line, on-camera work, but this is a *type* of performance, in a way, and I'm confident that with the assistance of our literary branch and our in-house counsel we'll secure you the best possible deal."

"I have no idea what you're talking about."

"All the big publishing houses are interested in a tell-all. Memoir. Autobiography? I can never remember the difference. Anyway, they're floating six figures."

"Ha! No, you must have misheard. The offer was for a hundred fifty dollars. From an e-publisher named Jinx. Call them back and tell them they might want to consider changing their name; it's not exactly confidence-inducing. Besides, I turned them down already."

"Jinx? Never heard of them. This is the big time. Your rise to stardom this week was a perfectly calibrated submission. Your presence on Reddit, J. J. bringing you up on that talk show, all the magazine articles, trending on Twitter. You blew up this week."

"A memoir, though?" It was a strange word, and forming it in my mouth only made it more so. *Mem-wah.*

A chance to set the record straight.

A stone dropped into my stomach, sending ripples across my insides.

Didn't part of me always know if I wanted to sell a book, all I had to do was make it nonfiction? If I wanted people to give a shit about my writing, all I had to do was write about real life. Write about me.

And by *me*, of course I meant *them*.

"And today, the video..." He sounded giddy.

My blood shivered in my veins. "What video?" I demanded. "I've been traveling and haven't had access to the internet." *My jailer/boyfriend/tentmate only lets me on fifteen minutes a day.*

"Okay, Danner, hang up and go on YouTube. There's a video of you from last night at some stand-up club and it's gone viral. People are responding to your self-deprecation. All that woe-is-me-I'm-a-loser stuff. Watch it and call me back."

I proceeded as told.

Thom cocked his head to the side like a confused puppy.

"I know you were joking about me being a YouTube star, but according to my phone call, the joke's on us."

Seconds later we watched me in last night's performance. The homemade video opened with a hobbled-together "montage" of my "life": tap-dancing on *Diego*; then the snippet of J. J. mentioning me on *Jerry Levine* (BECAUSE APPARENLTY NOTHING HAPPENED TO ME DURING THE INTERVENING YEARS); then a clip of some ancient *Jeopardy!* episode heretofore unknown to me in which I was the answer (er, the question) and none of the contestants got it right; and lastly, my "nightclub act."

Guess who randomly showed up at my favorite happy hour place last night??? J. J. Randall's ex-girlfriend! #PickupthephoneHolly, crowed the text. Then it cut to the MC introducing me by name. The audience's laughter throughout my impromptu set sounded thinner and higher-pitched than I remembered it, but it might have been due to the phone's tinny speakers.

After I exited the stage to decent applause, the video jumped ahead to the winners being announced. There I was, presented with my second-place envelope and bouncing offstage, pleased.

If it didn't cut off soon, if the camera kept following me, it was going to see... yep, there it was. Me and Thom kissing.

So *that* was on the internet.

I shot a guilty look at Thom, whose expression was unreadable. The saving grace was that the club hallway was dark and there was no way to identify him from the video.

It had fifty-four thousand thumbs-up and seventeen thousand thumbs-down. I was savvy enough not to read a single comment and instead hit redial to Geoffrey, who answered on the first ring.

"I didn't have to do a thing, the calls came to me," he said by way of hello. "'Where have you been hiding her?' they all wondered."

If you didn't have to do a thing, why should I be giving you a commission?

I rewound our conversation in my head and paused on the term *six figures*.

"Are we really talking that kind of money?" I asked.

"If there's a bidding war, it'll go higher," Geoffrey said casually.

Higher? I thought in a daze. What was higher than six figures?

Oh.

A million.

A million-dollar book deal.

"First things first: Will you be at the anniversary tonight?"

"Yes. I'm on my way there now."

"Excellent. Because I've been getting calls about *that*, too. I'll let them know to expect you and to have wardrobe and makeup ready. Secondly, the interested parties have made it clear they want dirt. The show, your lives after the show, the highs and the lows and scandals, everything. Do you know where the bodies are buried?"

"Geoffrey," I replied. "I *am* the bodies."

"Great, I'll let everyone know you're willing to play ball. Finally, and it's the most important, you have to announce that you're writing a book tonight on national television. You'll never have a bigger audience, and that'll help us negotiate from a place of strength."

"Wait, hold on, I'm not sure if I—"

"You're not sure about what? Look, it's a lot to take in, I understand. But the good news is, you have time. You have hours to think about it. And you'll have four to six months to write it. Is that doable?"

"Yeah, yeah..." I trailed off.

"Excellent. We'll talk Monday."

We clicked off.

It seemed silly to return any other calls after that one. What could they possibly matter?

Thom waited until I looked over. "What's this about a memoir?"

23

"I thought you didn't have any reps," Thom said, after I explained Geoffrey's call in detail. It wasn't exactly the climactic response I was going for.

"It's been a decade, but he never officially broke things off. That's how Hollywood works. They might stop returning your calls, but they never want a permanent severing in case something like this happens."

"So now he's back, trying to make money off you, assuming you'll be so grateful you'll forget that he hasn't spoken to you in years? Don't you think that's tacky?"

"Nothing tacky about six figures," I pointed out.

"Ask for a two-book deal. A memoir *and* something fictional. Get them to agree to publish one of your other books first."

"That's not how this works. If you demand too much, they'll drop the whole thing."

He was silent, watching the Amish farmland move past us. A combine harvester and other farm equipment looked like something out of a storybook. The light hit our train window in such a way that I could see his reflection as well as the countryside, depending on how I focused my eyes.

"I thought you already turned down a book offer," he said.

"That offer was insulting. Come on, you know that."

"So it wasn't the tell-all you objected to. It was the price?"

"Hey, I haven't agreed to it yet. But if I'm going to do it, Geoffrey wants me to announce it tonight, onstage."

"That makes sense," he said. "I guess."

"Thanks for the support," I muttered.

We looked at each other through the reflection in the window, as though from an impossible distance.

"Without distractions, I could crank it out in two or three months I bet," I said.

"So let's say you do it. You write some trashy tell-all."

"It doesn't have to be trashy," I muttered, but we both knew that was a lie.

"What happens after that?" he asked.

"What do you mean?"

"They'll never speak to you again."

"They don't speak to me now!"

"You might not care at the moment, but someday…"

"Never thought I'd see you take their side."

"I don't care what it'll do to them. I care what it'll do to *you*."

I crossed my arms. "What will it 'do' to me?"

"It'll make you think this is all you are."

"Pretty sure the universe has been telling me that for a while. May as well make money off it, right?"

He motioned for me to sit next to him, and I did. His words came out gently, and I could tell they were carefully considered. I found myself leaning closer to hear him.

"You could have written a book about them anytime during

the last decade, but you didn't. You chose not to. That should tell you something."

"I was dating J. J." As if he needed any reminders.

"Not the last five years you weren't," he retorted.

"No one asked me to write a book before. Today they're asking me."

"You'd be wasting your talents."

"What talents?" I roared.

"Your sense of humor, your way of looking at the world, your ability to get an audience invested. You have great instincts, you're smart, you're creative. Write *your* book, not theirs."

I shook my head, not listening. "I've never been less certain about what I'm supposed to be doing with my life than I am right now, and this saves me. I don't understand why you don't see that."

"You must have had a plan for yourself, some idea of what you wanted to do when you quit watching Lainey. What did you have in mind when you told your sister it was time for *you* now?" His words were soft, gentle, coaxing.

My heart slammed in my chest and my throat went dry.

Thom laced his fingers through mine, concerned. "Hey, you okay?"

I took a slow, deep breath. "Can we talk about something else?"

"I just...I hate seeing you sell yourself short."

"Noted," I said. "And appreciated." He wrapped his arm around my shoulders and we kissed. Nothing had been resolved—we were on opposite sides of the fence as far as the book was concerned—but kissing was a good start.

"What should we talk about?" Thom asked.

"First crush: Go."

"Winnie Cooper. You?"

"Michael from *For Better or For Worse.*"

He had to think about that for a second. "The comic strip?"

"He was perfect and our love was pure," I declared. "Every Sunday, in color."

I was reminded of Thom's *Calvin & Hobbes* wrapping paper, the months he'd spent cutting out the strips for his friend. He was such a fundamentally decent person. No wonder he recoiled at my eagerness to sell out.

"A hand-drawn boyfriend and a pop star. Pretty hard to live up to," he muttered.

His tone was fairly light, but it reminded me of the way he'd interrogated me at the start of our road trip, about whether I made guys "compete" for my affection. I didn't have the energy to explain to him he needn't fear a long-ago funny-pages character stealing my affection.

I plunged ahead with a different topic. "What's the worst movie Sammy became obsessed with?"

"*Land Before Time.*"

"What? That's a good film."

"Ahh, you didn't let me finish. *Land Before Time: Journey of the Brave.*"

"Oh." I nodded. "A sequel. They *always* prefer the subpar ones. Lainey was obsessed with Daniel Tiger. Did you ever see the episode where Mom Tiger is by herself for a split second and she sings a song about cleaning up—'Clean up, pick up, put away, clean up every day'—and it's not even the main song of the episode? She wasn't imparting wisdom—this was *her life.* Something she sings to herself when she's alone in the house. They circled around to it later in the season and expanded the song so it could be reconfigured as the main one everyone sings to the kids, but it started as a cry for help from a desperate woman."

He laughed. "Think you might be projecting a little?"

"I had a nightmare about it, once."

"We were more of a *PJ Masks* family. Until about two years ago."

"Actually," I pointed out, "he still loves it."

"Says who?"

"He told me on the phone. We're very close, Sammy and I," I said teasingly.

"He told me he's over it," Thom protested.

"He might want you to *think* he's over it, but he's not. Everybody thinks kids want to grow up as fast as possible, but they're as nostalgic as the rest of us. And their memories of being younger are fresher and closer, they're the only memories they've *got*, so it's even more painful that they can't go back."

"I never thought of it that way."

We sat in silence for a while, watching neighborhoods go by. We'd left the countryside behind, and downtown Philly was a blur of red-brick buildings, a leaden gray sky, and thick billowing clouds. If we got caught in a rainstorm, I'd look like a drowned rat for the special.

"Is that...what the whole book thing is about? Nostalgia for childhood?" His eyes were soft as his fingers laced through mine. "That's understandable, but..."

I pulled my hand away. "You know, we're not in group therapy anymore, you don't have to analyze me."

We were both too stubborn to continue talking after that. We rode in silence for the remainder of the trip, until the loudspeaker informed us we were nearing Grand Central.

As we departed, it hit me how immature I was being. "Hey,

I'm sorry. I meant what I said last night. I want us to have our rain check. I want to meet your family, come stay at your place tonight. All of it."

His face relaxed into a smile, the shy one I'd begun to long for. "That's a relief. Because I have a surprise for you."

24

"Daddy!"

We exited the terminal and squinted against the late-afternoon sunshine. As our eyes and ears adjusted to the movements and sounds of 42nd Street, three figures loomed into our sight lines.

I recognized them from FaceTime. Thom's parents and son had come to pick us up.

"Daddy!" Sammy's voice was loud and insistent, yet he hung back, flanked by his grandma and grandpa. I didn't want to stare too hard, but the child was beautiful. Enormous eyes, thick dark eyelashes, messy light brown hair.

Thom dropped his bag with a thud and squatted down so he was eye level with Sammy. He held his arms open.

We all watched to see what Sammy would do. After a painstaking moment in which none of us seemed to breathe, he launched himself toward Thom, who wrapped him in a hug and managed to lug him upward, one-armed, and spin him around. It was crazy and off balance and scattered. Sammy's sneakers flew past in a loop as Thom swung him.

Thom's mother, silky hair in a bob, offered me a smile of my own and held out my...

"Purse!" I cried. It must have arrived that morning from Renee.

I took my beloved from her proffered arms and spun it around in a circle like Thom and his son. Everyone laughed, as though inviting me to join their team.

Sammy had picked out a pizza place the next block over, so we walked in that direction while I flicked through the contents of my purse to confirm my credit card was there. When we arrived at the restaurant, I said my goodbyes to his family. As I thanked them for picking us up, I raised my hand and prepared to hail a cab.

"We're glad you took Thom up on his offer of spending the night," his mother replied with a smile.

"It'll be great to get some time to chat with you once all this craziness is over," I answered.

"You guys go get a table," Thom told his parents. "I'll be right in."

"Why is Daddy not coming?" Sammy asked as his grandpa ushered him inside the pizza place.

Thom and I smiled at each other. "I better head out." I shrugged, standing on my tiptoes to give him a kiss.

He held my hand. "Crazy thought: What if you didn't go?" he asked. "What if you stayed?" Before I could answer, he forged ahead. "We could take Sammy to a movie, see the city at night, take a late train home, let him fall asleep on the way back. What do you think?"

I smiled perfunctorily. "Heh." Was this a lame attempt at a joke?

"I'm really asking," he said.

"I don't—that's why I'm here, that's the whole reason I came on this road trip." I tried to make light of his behavior by lifting his wrist and peering at his watch. "If I don't get going, it will have been for nothing, so..."

"But it's turned into something else. Hasn't it? It's turned into you and me. Right?" His need for reassurance was so unlike him—as far as I knew, at least—that I couldn't wrap my head around his behavior. His confident veneer slid open like automatic doors, revealing a man who looked completely out of his element. "Not you and *him*."

Oh.

"You're worried about J. J.?"

"You told me yourself, multiple times, that you guys always get back together, that no matter how long you're apart, you always find your way 'home.' I'm afraid he's going to manipulate you, and..." His voice dropped so low I struggled to hear it. "And I'll never see you again."

I knew it took guts for him to say that; to be open and honest about his fear. And if I hadn't been minutes away from the anniversary, I would have taken time to reassure him. But all I could think about was how far we'd traveled and how difficult it had been to get there, and how Thom of all people was the one standing in my way. His timing was atrocious.

I did the worst possible thing I could in that scenario. I rolled my eyes.

"You're being absurd. I'll see you later, okay?"

Before I could hail a cab, Thom's fingers lightly encircled my wrist. He tugged me to a private alcove under the awning of a shuttered corner store.

"Can you see it from my point of view?" he asked. "Why I wouldn't want you to go?"

"Can you see it from my point of view, by which I mean the *expression on my face*, that I'm in a hurry?"

It came out way harsher than I intended. We stared at each other.

"I get it now," Thom said finally. "Yeah. I should've known."

"Should've known what?"

"That you couldn't date regular guys after J. J. Randall."

"That has nothing to do with—"

"I think you're excited to see him tonight. Maybe all the attention you've been getting, all the social media love, has made you feel like you're on his level, and now that it's so close—being famous is so close—you can taste it. You can be one of them, at last! You've railed against them for weeks but the moment he acknowledges you—the moment he expresses the tiniest interest in you, you run back to him—"

Tears filled my eyes. "Enough."

The air around us was charged with anger and confusion, a sense of unreality.

"Reddit and going online isn't your addiction," Thom continued. "It's him. Him, and fame. I've seen pill heads my whole life, I know what chasing a high looks like."

"I hear it's a lot like gambling," I said sharply.

We stared at each other, our breaths rapid, colliding. I regretted my words instantly. "I'm sorry, I'm really sorry, but I need to go. I'll see you after. I want to see you after, okay?"

"I don't."

His words hung in the air.

My face tightened, every nerve in my face hot and sore. I could hardly breathe. The world around us seemed to be buzzing; a droning sound drowning out our words and the ways they harmed each other.

"Why are you doing this?" I pleaded.

"Go get your man. Go get your old life. I don't have anything to offer you so let's stop pretending this was ever going to work," Thom said.

Sammy exited the restaurant, head swiveling as he searched for us. He literally bounced off the walls, plowing into every available surface—brick wall, grandparents—and back again like a Ping-Pong ball. Thom's dad gripped the boy's shirt collar to prevent him from smacking into a passerby. Sammy struggled against the restraint and yelled, "Stop it, Grandpa."

Thom sent them a pleading look. Seeing him torn between intervening or finishing our conversation, I tried to be patient, tried to see past his hurtful behavior to its underlying cause.

But I didn't have time.

A taxi pulled up and I dove for it, sadness and anger warring within me. To think, I'd considered building a *life* with this person. How was it possible I'd fallen asleep with my head on his chest last night, his heartbeat steady and strong and so, so right?

"Don't you worry, Thom," I said in a loud, cheerful voice, "I'll pay you back every cent of this trip. Check your mailbox next week for a check."

He looked pale now. Shaky. "You don't have to do that."

"It's no problem. I'll be coming into a lot of money soon."

His confused, hurt expression made me even angrier; propelled me to new heights of belligerence and spite. "I'm announcing the book deal the moment I hit the stage."

PART III

1

In the backseat of the cab, I jammed the seat belt clicker into the wrong slot, over and over, until I realized it belonged in the one beside it. I pushed down so hard I pinched my finger and cursed a blue streak.

"Where you goin'?" the driver asked.

"Rockefeller Center, please."

"We'll have to circle it. There's something going on tonight and there's a big crowd outside," he warned me.

"Yeah, I know," I said through the pain, shaking my hand out. "Just drop me the closest you can get without killing anyone."

The driver's uncomprehending eyes met mine in the rearview mirror.

My purse seemed endless. Where were my credit cards? *So help me, Renee, if you forgot to*... wait, I already found it when we were walking from the train, so it had to be here somewhere. Had I moved it into the other pocket? Goddammit. Wait, there it was.

I wiped uselessly at my eyes and pulled my knuckles away, wet.

Fuck. I was going to have puffy eyes for the cameras. I was going to look like a fucking HAG. Thanks, Thom.

Oh God. Was it really over? How could we go through all the things we went through and have it end so abruptly, so nastily?

The events of the past seventy-two hours flickered through my mind like an animated flipbook. The car breaking down. The skate park and the Hilton. Kissing.

The tent.

Listening to his heartbeat.

And within all those things, winding around them like scarves, pulling tight to bind them together: laughter. Yes, we'd talked about painful and difficult things, serious things, but within the pauses there was always laughter, and I remember thinking, *I could talk to him forever*, and needing to find out his opinions on everything because so many things in the world seemed new to me again, with him beside me.

So why couldn't he support me?

Fresh, angry tears slipped down my cheeks.

I thought back to joking around on the train about our first crushes. Winnie Cooper for him and Michael from *For Better or For Worse* for me.

"What chance does a regular guy have?" he'd muttered. He was preoccupied with my past, convinced he wasn't enough for me, and worse, he seemed to believe I expected my boyfriends to be two-dimensional pinups who came with private jets and personal chefs.

What he didn't know was that for me, a "regular" guy was all I'd ever wanted. I adored the fact that he ran his own business and worked hard to take care of himself and his son, instead of employing a team of yes-men to blow smoke up his ass and cater to his insane whims. Give me an anonymous, nose-to-the-grindstone guy over a celebrity any day. In my life, that was rarer. I should've told him that. Would it have killed me to acknowledge his fears in a sincere way, instead of joking about it? Why did I have to be the class clown all the time? Why couldn't I have been kind when he needed me to be?

Even as I wavered, a tsunami of anger washed away the guilt.

He had no right to make decisions for me or accuse me of being a fame-whore. And the fact he thought he *did* have that right made my stomach roil as the car jolted to a standstill.

The taxi driver hadn't exaggerated: The crowd outside Rockefeller Center seemed a mile deep. I quickly paid and threw myself out of the cab. My slip-ons flapped against the pavement and the world went sideways.

I'd tripped and fallen, in front of a line of ticket-holders. Sprawled on the ground, eyes closed to squeeze out the world, I could make out a few conversations swirling above me like lassos. I wished one of them would loop around my neck and squeeze. Just put me out of my misery.

A rush of voices grew louder, nearer. "Is that..."

"Yeah, she's here, she made it."

"It's Holly Danner!"

"Who?"

2

By the time I was dusted off, checked for injuries, and ushered inside through a back entrance by a khaki-clad, no-nonsense woman (the AD) wearing a headset and carrying a clipboard, the special had already started. Groggy and dull-eyed, it dawned on me I hadn't made it in time. Oh, and I had a scuff mark on my FACE from wiping out on the sidewalk.

"We're glad you're here, honey, but you know we're filming this live, right?" the assistant director asked. "Where have you been?" I didn't blame her for wondering. Everyone else had arrived by limo and no doubt worked the red carpet, posed for photos, and signed autographs before sitting down onstage with Cindi Cooper, the investigative journalist moderating the Q&A segments. She must have picked the short straw at the network—a woman who'd spent months in wartime Bosnia shouldn't have been overseeing the ultimate fluff assignment.

The AD shoved a bottled water in my hand and attempted to smooth out my hair. "How come you didn't arrive early for hair and makeup?"

"I've been traveling. It took a lot to be here today. I wasn't sure I'd be on the roster; I...I thought I might be turned away."

"Are you kidding? You're all they talked about the past hour. Wondering if you'd come, where you were..."

"Hmm." *Doubt it.*

"Anyway, the first segment is the longest. Twenty minutes. Then break for commercial, then five segments of ten minutes each. Kick back and I'll escort you out once I get the all-clear."

I took a deep breath and closed my eyes. I transported myself back to the set of *Diego and the Lion's Den*. The smell of sawdust. The flimsy plywood sets, the freezing air inside the soundstage. The three-quarter-size furniture, so we wouldn't look swallowed up. (Talk-show sets were the same way; desks and chairs were customized, petite but proportioned, so the talent would stand out, dominate.) You don't recover from something like that, I don't think: Having reality bent to your benefit. Being and looking larger than life.

Which was why it jarred me so much to look out from my hidden spot in the wings and see them sitting on regular folding chairs on a stripped-down, undecorated stage.

There they were: the people I'd both loved and hated, railed against and adored. There they were, primped, plucked, pulled apart, and rearranged for ultimate consumption by a ravenous public.

Who even were they?

I used to know. Now I wasn't sure anyone did. Or if it was even possible.

On TV, the radio, and movie screens, they loomed larger than life because they were designed to be. But in person, the only way to describe actors and other celebrities was "doll-like." Their exquisite features and insidious perfection seemed carved out of lesser humans. If you had a personal staff attending to your skin, follicles, teeth, body-mass index, makeup, wardrobe, hairstyle, exercise regimen, and more (Swag Coach; personal tattooist; Reiki specialist) you would hover above the earth, too. Untouchable. Just out of reach.

How did I forget how tiny they were?

I took them in, one by one, down the line, and envisioned each of them at their lowest moments. Because those were the things I'd need to write about soon. No sugarcoating their lives, no being coy. A detailed hit job. Multiple-choice questions about which one(s) had anal herpes wasn't going to cut it.

Should be easy. They'd spilled their guts to me over and over, like trusting little bunnies.

Kelly Hale: My second older sister. The nicest teenage girl you could ever meet. One night, when we were all stuck inside because of a rainstorm, she confessed to us that at her high school in Muncie, Indiana, she'd had no friends. Not a single one. She belonged to tons of groups, yes, but they were people in Cheer and Dance she was forced to see. No one ever made plans with her outside those activities. Kelly Hale, a would-be prom queen in search of a prom. The first of the group to be emancipated from her parents, with the others following her lead based on their own career necessities and/or level of dysfunction in their families. *Honeypot*'s showrunner, a nerdy, wispy-haired married man and father of two, was famous for his feminism and for writing "strong female characters," yet he had bedded every actress on his show. He told Kelly his personal tragedy was the kinship he felt for the Roman god Janus, who was considered two-faced. (Oh, the guilt. Oh, the agony of cheating on one's wife. Oh, spare me.) In the same breath, he reminded her Janus was also the god of beginnings and transitions, of gates, doors, doorways, endings, and time. In other words, he owned her. He alone could open or close the doors of her career, and he'd love nothing more than to write strong female characters for her forever—so long as she was discreet and accommodating. Which was why she'd had two abortions at twenty, the same year she received a Golden Globe for Best Actress in a TV drama.

Brody Rutherford: the loudmouth good ol' boy from Texas who was so convinced his career would wither if he came out of the closet (and he may have been right) that he doubled down on over-the-top romances with Melody and Tara. Who pushed away anyone who encouraged him to be his authentic self and required everyone who spent more than five minutes in his presence to sign an NDA that forbade them "and their heirs" from discussing their interactions. I couldn't out him for the book—it would turn readers against me—but I had other gossip that would do the trick. For example, his twin sisters had tried to follow in his footsteps with their own pop careers. He pretended to be supportive—even produced one of their tracks—but when their hokey, embarrassing efforts were savaged by every music critic who counted, he asked his record label to drop them because their lack of talent was scooping up all his good press. They never knew he was responsible for the end of their fizzled dreams. But I did, and when he revealed this in halting stops and starts over beers at my parents' restaurant, I assured him it was a difficult position he never should have been put in.

Ethan Mallard: the indie darling, the sensitive, quirky artiste and auteur, troubled by the attention, yet never actually willing to leave it behind. The boy who once joined a cult called Pöorify in which members deliberately ate spoiled food so they'd vomit it back up in a "cleansing" and become "purified" (and lose weight). Known for fully immersing himself into his roles, to the point of living on skid row with heroin addicts for a month. Citing privacy concerns and a fear of glamorizing drug use, he politely declined all questions about the experience, and the framing worked as it was meant to; no journalist dared broach the subject. They certainly didn't know how he'd done justice to such a brutal, unsympathetic character, a murderous junkie—but I did. He had a baby with one of the homeless addicts. And every film role since had garnished his wages for alimony.

Melody Briar: Where to begin? The tricky thing was, most of her scandals were readily known; she'd be the toughest one to dish the dirt on. Shaved heads and car crashes were pretty Meh at this point. But there were still some hidden scandals that never hit the press, because they happened when she was with my family. The Christmas she lost custody of her son and daughter, she decided to take a handful of sleeping pills and lie down in the middle of traffic. It was a story with a happy ending—she had joint custody now, so long as she kept her nightly gig at The Palazzo and proved herself a capable mother.

Tara Osgood: Desperate to maintain her reputation as a proper English rose from the stage, she struggled like hell when her cousin Luther, reportedly a Manchester football hooligan, was convicted of deadly assault in a brawl during a soccer game in Madrid. He languished in prison to this day despite evidence that he may have been falsely identified. What did that have to do with Tara? Nothing much, except it was personally painful, and everyone loves famous people in pain, caught in lies of omission.

J. J.: What could I write about J. J. that wouldn't also be

about me? Would I be willing to discuss the one hard truth of my life, which was if I'd converted to his specific brand of Christianity we'd have gotten married ages ago, complete with kids and an influencer Instagram designed to make people like Marjorie at Prevail! feel like crap? How at age twelve, he worried incessantly that God was angry about his enjoyment of Whitney Houston's "The Greatest Love of All" (which celebrated loving oneself rather than loving Jesus) and was punishing him with agonizing headaches? My parents and I tried to tell him the headaches were caused by caffeine withdrawal, but he never stopped believing. Would I be willing to discuss his drug use? His family? How he'd revealed to us that his baby cousin had died because his fundamentalist aunt and uncle refused to give him antibiotics, insisting that if their faith were strong enough, they wouldn't be necessary?

Just then, Kelly saw me sitting in the dark nursing and cataloging horrible thoughts, and waved.

"Where you been, kid?" she called. Everyone swiveled their heads to look. "Get out here!"

"Hol-ly, Hol-ly," chanted Brody, which meant soon the entire audience joined him. It sounded like a thunderclap, a roller coaster.

"Should I... can I..." I asked the AD.

"Go right ahead," she said.

Which meant there was only one thing left to do.

I took a deep breath and walked onstage.

3

J. J. stood and pulled the one vacant chair closer to the group. "You made it," he whispered. I didn't trust myself to talk to him. I nodded instead and slid onto the chair.

"Are you okay?" he spoke in my ear. The optics made us look intimate; romantic. I hoped Thom wasn't watching and misinterpreting it. Then I realized how dumb that was, and part of me hoped he *was* watching.

"Thank you for joining us," said Cindi Cooper. I nodded, unable to speak. She probably thought I had stage fright, but that wasn't it. I was afraid if I opened my mouth I'd start wailing and I wouldn't be able to stop.

After introducing me and showing a five-second clip from *Diego*, Cindi asked us to share our most vivid memories of that time.

"How about Brody trying to score a free pizza every Sunday," Tara said.

"Brody? Care to elaborate?" Cindi asked.

"Oh yeah, I forgot about that," Brody said. "Gather 'round, children, and I'll tell ye a tale of olden times: In those days,

Domino's Pizza had to arrive in thirty minutes or less or you got your order free."

On Sunday evenings, the cast and their guardians always came over to my parents' house to watch a movie. We'd order six large pizzas from Domino's and a couple liters of Coke (one entire bottle of which was for J. J.). Brody would flag down the delivery car at the end of the street, fake a bike injury, and try to stall them before they got to the house. (The policy ended in 1993.) He managed to delay them enough to qualify for free food, but my mom was always so aghast by his behavior that she paid them anyway, and added a big tip.

"You think that's bad, you know what else Brody did?" said J. J., reaching across me so he could flick Brody's ear.

"Ow. What's that, bro?"

"You stole my dance move, *remember*?" J. J. asked mock-bitterly. He turned to the audience. "I came up with this sweet move one day during rehearsal. I called it 'The JJ' for the Jason Jump. And he ripped it off and performed it on *Star Search* during hiatus."

"It was different! I called mine the BJ. The Brody Jump. They wouldn't let me say BJ on air and I never understood why."

"I did," Kelly said. "I understood."

I laughed. I couldn't help it. It came out as a honk, like a startled goose.

Brody wanted the last laugh to be his. "I still don't get it," he said.

"I'll explain it to you later," Tara said, patting his hand.

The audience was eating out of the palm of their hands.

"Holly, what about you? What's your most vivid memory?" Cindi prompted me.

I immediately looked at J. J. I wasn't about to tell the

audience about any intimate moments, so I picked something humorous and benign.

"The time J. J. and I stayed up all night eating Jell-O powder."

"Gumdrops," J. J. corrected me.

"Excuse me, yes, gumdrops."

"From science," he clarified.

"We had this book called *Mr. Wizard's World*, and there was a recipe for gumdrops in it."

"All you had to do was pour some Jell-O powder in a bowl and..."

"Who's telling this story?" I teased.

"Go ahead."

"Jell-O powder in a bowl and add a few drops of water."

"Preferably with a dropper."

"Right. We probably went through six boxes of pure gelatin sugar. Didn't sleep a wink and we had to be on set at four the next morning."

"Was that the day J. J. threw up near the seal exhibit?" Kelly asked.

"And I fainted," I said. "It also happened to be the day the *San Diego Tribune* came sniffing around." I giggled. "They reported what they saw as an exposé on child actors being pushed too hard."

"It was the Jell-O!"

Cindi Cooper read from her notecard. "There's an old fan club membership kit from the first season of the show. It came with a Q and A you all filled out that would be sent to the children of PBS subscribers. I thought we could all go down the line and see what you wrote. The question was, 'What's your favorite part of being on the show?' "

She handed out the sheet.

Tara read: "'The singing.'"

Brody read: "'Craft services.'" He sent a shit-eating grin out to the audience. "That means the snacks, yo."

Pause for laughter.

J. J. read: "'The dancing.'"

Kelly read: "'The acting.'"

And I read: "'The friendships.'"

My voice cracked. Tears washed down my face, turning it into a mascara-streaked mess. I let the tears fall. If I tried to rub them away, tried to pretend they weren't there, I'd make things worse. And who cared, at this point? Who cared how many people were watching me? *Who cared, who cared, who cared?*

I was turning down a million-dollar book deal. I'd lost Thom. I had no job, no prospects. But somewhere back in time, my eleven-year-old self knew I was doing the right thing. It was her I'd saved; not the wildly overcompensated celebrities out there, but *me*, and the kids I once knew. The kids who had been my very best friends.

I got up, set the paper down on my vacant folding chair, and left. I just left the stage. I could barely see for crying by the time I got backstage.

A fuzzy, glowing red sign in the distance indicated the EXIT. I staggered toward it.

I was done.

I was done, now.

Coming here, seeing them—it was something I'd needed to experience, and it was wrong of Thom to try to rob me of it. Certain things couldn't be described to us—we had to feel them—and this was one of them, for me. Maybe even the most important one.

Besides, if I were the kind of person who'd been capable of betrayal of that magnitude, I didn't deserve Thom or anyone else in my life. Whatever issues I had with them were exactly that: issues between *us*, not an excuse to reveal a litany of the heartaches, abuse, and private regrets they'd gone through to a vicious readership.

My tears turned into a hacking cough as I reached the exit and pushed myself against it.

"Wait." (J. J.)

"Holly, don't go." (Tara.)

"Hol, come on..." (Brody.)

"Get back here." (Kelly.)

"Don't go." (Ethan.)

I stayed where I was, not moving, not turning around.

So they came to me. They surrounded me.

"Makeup! Oh my gosh, y'all, where is my team?" Melody shouted, swooping in last.

She reached me in a few steps and wrapped me in a hug. She smelled like cherry blossom Lip Smackers. "That's why you took off, right? You need a touch-up? We'll get my guys to fix the bags and smears."

I released a soggy laugh. "No, that's not why I left."

"Maaaaake-up," she called again, and headed off in search of her team.

Kelly took my hands in hers. "We're not going back out there if you don't come, too."

I squeezed her hand. "It's okay, you guys. It's you they came for. I'm okay with that; I really am." For the first time, I believed myself. Because for the first time, I was telling the truth. I didn't belong out there with them. And that was all right. "Nobody came here for me."

"That's not true," said J. J. passionately. "We did." His eyes shimmered with tears, too. He'd always had a tough time keeping it together when I fell apart. Sometimes, I'd wanted him to be stronger. But right now, it was familiar, and kind. It was good. It showed me he meant it. "Why do you think we chose GirlsWrite as the charity?"

"I have no earthly idea."

"Your sister said that you were going through a hard time. We know how much you love writing, and we thought, maybe if we donated all the ticket money to them, you'd come."

GirlsWrite, GirlsWrite...

Every time I'd checked my email during the last few days, new messages from that group were there. I'd assumed they were pleas for cash at a time when I had none. I groped for my phone and opened my inbox. Typed in a search and scrolled down to the first one, sent the day before I arrived at Prevail!

"Upcoming Fundraiser," read the subject line. The body of the text went into specifics: "Can you believe it's been 25 years since 'Diego and the Lion's Den' premiered on select PBS stations? We can't, either! We're emailing to invite you to the 25th anniversary of Diego and the Lion's Den. Ticket proceeds to benefit GirlsWrite."

They had invited me.

I didn't have time to process that piece of information before Melody shimmied back over.

"Everyone," she whispered heatedly. "Mikes *off*. They can hear us out there."

Horrified (all of them had been nailed by hot-mike scandals in the past, and now I guess I had, too), we simultaneously freed our collars of our mikes, like we were unplugging our IV lines and busting out of the hospital.

"What are we doing?" Melody asked. "Are we having a secret meeting?"

"Your mike's still on," I muttered.

"Why won't it turn off?" Melody complained.

"Still on."

Melody struggled with the wire and flung it down.

My tears had dried. It was time to finally say what I'd come here to say. "I appreciate you organizing things with the charity. But it doesn't change the fact that you guys have never been there for me. After J. J. and I broke up, no one reached out to see how I was handling it. But you still thought you could use me for a safe house! I got sick of you popping in and out of my life, in and out of my parents' place whenever you needed an escape, but never to check how *I* was holding up, or whether *I* needed anything."

"You never understood how difficult it was to be us," Ethan said.

"I can't even go out to eat with my kids unless the place is shut down for the night," Melody pointed out. "I can never be spontaneous, or enjoy anything unless it's been planned for and paid off in advance. I go from people touching me all day and shouting questions at me all day to silence. I'm completely alone."

Kelly gave her a hug.

"You don't know what it's like to have a chick you've never met try to sell your sperm to the highest bidder," said Ethan.

"I can't even go home for Christmas or other holidays. My aunt created a tour company in my hometown and they drive a mini bus past the house every hour," J. J. said.

"Your family hasn't sued you, or sold off your childhood bedroom piece by piece," Brody added.

"Are you mad at me, too?" Melody asked.

"The last time I saw you, you told me I was the lucky one. You told me, 'It doesn't matter what you do because nobody cares.' Why would I want to hang out with you after that? With any of you?"

"I meant it as a good thing. I was jealous," she said.

"Do you know how insulting it was? How condescending? Whenever you showed up out of the blue, it was always about you. It could never be about *me* and what *I* was going through."

"Maybe we didn't ask about you because you seemed fine," Melody protested. "You had a good family, you had freedom, you could go anywhere, do anything, without the entire freaking world judging your every move."

"And you loved being a part of my life, and my family, whenever things were tough, but then—but then—"

"But then what?" said J. J.

"You always left! Just when I'd gotten you back, just when we'd had a fun week together, just when things were the way they used to be, you'd leave."

"What were we supposed to do?" Kelly said. "Live at your parents' house forever? As far as I can tell, *you* cut *us* off."

"Because of the way you treated me!"

"People drift apart. That had nothing to do with us being famous."

"Bullshit."

"People leave, and they have their own lives, and they drift apart. It wasn't an us-versus-Holly thing."

"But..."

"What did I do that was so bad?" Kelly insisted.

"You didn't do it to me. You did it to Renee. When she gave

birth, and all the problems she had afterward, she *needed* you, Kel."

Kelly and I locked eyes. After a moment, she averted her gaze.

Renee and I had always been her support system. She couldn't deny it, and if she tried, I would lose my shit, potential hot mikes be damned.

"You're right," she said. "Can I call her sometime?"

My rage deflated like a popped balloon. To think, that was what I'd needed. What I'd come for. I didn't want to be a star. I'd wanted my friends back. I'd wanted acknowledgment, not that I'd been on the show, but that I'd been *one of them*. A friend, that they'd treated poorly. Perhaps I'd treated them poorly, too. I hadn't respected them enough to explain my side of things and given them a chance to either apologize or explain their perspective.

"Yes, I think she'd appreciate that," I told Kelly. We hugged, and she carefully pulled her hair out of the way so it wouldn't get mussed. I read somewhere she'd had it insured for a million bucks.

A million bucks. I laughed. I'd given up a million bucks just to hear Kelly say, "You're right."

She gave me a curious look. "What's so funny?"

I thought fast. "Anyone else feel like Cindi Cooper's annoyed with us? She sounds like Baroness Schraeder. 'My dear, is there anything you can't do?'" I mimicked the character's soft lilt from *The Sound of Music*.

"What happened to your cheek here?" J. J. asked, lightly touching the scrape on my face.

"I wiped out when I exited the taxi. Fingers crossed someone in line captured it on camera," I said sarcastically.

"I know a place you can hide out till the heat dies down," J. J. said with a wink. God, he was still so cute. But he was closing in on thirty-seven and still wearing clothes for people in their early twenties, trying to freeze time, hang on to boyhood forever. Thom had been a dad for eight years already. A single dad, no less. J. J. and Thom may have been the same age, but only one of them had grown up.

"I think we should fix your face," Melody said. "Also maybe try to hide your hands from the camera; your nails are ragged."

I'd been chewing them for three days straight, what did she expect?

"Oh good, they're here," she finished, relieved.

Melody's team fluttered around me with powders and creams, horror-struck. They squinted at me as though my nearness pained them.

"What can we do?" J. J. asked. "To fix our friendship?"

"Nothing. You don't have to do anything," I said honestly.

"But we want to. God knows you've helped us," Mel added.

"There is one thing. Could you have your publicist send a couple of autographed photos to the Hilton in Harrisburg, Pennsylvania?"

"Of course."

Melody's makeup guru wasn't pleased with my squirming. "Hold still."

The AD listened to her headset and then flicked it off and snapped her fingers at us. "We're back in two minutes, get out there, get out there."

I nudged Kelly in the ribs with my elbow. "TVs are rolling, Kel."

"TVs are rolling," the group repeated. I put my hand in the middle of the circle. Ever since her frantic warning on our first live tape day, captured forever in that blooper reel, we'd used that as our personal mantra before showtime. The others followed suit. We huddled up and lifted our hands. "TVs are rolling!"

Kelly smiled back at me, and the years melted away, as though no time had passed since our first live show and this one, as though no time had passed since that chaotic, bumbling beginning.

4

The next segment took a serious turn.

"Tara, could you speak to your experiences during and after the show, and how they may have contrasted with the others' due to your race?"

Tara sipped her water. "How much time do we have?" she asked, which got a laugh. "It was definitely tougher, I'd say, for me to get work than for anyone else here. It was like, 'We have a recurring character on *one* other show who's black, so . . . maybe next year.' " She rolled her eyes. "Is it getting better? Slowly, yes, I think it is. But there's still a long way to go."

Brody shook his head in disgust. "You've had to work twice as hard as the rest of us to get half as much."

Tara kissed his cheek. "Thank you."

The audience *aww*'d at their PDA.

Cindi took this as permission to "go there."

"You two are together . . . " she pointed out.

"We are," Tara confirmed with a wide grin. "Two years this June."

"I'll get angry letters if I don't address at least a *few* of the tabloid aspects of your lives," Cindi remarked.

"Here we go," Melody lamented, which got a big laugh.

"The love triangle," Cindi began.

"It's not like we planned it that way," Brody protested. "We didn't get together in a back room and say, 'I know, let's have a love triangle.'"

It took all the willpower I possessed to keep my expression neutral. That was literally what they'd done. The Seven-Year Plan. And written a low-down, dirty soundtrack to go with it.

"Still, was it painful, Melody? Did it hurt to see him move on with your former co-star and bandmate?"

"Manchot was a beautiful time in our lives," Melody said.

Okay, *now* it took all the willpower I possessed to keep my expression neutral. Manchot had been a clusterfuck from start to finish.

"It's all good," Melody assured the audience. "If I had to lose, better to be to my duet partner than anyone else."

Tara ejected herself from her seat and gave Melody a big hug, and the audience rose up for a standing ovation. If a camera had happened to catch my expression right then it would have been a rictus smile.

Cindi moved on to a new topic. "Kelly."

"Yes?"

"While researching for this special, I ended up in a, what do people call it, a rabbit hole? A YouTube spiral?"

Kelly covered her face. "I know where this is going..."

"During this YouTube spiral I discovered a conspiracy theory about you—or rather, your *Lion's Den* character..."

"It's so meta that they let us keep our names, right?" Ethan said.

"Not me," Brody said proudly. "I was Diego."

"We know," we all yelled back.

"First off," Kelly said, "it was a dream sequence in a fairy-tale episode, like the Scooby-Doo episode. So even if I had licked a toad, it was part of a fantasy scene, it was never real. But I *didn't* lick a toad! I kissed a *frog* to see if he was a prince. Fairy tale, remember?"

"So to put my mind at ease, the remaining episodes of the show's run were not a hallucination occurring in Kelly's mind."

Kelly laughed. "No. Where does this stuff come from?"

"She has to say that, though," J. J. teased. "She has to steer you away from the truth."

For a gag in the next segment, everyone put their names in a hat, and the person who drew it had to perform the other one's biggest hit. Ethan sang a strangely haunting, a cappella version of "Sock Me in the Face (Right Now)," Kelly and I sang OffBeat's "Bubblegum," and Melody performed a monologue from one of Ethan's indie films where he was in love with a sock puppet.

As the others answered pre-vetted questions from the audience, my mind wandered and I decided not to think about what the future held. I decided not to speculate about whether I'd see anyone on this stage again, or if we'd drift away for good—softly, this time; in the natural due course of life, not an abrupt severing like we had five years ago.

Because there was only this moment. There was only this time.

Which was why I made us perform "Cabbage-Leaf Rag."

"You guys are about to see something that never aired on *Diego and the Lion's Den*," I announced. "Something so wrong, it came all the way back around to being right."

J. J. was the only one who remembered the moves, so he performed it properly while the rest of us fumbled. I sank into the memories of him and I. He'd been our strongest dancer—holding me up, coaching me through the moves, in the hallway of my parents' house; in the San Diego Zoo itself; at the soundstage. When he'd guided my hands and feet, I'd never felt more capable. Never felt more graceful.

"Didn't you have this skirt in high school?" J. J. said, then turned to the audience. "Y'all, she's had this skirt since high school and she still fits in it."

"Niiiice," said Ethan jokingly, and high-fived Brody.

"That reminds me," Cindi Cooper pointed out. "Footage captured earlier today shows you panhandling at a train station in northeast Pennsylvania. How much of a financial hardship was it for you to get here, Holly?"

I shook my head. Of course. *Of course* someone had shot a video of me. They weren't kidding about the world judging their every move. It had only been three days of attention and I was so, so over it.

It occurred to me that despite her meltdowns every other year, Melody was well adjusted considering she'd been under a microscope more than half her life.

"Do you often take to the streets to earn money?" Cindi pursued me like she'd gotten me in her crosshairs. *Thanks, Cindi! You've proven your journalistic chops for sure now.*

"No, Cindi, I do not. But I do have another good memory from the 'nineties if you want to hear it."

"By all means."

"During the last episode of the first season, the Studdards—they were the producers of the show—didn't know if we'd be renewed for a second one. The show was on the bubble, so they posted a caption over the credits that read, 'Write to us and tell us what you think!' But they *forgot to include an address.*"

Tara busted up laughing. "Madder than a bag of badgers."

"Keep in mind this was before the internet, before fans could join together or create hashtags and aim them at the people in charge."

"Yeah," Ethan added, "Netflix wasn't around to revive it like *Gilmore Girls.*"

"In a way, the Studdards were ahead of their time, and who knows, maybe they would have been inundated with letters. Except for that not-including-an-address part."

The rest of the evening went smoothly and quickly, and before I knew it, we all held hands and bowed, to a standing ovation.

"Write and tell us what you think," Tara shouted amid the applause, and the cheers and laughter grew in volume.

Backstage again, J. J. and I gravitated toward each other.

His soft, deep-brown eyes connected with mine. Bonelessly, I fell into his arms and we hugged for a long time. His warmth and strength were so familiar to me, it was like slipping into the past, accessing a time line that had veered away from me yet also existed forever. I honestly think that, for a time, I knew his body better than my own. We were extensions of each other, with so many overlapping experiences, it was difficult to know which memories were his and which were mine.

My eyes were wet again, and half my vision was blurry, as though I wore bifocals. I'd had a late-night talk with Renee the day after J. J. and I had had our first kiss.

"What if we don't work out?" I worried. "He's my best friend. I don't want to lose that."

"Holly," Renee said patiently, "what do you think love *is*?"

I had a new definition of love, now. Love was acknowledging mistakes, and how much they hurt, and trying to do better next time. If there was a next time. If there could be one.

Thom had been right. This was a high school reunion. It wasn't my life anymore. I had a different one now, one that I desperately wanted to return to.

"I have a train to catch," I said apologetically, pulling away.

He looked disappointed. "You're not staying for the aftershow? The Jerry Levine special?"

"No. I'm going to leave that to the experts."

"I know you were mad at us for not checking in with you, and I get that. But you know, a lot of things happened during the past five years that were tough for us, too."

"Really?"

"Yeah. Tara had surgery on her vocal cords. She was terrified she would never sing again. Ethan adopted the baby he had, you know, back then, and the baby's sibling, because he knew they weren't growing up in a good environment. And—"

"I heard about some of it after the fact. But I was busy raising my niece. I didn't Google you guys for years."

"What changed? Why did you decide to look us up *now*?"

"I don't remember exactly," I fumbled.

"If you didn't Google us, how did you even know about the anniversary?"

Every cell in my body lurched. "I happened to be online and it was on a news ticker or something."

He looked at me.

He could tell I was lying.

But he let it go.

"So, are you with that guy, now? The one you were kissing on YouTube last night?"

It was bizarre hearing him ask that. It was as though we'd picked each other's names from Cindi Cooper's hat and swapped roles.

"I'm not sure. I'd like to be. But we had a big fight before I got here." The evening was a success, ultimately. But a wave of sadness approached me, getting closer. I hastened to leave.

"What we had... I wouldn't trade it for anything," he said.

"There was a time you wanted to," I reminded him.

"I was going through a crisis of faith and I shouldn't have taken it out on you. That's what I wanted to tell you on the phone when I called you. I mean, I was going to ask you about the anniversary, but I also wanted to invite you to my baptism. We had a whole ceremony. My parents even came to it," he added with unmistakable pride.

"I'm happy for you." They'd always been so tough on him; so unrelenting in their expectations of the way he ought to live, and how exactly he should show his devotion to God. I wasn't sure if his adult baptism meant his parents had "won," or whether it was more hopeful than that and meant J. J. was finally at peace with himself. But it wasn't my problem anymore.

It had nothing to do with me.

I squeezed his hand one last time. Then I said goodbye to the boy I'd once loved, so I could try to make things right with the man I needed.

5

Two Months Ago

It was supposed to be temporary. Of course it was. Watching Lainey.

When I quit college and moved into my sister's apartment to look after my sister's baby, the circumstances were frightening. But it was only going to be for a few months. It was exhausting, taking care of a baby. But it also gave me a sense of importance. I was *vital.*

Then Renee opened her bistro and needed me to stay on a little while longer while the restaurant got on its feet, so I did. A few years passed, and the restaurant became a success. We moved into a house with a little yard and a guest cottage out back, where I could have some privacy. When I began charging, it wasn't much—around $5 per hour, because Renee supplied the housing, food, and everything else I could need.

I loved that little girl like she was my own.

But that wasn't the tough part. I could have survived it, if it was one-sided like that. The tough part was that she loved me right back, as though I were her mom.

We didn't analyze it when she was a newborn. Babies don't remember much before age three, only whether they felt loved and protected, which I was able to provide for her. I fully intended to get out of there before her memories started to form as a toddler, because even though that would have been difficult for me, it would have been worse for her and Renee if Lainey came to think of me as her mother.

But then Ian, Renee's husband, returned from Iraq with injuries that were physical *and* emotional, and I knew if I left, they wouldn't have been able to cope. When Renee and Ian divorced a few years after *that*, I remained where I was, because it would have been unfathomably cruel for me to up and leave, too. Lainey and her feelings and her recovery were the most important things, and I was the linchpin that held it all together. I was her constant.

As a result, Lainey rebuffed Renee's help during any transition in her life. It was me she wanted to sing her to sleep after a nightmare, me she insisted on hugging before bed, me who had to drop her off on the first days of school, me she wanted to read stories to her with my funny voices.

We didn't allow her to call me Mommy, we put a stop to that early on at least, but Lainey came up with a nickname for me: Molly. Holly, but with an M for Mommy. A way for Lainey to feel she had control over the situation.

It drove Renee crazy. "That's not her name, Lainey. Her name is Holly. Please call her that."

"Her name is Holly, but *I* call her *Molly*."

We gradually reduced my role. Lainey signed up for lots of after-school programs and I took freelance writing jobs to keep busy during the day, but I still lived in the guest cottage. I was still there for dinner and playtime and visits to the zoo and birthdays and playdates on weekends. I was still there.

Until a final breakthrough with her therapist caused Renee to realize she would never become the mother she wanted to be, or have the relationship she yearned for with Lainey, unless I left.

So two months ago, she asked me to come have a chat in the kitchen, and she explained that it was time.

There is no easy way to say, "I want my child back."

So she couched it in other terms.

She laid it out as nicely as she could. She was firm but flexible. She said it was time for me to go, especially now that Lainey had so many after-school activities, and that I needed to move out, do my own thing, for my sake as well as theirs. I needed to have my own life.

She said I had saved hers, and Lainey's, and it hadn't been fair to me. She said she owed me more than she could ever repay.

I nodded and said she was right and walked outside in a daze. I didn't deviate from the path I'd taken prior to the conversation. I didn't go out that night or make plans with friends (what friends?) or start a list of things I wanted to do.

I walked back to the cottage, and I stayed there.

I spent every day in my pajamas. I didn't come inside the house; didn't want to bother the family that lived there. I had food delivered. I stayed in bed.

I went online.

I wondered what the last ten years had taken from me, and what they'd given me in return. Before, I could say I'd been noble. I'd been helping. Now they wanted me gone and I had nowhere to go. No degree. No real skills. Nothing to show for it. It was like I'd woken up from a long nap, and I should've been back in college, on opening night for *Into the Woods*, playing the role of Little Red Riding Hood. Couldn't I get a do-over? Couldn't I go back, and start over?

Better than that...couldn't I go back to *Diego and the Lion's Den*?

Lainey would be turning eleven in a few months. The same age as me when I booked the show. How could that be? She was so young.

What had I looked like, back then? What had all of us looked like, so long ago?

Easy enough to find out. I started with a Google image search and looked up my castmates. Instantly, hundreds of cast photos of us as kids lit up my screen.

I immersed myself in the past. In the lost opportunities. But soon I tired of the photos, the fan sites, the episode summaries, and Tumblrs about that bygone era.

I wanted current information.

I moved my cursor up to the link for NEWS.

Diego and the Lion's Den was having a twenty-fifth reunion, and I hadn't been invited.

6

By the time I arrived in Greenburgh and knocked on Thom's door, it was eleven p.m. It was no problem finding his address, as he'd written it in an email to Renee in my sent folder. I knew what I wanted to say, I'd practiced it quietly to myself on the train ride, but I didn't know how Thom would react.

The address corresponded to a classic Colonial home with a wraparound front porch and columns. There was a swing on the porch, a couple of worn wicker chairs, and a beanbag, too.

His mother opened the door when I rang. I smiled nervously and told her I hoped I hadn't woken Sammy. I was so dead tired, I would've happily curled up on the kitchen floor and fallen asleep.

"No, you haven't woken anyone. He and Thom aren't here."

"What? Where are they?"

"They stayed in the city, looking for you."

"Sammy, too?"

"It's a late night, but he can sleep in tomorrow. They went to the taping. *The Jerry Levine Show.* We've been recording it, if you'd like to see. We can start it again from the beginning."

I followed her into the living room, passing framed artwork from school projects Sammy had made with painted handprints on construction paper: Turkeys, Christmas trees, reindeer antlers.

Thom's dad was asleep on the couch, snoring intermittently.

His mother asked if I wanted anything to eat or drink, and when I declined, she pressed the buttons that would return the show to the beginning.

My co-stars were back to looking larger than life. The couches and chairs were customized to make them look bigger and brighter and better than regular mortals.

Each one was interviewed separately by Jerry, except for Tara and Brody, who emerged holding hands and promptly upstaged everybody else by announcing that they were engaged and expecting their first baby.

I let out a guffaw. And here I'd been thinking I'd shock the world and win the hour by announcing a *book deal.* Leave it to the experts to out-drama me. At some point in their lives post-*Diego*, they had concluded no amount of fame and adoration was enough. There was always room for more, and this was how they'd collectively achieve it. Every move was prefabricated for clicks, and I was glad I'd finally walked away from it.

I knew what was real in my life: He was onscreen. Not onstage; in the audience.

Every time the camera turned its gaze to the live viewers, Thom and Sammy held up a sign in the front row.

The first one said, I HAVE BAGGAGE.

The second one said, AND YOU HAVE BAGGAGE.

The third one said, BUT TOGETHER, WE'RE A MATCHED SET.

The fourth one said, I'M SORRY, BUCKAROO.

And there I was thinking I'd used up my quota of tears for the day.

I covered my mouth with my hand and tried to muffle the sounds I couldn't prevent from spilling out.

Thom's mother handed me a tissue and gave my shoulder a squeeze on her way past.

"I'm going to call it a night." Thom's dad had already headed upstairs. "Are you sure I can't get you anything?" she asked. "The foldout couch is real comfortable, and there are sheets and other linens in the hallway."

"I think I'll wait up for them, but thanks. Thank you so much."

"For what?"

"Raising an incredible son."

7

Two hours later, a key rattled in the lock and I roused myself from half slumber.

The front hall light flicked on and Thom stood in front of me, surprised. Sammy was asleep in his arms. I lifted my hand in a wave.

Eyes wide, he raised his hand and made a just-a-second gesture.

He walked upstairs, carrying his sleepy boy. One heavenly, halting verse of "You Are My Sunshine" later, and he was back downstairs. Thom had only pretended to have a terrible voice earlier.

"You owe me a royalty check," I said. "You stole my line."

"No, no, you're mistaken. That was an example of a sign I would *never* write."

We smiled tentatively at each other, uncertain how to proceed.

"Should we talk outside?" Thom asked. He looked as nervous as I felt.

"Sure."

He gestured for me to walk ahead of him. I opened the front door and stepped out into the cool air. He closed the door behind him and shoved his hands in his jeans pockets. The porch light was still on, and we stood there in silence for another moment.

"How did you get in the audience?" I asked tentatively. "Didn't you need tickets?"

"Nah, we name-dropped you."

"Seriously? I've never been name-dropped before."

We both spoke at once, urgently.

"I need to tell you something—"

"I'm so sorry," Thom blurted out. "I wouldn't blame you if you never wanted to see me or talk to me again. I was being a controlling, jealous asshole—"

"You were right, though," I repeated. "About the book."

"No, I was wrong—"

"I was never going to write it. Not for any price."

"Because you're a good person."

"I don't know about that."

"I do. You gave up your own dreams to raise a kid. You didn't have to, you *chose* to. I know you think that means you didn't do anything with your life, but you were there for a little girl who needed you, for a sister who needed you, and I think that's incredible."

"I lied to you," I said, my throat clogging up. "I lied about quitting my job. The truth is, *Renee* fired *me*. I never would have left on my own. Renee told me it was time, that for all our sakes I had to leave. What I'm trying to say is, all of this, all of it—getting treated at Prevail!, feeling angry about the anniversary, dragging you on the road trip, *everything*—was because I didn't know how to say goodbye. But I know it's the right time. I know I have to do it. Even though it's hard. And tonight I said goodbye to everyone from the show, I said goodbye to my oldest friends, and if I have to say goodbye to one more person I love tonight I don't think my heart can take it."

He pulled me into his arms and held me tightly while I let it all out. My grief over losing Lainey, my happiness at getting to the anniversary, my hope for a future that included Thom.

"A person you love?" he asked.

He looked so hopeful and so hesitant I knew I had to be 100 percent honest with him, even if it was terrifying.

"Yes," I whispered.

"I love you, too. I never should have tried to stop you from going. I never should have tried to guilt-trip you or pressure you into staying. You had every right to go, and every right to see J. J., and I should have trusted you, trusted *us*. It's not an excuse, but all I can say is I panicked."

"I could tell," I replied, reaching up to wipe his face with my fingertips. "And I should've spent more time talking with you about it. If I hadn't been in such a hurry to leave, I would have."

"What happens now?" He tucked a strand of my hair behind my ear.

"I'm going back to Prevail! I want to finish the program, see where it'll take me. Without you there—being distractingly handsome—I'm going to start writing a novel. I think it'll be about a woman who doesn't think she belongs anywhere."

"Does it have a happy ending?" Thom asked.

"Very," I assured him. "Will you write me letters?"

"Every day."

"Lisa is going to flip when she sees me."

We sat on the bench and held each other some more.

"I lied about something, too," he said.

"You don't have to—"

"With some people, you meet them and you know, 'This person is going to change my life. I'm already different, just from having met her.' When we almost had sex in your room, I was scared if we took that step, something big was going to start, or maybe it already had. I knew I would want to fit you into my life, and I was afraid I wouldn't be able to."

"Because of Sammy?"

He nodded. "I was afraid if I tried to grab some happiness, if I tried to have something that was for me instead of for him, something bad would happen."

I kissed him. "I used to think fame was the same as happiness. That it was something I got to borrow every once in a while, but I always had to give it back. I never got to keep it. I get the feeling you don't even let yourself borrow it, do you? Happiness. But I promise you can have happiness if you let yourself."

"I'm trying right now," he said quietly.

We kissed as we moved through the front door and down the hall into the living room again.

"I forgot, my parents are in the master bedroom, and the bed in the guest room is creaky..."

I interrupted him with more kisses. "Couch it is," I said, lifting his shirt off.

Clothes flew. He pulled me down on top of him on the couch. "I'm sorry this isn't a tent," he said.

Our laughter turned into kissing and the kissing turned into sex, and we found out the truth. Third time really was the charm.

Three Years Later

FOR IMMEDIATE RELEASE

San Diego, California

Hometown Author Visits Local Bookstore

Debut novelist Holly Parker was in town this weekend as part of a five-city tour to sign copies of her first book at Turn the Page used-book store on Main. Her fourteen-year-old niece, Lainey, introduced her to the crowd, noting that Aunt Holly used to oversee the Saturday Storytime when Lainey was in elementary school. Her free, hour-long events proved so popular back then (Ms. Parker is skilled at character voices), Lainey explained, that she made it a condition of attendance that customers purchase at least one book or she would stop reading at cliffhanger moments and then hide the book somewhere in the store.

Though she now resides in upstate New York with her family, Ms. Parker was born and raised in San Diego. As a child, she spent many hours at the zoo.

ACKNOWLEDGMENTS

A big thank-you to my agent, Victoria Marini at Irene Goodman, for her expertise and encouragement. You rock!

Maddie Caldwell, editor extraordinaire at Grand Central, you are a genius who makes everything better, funnier, clearer, and more emotional. I continue to learn from you and I'm grateful for your tireless help, hard work, and insightful ideas. Also at Grand Central and Hachette Book Group, I'm indebted to the fabulous publishing team of Beth DeGuzman, Bob Castillo, Erica Scavelli, Brigid Pearson, Nancy Wiese, Kamrun Nesa, and Alana Spendley. Thank you all!

Kiana Davis: Our stories and phone calls throughout junior high and beyond helped turn me into the writer I am today. Such fond memories and love.

Sarvenaz Tash: It's a delight and honor to be your friend and collaborator. I'm so glad we bonded over our shared adoration of 1990s TV. Thanks for your enthusiasm and help with this project.

Early readers include the aforementioned, plus Rachel Murphy, Amy Spalding, Maggie Lehrman, Dana Davis, Lynne Kadish, Kathy Foley, and Mark Herder. Thank you so much!

The Santa Clarita chapter of RWA (Romance Writers of America) has kept me going and growing as a writer the last few years. Thanks especially to Lisa Gail Green, Leslie Rose Sullivan, and Katharyn Sinelli for always being up for a meal and a chat.

Thanks as ever to my parents, Earl and Ros, and Lydia and Richard, for their continual support. My wonderful husband, Joe Skilton, makes my writing life possible. You and Elliot are my world.

Thanks to my aunt Carrie Lapham, for knitting me such a lovely pair of fingerless mittens. I use them for all my typing, and they help keep tendinitis at bay. Speaking of Carries, ever since I read Carrie Fisher's *Postcards from the Edge* as a teenager I've wanted to set a story in rehab and now I finally have!

Researching for this book was a multiyear process. References include, but are not limited to: *The Song Machine: Inside the Hit Factory,* by John Seabrook; *Why? Because We Still Like You: An Oral History of the Mickey Mouse Club,* by Jennifer Armstrong; *The End of Absence: Reclaiming What We've Lost in a World of Constant Connection,* by Michael Harris; *Dreamland: The True Tale of America's Opiate Epidemic,* by Sam Quinones; and the article "Making Mickey Proud" (*Chicago Tribune*, November 5, 2007, by Newsday).

Last, thank you to the *All-New Mickey Mouse Club* (special shout-out to the 1989 season), the short-lived but memorable teen soap *Swans Crossing,* the 1990s in general, and every tabloid ever for helping inspire this story.

ABOUT THE AUTHOR

Sarah Skilton is a book blogger with Barnes & Noble as well as the author of two young adult novels, *Bruised* and *High & Dry*. Her first adult novel, *Club Deception*, was published by Grand Central in 2017.